MURDER ON THE MOTHER ROAD

Brenda Weathers

New Victoria Publishers
Norwich, Vermont

© Copyright Brenda Weathers 2005

Published by New Victoria Publishers Inc., PO Box 27, Norwich, VT 05055, A feminist literary and cultural organization founded in 1976.

Cover Design Claudia McKay

First printing 2005

Library of Congress Cataloging-in-Publication Data

Weathers, Brenda, 1936-
   Murder on the mother road / Brenda Weathers.
       p. cm.
   ISBN 1-892281-23-6 (alk. paper)
   1. Women travelers--Fiction. 2. Murder victims' families--Fiction. 3. United States Highway 66--Fiction. 4. Recreational vehicles--Fiction. 5. California--Fiction. 6. Friendship--Fiction. 7. Deserts--Fiction. I. Title.
   PS3573.E147M87 2004
   813'.54--dc22
                                        2004023700

To Vicki,
for all the roads we've traveled.

CHAPTER ONE

The Knight's Rest Motel and Café sprang from the desert floor like a pop-up greeting card. The low buildings leaned into the wind at the bottom of a small rise, pink paint peeling in the Mojave sun.

On a whim I had ventured off Interstate 40 just outside Barstow and headed east on Route 66, now just a ghost of a road, a faded shadow of its gaudy past.

For several miles I had been driving toward a large sign advertising GAS, which poked into the cloudless blue of the October sky. The needle on my temperature gauge was creeping to the right just a bit, and I wanted to have my water level checked. When you are female and traveling alone along deserted highways in a thirty-two-foot RV, you're well advised to pay attention to your dash instruments.

When at last I reached the GAS sign, I was dismayed to see that the station attached to it was closed and had been for years, if not decades. On the opposite side of the road, however, the Knight's Rest Motel and Café stood open for business.

The motel was just a string of four pink stucco cabins with a small office at one end and a larger building at the far end serving as the café. The establishment sported a sign on a tall metal pole similar to the one over the defunct gas station, though not as tall. The sign was cut in the shape of a castle and, when the paint was new, the picture had probably been meant to resemble the large stones of a fortress wall. Now the image looked like a wad of smudged substances best left unmentioned. Perched atop the fortress wall was a cutout of the helmet of a suit of armor. The sign was still ringed with flickering pink neon,

5

although the 'C' in Café had burned out ages ago.

The entire place gave new dimension to the term seedy. Two metal lawn chairs in front of the office were secured to a wilting and stunted palm tree by a length of thick chain. A sign on the motel window admonished NO PETS NO CREDIT. I swung my rig around, crossed the road and eased to a stop. My little detour on Route 66 was already starting to feel like an adventure.

I pull a little Honda behind my motor home and I'll admit that managing the tow bar and hitch single-handedly is a bit of an effort, but I'm getting better at it with each trip. We call those cars hitched to the backs of the rigs our 'dinghies' and I wouldn't be without mine. Traveling with a dinghy allows me mobility but does require that I park in places where I don't have to back up when it's time to leave. I noticed a long empty space at the periphery of the parking lot and eased my rig into it, pulling directly behind an old Winnebago.

I decided to let my engine cool a bit while treating myself to what I hoped would be a steaming cup of good old-fashioned Route 66 java.

I couldn't help but notice the Winnebago I'd parked behind, possibly because we RVers spend such an inordinate amount of time sizing up one another's rigs. We throng to RV shows, and even while traveling scrutinize one another's stabilizer jacks or satellite dishes or, for the aesthetically challenged, even mud flaps—or worse.

The Winnebago was downright shabby. Decades of rust had made a lacy filigree of the lower panels and had established thriving colonies of reddish stuff around the windows and over the grill. The once shiny paint had faded in uneven patches. The sides and rear were covered with dents and scratches, evidence of numerous encounters with roof eaves, trees or even the rain gutters of the driver's own garage. I divulge the latter from unhappy experience. My heart went out to the poor guy, probably one of the army of retirees living and traveling on a limited budget.

The parking lot wasn't crowded. I threaded my way between a pick-up and an older semi toward the tiny coffee shop. It was a little past noon and blazing hot. The asphalt felt soft under my feet. Even with the heat, I had an extra bounce in my step. I love the thrill of discovery, the eager moment just before stepping through an unfamiliar door.

As I approached the café, I noticed a tall, patrician-looking woman standing on the curb staring out across the macadam. She appeared to be near my age, maybe a tad older, meaning neither of us would ever see forty-nine again. She faced away from me and, just for an instant, I thought I recognized her. I quickly let the feeling pass. One of the oddities of so much traveling is that after awhile strangers begin to resemble people one knows from home. I've long ceased dashing about and yelling "Oh! There's Marge from the bakery" or "My God—Danni— Whatever are you doing here?" only to be huffed at or given that look that's meant to indicate I'm a couple of hot dogs short of a wiener roast.

I paid no more attention to the tall woman in the parking lot and did not think of her again as I entered the coffee shop and made my way toward the only vacant stool at the counter. A large pie-shaped wedge of red vinyl covering on the stool was ripped but had been salvaged by a generous overlay of duct tape. At least the café made some effort toward theme coordination—there were four booths along the front wall done in matching duct tape on red vinyl.

A painting of Elvis embossed on black velvet dominated one wall— a jukebox that played old 45s, the other. An electric beer sign poured an endless stream of neon water through a painted-on forest.

As I entered, a large imposing woman, probably in her early forties, eyed me with suspicion. Her dark, unruly hair was pulled back and held in place with a red bandanna. She wore a dirty white T-shirt, faded blue jeans and a prominent tattoo of a rose on her bicep. A plastic nametag identified her as the Knight's Rest's proprietor, one Hazel Tutt.

I took a seat at the end of the counter just as a man who appeared to be the driver of the semi rose, dropped money under his saucer and sauntered toward his truck. Another customer, a harried-looking woman with three young children in her wake, busily wiped a nose and

7

encouraged a small girl to finish her tuna-fish sandwich.

Hazel Tutt came over and brusquely wiped the counter in front of me. "Hot enough to fry dust, ain't it? What'll you have?"

I ordered coffee, and when it arrived picked up the cup and blew over it, smiling my appreciation. The brew was a dark french roast, a Starbucks kind of taste. So far Route 66 was keeping to her tradition of quirkiness and surprise.

"That your rig?" Hazel hitched her thumb over her shoulder in the direction of my Airstream. Like many, I was glad when the Airstream company expanded operations from their signature silver bullet trailer into the much more commodious motor home. Quality counts, especially in a condo that you drive.

I nodded. "By the way, where is the nearest place to have my water level checked? I see the gas station across the road is closed."

"Back in Barstow's a pretty good bet. Ain't nothin' out here but dust and rattlers the size of crocodiles. I'd head to Barstow, if I was you."

"Oh no, I don't want to turn back. I'm in a hurry to be on my way. I can check it myself. Do you have a hose in case I need a top-off?"

"No problem." Hazel gazed out the window. "That rig looks brand new," she said with a huff. "We don't get too many rigs nice as that one out here."

I thanked her for the compliment although it sounded more like a complaint.

"Where you headed in such an all-fired hurry?"

"Albuquerque. For the Balloon Festival. I'm meeting friends there. I was traveling over on I-40 but at the last minute decided to take old Route 66. The interstate is such a bore."

"Honey, you ain't seen boring till you've hung out here for a while." Hazel stared at me for several long moments before turning around to slice a couple of pies and place them in the refrigerated case.

After satisfying herself at the arrangement of pies on the shelf she turned toward me and leaned over the counter on her elbows. "I don't mean to pry, but that's a pretty big RV you got there. You handling that thing all by yourself?" Her brows knotted in puzzlement. "Ain't you traveling with anybody?"

The simple answer is almost always best. "Nope," I said and smiled. "Just me, myself and I." There was scarcely a chance in the world that Ms. Tutt really wished to hear about the Year From Hell from which I had mercifully and recently emerged.

"Hmmmm," said Hazel with the first trace of a smile. "So. You're just out and about doin' whatever you like, traveling and all, I mean."

"That's about the size of it." The part about traveling was right on the money. The part where I performed this feat alone was most certainly not the case. Ah well. One plays the hand one is dealt. I fished money from my bag and handed it across the counter along with the check. "I really enjoyed the coffee. Thanks. I'll be getting on my way now. I'll let you know if I need the use of your hose." I smiled and stood.

I was almost through the door when Hazel called, "Why'd you do it? I mean, what made you decide to strike out like that?"

My lover up and left me one day for a woman half my age, was what I started to say. I checked the urge. "Oh, I don't know. I just woke up one morning and realized that I've lived a pretty good number of days and I've never really been anywhere."

"Why not take a plane? It's faster."

I stepped out into the incredible heat. "I'm afraid to fly," I called back to her, giving Hazel a smile and a goodbye wave.

The woman I had noticed earlier was still standing on the concrete walkway in front of the café. That seemed odd. She hadn't moved, changed her position, or, even more important, taken any kind of action to get out of the sun. From the back I could see that the woman's hair was mussed. The aqua polyester pantsuit she wore appeared slept in. A scarf sporting red roses on a bright yellow background was knotted around her shoulders. I continued looking. Something was very familiar about her, and very wrong.

Most people think twice before butting, uninvited, into the business of others, myself included. I thought twice. And thrice. Still the woman didn't move. I couldn't help myself. I reached out and tapped her on the shoulder. She turned slowly and focused her wide, pale eyes on my face. The woman stared without uttering a sound and I stared back. We must have looked like a couple of cats staring at each other across the backyard fence.

After a few more moments of determined staring, the realization hit home. I did know her!

Standing there on the burning asphalt, her eyes wild and searching, was none other than Janet Witherspoon, my old college sorority sister. I could scarcely believe it. I mean, what are the odds?

We hadn't been all that close all those years ago. She had been a queenly senior my freshman year. But I had no doubt that this was Janet, of the Pasadena Witherspoons. We had lived on the same floor of the sorority house. My most vivid memory of Janet was her long legged stride in the hallways or across campus, a black beret pulled low on her head, a long cigarette between her fingers, a volume of Ezra Pound or Jack Kerouac under her arm.

She was standoffish and aloof, but I don't think it was because of her money, which she seemed to disdain. She was just an odd duck, preferring the company of poets, beatniks and the occasional anarchist to the others in the sorority. I was a bit in awe of her and had admired her from afar. Until that day she had loaned me her dress, I figured she barely knew I existed.

"Janet!" I reached out and touched her bony shoulder.

I waited for the joyous look of surprise when she recognized her old college chum. "Libby," I waited for her to squeal. "Libby Merchant. Oh my god!"

Nothing of the kind transpired. For the longest time, Janet's face remained impassive, except for her eyes. Suddenly her expression contorted into a twisted, feverish attempt to smile. She extended a trembling arm. I noticed she wore one of those plastic identification bracelets used in hospitals. I took her hand and turned it so that I could read the name. Janet Witherspoon, it said. I had no further doubt that this wraith before me was my sorority sister. I folded her into an embrace. She still had not spoken.

Janet had obviously lost her ability to speak and, judging from her horrible grimace, I'd have to say she couldn't communicate by facial expression very well either. The first shocker was that she had clearly suffered some kind of stroke. The second was that both of us had reached the age where such a thing was remotely possible. One usually thinks of stroke victims as being elderly, and we were still in our fifties.

She had to be traveling with someone else. She was hardly in any condition to negotiate this deserted stretch of road alone. But who? Janet cast her rheumy eyes between the parking lot and the café. Without letting go of Janet's arm for fear she might topple onto the pavement, I glanced back inside the café. The young mother and her children were still there. A couple of old-timers swapped tales and swigged coffee at a booth by the window. I tapped on the grimy glass, hoping one of them would look up and realize their aunt or sister had wandered alone into the heat of the day. But I received only blank stares from the grizzled men in the booth, and the young mother just looked puzzled.

The heat was furious. The sun beat down on us without mercy. I was sure I could feel my back getting a burn under the thin cotton of my shirt. Sweat ran in thin, ticklish rivulets down my side. I squinted at Janet who, judging by the redness of her cheeks, had been out in the sun far longer than she should have been. Could she have arrived here on foot? Perhaps she lived in the area and had gone out for a leisurely but ill- advised stroll.

At last Hazel appeared in the doorway. "Do you know this lady?" I asked.

"Nope," Hazel said gruffly, then pointed at the aging Winnebago at the edge of the parking lot, "but she was here last evening with some old duffer." She jerked her head in the direction of the Winnebago. "He said they were lost and waiting for a friend." Hazel squared her shoulders and glared at the dilapidated Winnebago. "Usually I don't allow no boondocking. Looks tacky. You wanna stay for free in somebody's parking lot, go to Wal-Mart. But," she shrugged her shoulders, "I felt sorry for 'em. Told 'em they could boondock one night."

Just then Janet grew agitated. She struggled to speak but no sound came out as her lips opened and closed. She kept at it and after a moment a sound did escape her. "Li...ee," she finally managed.

She remembered me! I nodded my head and grinned foolishly. "Yes. It's me, Libby. I hugged her to me, then held her out at arm's length. "Janet, what are you doing here?" I asked, as if answers might yet roll swiftly off her be-numbed tongue.

Suddenly her eyes grew even larger; her face froze in a mask of confusion. She grew unsteady on her feet, teetering on the driveway like a dropped penny. I was completely flummoxed.

Just when I thought she might actually tumble over, she grabbed my arm and took a few halting steps away from the café. I had no choice but to follow along, if only to keep Janet upright.

We wobbled out into the parking lot, I with my arm around her waist. Janet kept her eyes resolutely forward as her long legs struggled for purchase on the tarry macadam. We are both tall, so the task of supporting her was much easier than had either of us been shorter. Once or twice she even tried to walk faster than I could steer. She was unquestionably a woman on a mission from which she did not intend to be deterred and her mission was to reach the beat-up Winnebago.

Curious. The Janet I remembered from college could have purchased any RV she might have wanted. She came, after all, from old family money. In our college days, she exuded class and breeding, like the rest of us exuded sweat.

Her mother and father had lived in an ornate mansion, surrounded by acres of servants, antiques and prime real estate. They had made their money in lumber, as I recall. Environmentalists of today would label them robber barons and I'm sure they were. Maybe that's why Janet was always so closemouthed about her wealth.

I visited her once when the sorority sisters had been invited for a very posh birthday party. Janet had two brothers and the party was for one of them—her older brother, I think. His name was Clyde or

Claude—something like that. He was quite a bit older than Janet but they seemed very close.

Of course Janet and I didn't stay in touch over the years. I was at school on scholarship, while she was from the family that had endowed the library. Our paths were not destined to cross—until today. But I receive the alumni newsletter every year and I remembered Janet had been mentioned several times, always as a Witherspoon.

I had read something in one of the newsletters about Janet's younger brother. He and his wife were killed in a plane crash just a few years after their second child was born. Janet and her surviving brother, according the newsletter, remained at the family estate, raising their orphaned niece and nephew and devoting their lives to philanthropy.

What ever could have happened to change Janet's station so drastically? Suddenly my mind was alive with possibilities. Had her sibling squandered the family fortune, leaving Janet to fend for herself in the second-rate RV parks of the world? Or worse, reduce her to boondocking in the parking lots of shopping malls and grocery stores.

Whatever the case, I had a feeling I was going to learn a great deal more about the decline and fall of Janet Witherspoon than I had bargained for.

When we got to the Winnebago, Janet pulled open the door and tried to step up into the coach. The flip-down steps were not out, and she was too unsteady to step that high. But that seemed to make her even more determined.

She scrabbled for the handrail, making weak gasping sounds. I grabbed her right foot, placed it on the threshold, got behind her and pushed. She hauled herself up and slid through the opened door just as I was about to crumple from her weight. Panting, I hopped in after her.

I stood in the shabby, cluttered living area, adjusting to the dusky light. None of the windows was open and the heat was stifling. Janet slumped onto the small settee just across from the door, exhausted from the effort of crossing to the rig. She looked toward the rear. I allowed my gaze to follow hers.

"Oh good," I said softly, more to myself than to Janet. Her traveling companion was here after all. Happily, I spied a man lying in one of the narrow twin beds. Truth to tell I had begun to dread the consequences of becoming responsible for Janet. I was already anxious to be on my way. It would be so good to see my RVing buddies. We hadn't all camped together for several months. Frankly, I was looking forward to our gourmet potlucks and hours of good conversation.

"Oh no!" I heard myself groan. My hand flew to my mouth. There was not one happy thing about the guy tucked neatly into bed. Not one.

I took a few tentative steps toward the tiny bedroom. The man, half covered by a blanket, clad in striped pajamas. would not be much help with Janet. Judging by the rigidity of the corpse, the gentleman had been dead for some time. He looked like Janet: same nose, same chin. Her brother? A night table sagged between the beds, covered with the usual assortment of pill bottles, tissues and half-read novels. This was not a promising development.

CHAPTER TWO

Janet sat rigidly on the small sofa, her face frozen in confusion. She didn't seem to realize what had happened or, if she did, was unable to communicate her emotions.

Hoping she would be all right for a moment, I ran to my Airstream, grabbed the cell phone, and called 911. After a remarkably long time, a dispatcher answered and I gave the requisite information.

The Knight's Rest was located in an unincorporated township. The county sheriff handled law enforcement needs. An officer would be dispatched, I was told. All we could do now was wait. I returned to the Winnebago and sat beside Janet, placing my arm over her thin shoulder. She leaned into me like a frightened child. I patted Janet's head as she whimpered, muttering words of reassurance and compassion.

Suddenly, a shadow flitted across the floor through the open door of the Winnebago. I looked up then let out a small cry. A man loomed in the doorway, his face dirty and creased from sun and age. His beard was hardly a beard at all but rather patches of lank hair sprouting from his chin and sallow cheeks. "You better get out of here. You're interfering," he said in a gravelly voice full of accusation. "They won't like that." The man shook his fist angrily. His was a visage that might have frightened anyone, a Halloween card illustration of a bogeyman. His hair was long and matted and I could have sworn the topmost tangle was wrapped around some kind of metallic implement.

He reached down and scratched a leg clad in filthy fatigues without taking his gaze from me. His combat boots looked as if they had seen action in several wars, perhaps beginning with the Civil.

Janet noticed him too and pressed closer to me. "There, there," I said as I patted Janet's shoulder, hoping the apparition would be gone when I looked back to the open door.

"Go away," I said firmly. I did an internship at a metropolitan psychiatric hospital and knew that this man and his ilk could be very volatile. Or they could be mild in a distorted kind of way. Schizophrenia is like that. Often they were no danger to anyone but themselves, but you never knew which ones those were. When it was clear the man had not moved an inch, I added, "The police will be here soon so—"

Just then Hazel came up behind the man. "Otis," she said and gently took his arm. "Leave these nice ladies alone. Just go on up to the café and I'll give you a sandwich, OK?"

Otis grabbed a dented and rusty bicycle from where he had apparently propped it alongside the rig, mounted it and wobbled slowly toward the café. "Don't mind Otis," Hazel said lightly. She pointed her index finger at her temple and turned it in little circles. "He's harmless, really. Just a little tetched. Say, what's going on out here?"

"I'm afraid there's been an accident," I said and explained about the body in the bedroom and our wait for the sheriff.

Hazel scowled, placed her hands on her hips and craned her neck to peer inside. "Well, Jeezo-peezo," she huffed. "What next?" After a long moment she recovered her manners and offered to bring us a glass of water. I gratefully accepted. The heat was miserable. Before she turned to go I asked, "Was that an eggbeater in that man's hair?"

"Yep. Sure was. You see, Otis vows he can communicate with aliens from other solar systems. That there eggbeater is his antenna. Claims he can tune in different galaxies just by turnin' the handle. Like I said, he's nuts...but harmless."

Hazel brought water and I sensed she wanted to ask more questions, but just then a white and green police car pulled up to the motor home. From my position on the settee I watched a uniformed officer unfold himself from the driver's side. He was tall and thin as a bed slat. He hitched his gun belt with his elbows as he neared the Winnebago. The most striking aspect about him, apart from his height, was a handlebar mustache that would have done Pancho Villa proud. Thick brown facial hair festooned his upper lip while the downward tips hung in perfect precision just below his chin.

Deputy Harold Ramey smoothed first one bristly edge then the other between thumb and forefinger as he introduced himself. Every few moments, he spoke into the police radio clipped to his shoulder strap. Hazel stood by the door listening until another car drove up and she had to go take care of business.

I was able to overhear much of the conversation between the officer and his dispatcher. Somehow, a family had gotten lost in the mountains and, even as we spoke, search and rescue teams from around the area gathered to comb the forbidding terrain. The Ord Mountains rose over six thousand feet from the high desert floor and temperatures this time of year could fall to the thirties after nightfall.

Deputy Ramey barked something unintelligible into his radio, then yanked his notebook from the breast pocket of his shirt. The jerky, overly fast nature of his gestures left me to suspect the officer was miffed at missing out on the action up in the mountains. He frowned and asked, "OK. What happened here? Where's the body?"

I explained Janet's condition and led the officer into the Winnebago and pointed him toward the bedroom. I had no way to answer the first question but told him I assumed the deceased had suffered a heart attack. A few moments later Ramey emerged and, without speaking to Janet or me, called for ambulances—one to take the victim to the morgue, the other—to transport Janet to the hospital. Those details handled, he looked around the cluttered rig, and then flipped his notebook shut.

Deputy Ramey turned to where I sat beside Janet, my arm around her. She still had not uttered a single word. Ramey took another long pull on his mustache while he glanced back and forth between the two of us. "Sisters?" he asked

Even back in our college days, friends had commented on the similarity of our looks, Janet's and mine. We are both tall, green-eyed, high-cheek-boned, with rather chiseled features. I was holding Janet's hand at the time and the force with which she squeezed my knuckles at the question almost made me yell out. I turned and again saw those frantic eyes. Her fingers kept up the pressure on my hand and somehow I knew what she wanted from me.

I nodded in the affirmative. It was only a small lie, after all. What could be the harm? In truth, Janet and I are sisters…of a sort. Sorority sisters do pledge a lifetime allegiance, including a spoken and unspoken acknowledgment that we would be there for one another when the chips were down. "My sister…is ill. I'll tell you everything you need to know." I flinched at this statement, as in truth I hadn't the faintest idea what had transpired in the Winnebago.

The officer's face relaxed. I could see him subtracting the additional hours required to conclude the matter of the dead man in the Winnebago had the survivor been alone.

"Just one or two more questions." He looked first at Janet then to me. "You say your sister found the dead gu…ah, the body? Where were you? Were you traveling with them?"

"No, Deputy. That is…yes." I gulped and forced a smile. Now that I'd told the first lie, I could see that more were required. "Actually, I'm traveling in my own rig. It's the Airstream parked behind this one." At least that part was the truth. "I—that is—Janet and I met outside the coffee shop." Also true. "She was agitated. I was afraid something was wrong so I came in to check on things. That's when I found him." I could have stopped there, but didn't. Now I was caught up in playing the game. "My brother," I added brightly.

Now that I had decided to lie for Janet, it occurred to me that I was now committed to stay and help her out. To what degree, I was not yet sure. First, there would be the matter of notifying family, then waiting with Janet until one of her actual relatives arrived to take over.

The Winnebago posed certain problems as well. As far as I knew no RV parks existed in the immediate area. Hazel Tutt would not allow the rig to stay in her parking lot for longer than it would take to remove it to suitable storage. At the very least, I would have to call my RV buddies in Albuquerque and notify them of my delay. Too bad. Spending several days in the company of strong, determined women, all of whom drive large motor homes, is something I relish. Also, I had my heart set on seeing the balloons rising over the desert. Alas, the balloons might have to rise without me, the endless canasta games be forgone.

The ambulances arrived. One set of paramedics lifted the corpse onto a stretcher while I unhitched my car so that I could accompany Janet to the hospital. Deputy Ramey asked a few more questions before informing us that an autopsy would be done as a matter of routine. He promised to check back after the coroner had completed his examination. Deputy Ramey then departed in a swirl of sirens and red lights. I turned onto the road behind the second ambulance.

By the time I returned from the hospital the shadows had lengthened, the sky transforming from the white glare of day to the soft purplish hue that signals evening in the high desert. The temperatures had started to fall, the evening air grown chilly—a welcome respite from the heat of the day.

Happily back in my own Airstream, I sank into my swivel rocker. I dreaded the task of notifying the family. Death is such a difficult piece of news to deliver by phone. After notification of the relatives, I still had the job of finding proof of insurance for Janet. I assumed I would stumble on important papers among her belongings as I looked for names and phone numbers of relatives. Janet had taken her purse to the hospital but her insurance card was not there.

I wouldn't dream of traveling without identification. My sister, Sudie, who is far more conservative and fussy than I, still has a bit of trouble accepting my freewheeling lifestyle. Just after I sold my clinical psychology practice to my business partner and made it known I intended to travel most, if not all, of the time, Sudie insisted I tattoo her name and number on an inconspicuous portion of my anatomy. I rejected the idea out of hand. But I do carry a small safe with all my important papers and Sudie's name and number are in my wallet. Up until a year ago there was another name I carried as an emergency contact, but by now that piece of shredded cardboard probably lay disintegrating in some stinky landfill. And what better place, I say.

The evening chill had penetrated my motor home and I rose to turn on the heater. Just then I heard a knock on my door and jumped to see who had come calling. Deputy Ramey stood there, his face impassive.

"Have you found that lost family yet?" I inquired before he had a chance to say a word. I didn't want to engage in conversations with the deputy that might give away my lie.

"Not yet, but, we will. We have every Search and Rescue squad between here and Las Vegas out looking, every sheriff's department and most police departments from around here, too." He shifted his weight and tugged on a handle of his mustache. "I wouldn't be surprised if we didn't work round the clock on this one."

I felt a moment's pity for the lost family. I imagined them wandering cold, frightened and hungry, the mother trying to console her young ones.

Deputy Ramey had begun speaking again, so I directed my attention back to him. "See it around here all the time. Folks need to be more careful in these old rigs."

"I'm sorry. What did you say?"

"Carbon monoxide poisoning's likely what killed your brother. The doctor said that he had had a couple of major heart attacks, but that is not likely to be what killed him. We aren't treating this as a suspicious death yet—they still have to do a couple of preliminary blood tests. Most likely the coroner's report will list accidental carbon monoxide poisoning as the cause of death. Sorry to have to tell you like this." He shook his head. "As I said, so many of these accidents could have been prevented by a little routine maintenance. It's easy for you people to check the furnace vents to make sure they are open, no birds nests or the like clogging the airway. Important to check the heater flame, make sure it burns with a bright blue flame, not yellow or orange. Well, anyway, sorry about your brother and all, and you all remember to travel safe. If you need anything from the Sheriff's Department, here's my card. After the coroner issues the official death certificate, you're free to arrange to have the body transported back home."

He tipped his hat and blended into the darkening night, in a hurry to be on to more important business.

The news about how Janet's brother may have died gave me a chill. Carbon monoxide poisoning is the scourge of campers, RVers, anyone, in fact, who relies on a furnace burning in a small space. The deadly fumes can't be seen or smelled but can kill in minutes. I once heard of a young woman who died while bathing. An investigator later discovered that a family of mice had built a nest in the hot water heater's vent. Carbon monoxide, a colorless, odorless gas, had seeped in and killed the poor woman even before her bath water could cool. I vowed to check my heater vents first thing in the morning.

At the moment, however, there remained the matter of locating Janet's insurance card and the solemn task of notifying her family. Wearily I strode to the Winnebago. The light switch was located at about hip level on an entry bulkhead that actually formed the back of the dinette. That way, the ceiling lights could be turned on when entering the motor home and before stepping into the coach. On this particular model this was also the location for the twelve volt kill switch and the patio light. The lights flared, a sure sign the batteries had not run down and that I would not be obliged to conduct my search by flashlight. The sudden illumination made the inside of the motor home stand out in an almost macabre bas relief of disarray and collapse. Janet and Claude's living quarters appeared even messier than before, if that were possible.

I opened drawers and cabinets, poked around amidst dented pots, rusted Brillo pads and coupons clipped from magazines many years out of date. The small cabinets over the settee were filled with old magazines devoted to RVing, maps and well-used domino, cribbage and Parcheesi games—nothing faintly resembling the objects of my quest.

A search of the bedroom turned up more of the same. A wallet lay on the night table. I opened it, hoping for usable information. A California driver's license peered from a windowed slot. I breathed a small sigh of relief. I had perjured myself to the local constabulary, but at least I had gotten the victim's identity right. While he looked far better in the picture than the last time I saw him, the gentleman I found in the bed certainly was Claude Witherspoon. I reflected on the fact that this might be the sole instance in recorded history wherein a person actually looked better in the picture taken by the DMV than in life. Or in death, in this case, I suppose. I separated the flaps securing the bill compartment. Empty. I replaced the wallet on the nightstand and continued looking.

The carpet had not seen the business end of a vacuum cleaner in many a moon and the curtains were coated with a thick patina of dust. Even to part them for a general airing would surely create a health hazard to anyone with even mild allergies. The entire rig felt sad and old and cluttered with the detritus of a couple of older folks whose housekeeping skills had declined along with their eyesight.

What was I saying! Janet was a sorority sister of mine—an age peer. She just seemed so much older, with her diminished capacities, her dazed countenance. And Claude, her deceased brother had to have been only in his mid-sixties. Here I am out seeing the sights, while Janet exists in a twilight world of shadows and half-light. Bless her heart. Everything about this situation just seemed so sad.

Having found nothing resembling a file of important papers, it seemed a good idea to take a short break and just simply look around. I plopped down at the dinette and let my eyes wander around the messy rig at the almost total disarray. It wasn't long before a possibility occurred to me and, even before I rose and opened the fridge, I knew what I would find.

My sister Sudie is a writer. She cranks out romance novels at the rate of two or three per year. The garish covers always portray a half-clad hunk holding a dewy-eyed maiden in his arms. The maiden is melting with love, the hunk in need of a good haircut. Neither seem bothered that most of their clothing is nowhere in evidence. Despite the fact that Sudie's husband Wilbur is a gray, unassuming man, the kind you'd hardly notice in a crowd, Sudie writes passionate prose and does quite well. It's a hoot when you think of it. Maybe Wilbur was something of a studmuffin in his time, though. After all, they have those seven children.

Anyway, Sudie, who writes under the nom de plume, Marvel O'Day, stores her manuscripts in her freezer, or at least she did until the advent of floppy disks. Come to think of it, many full-time RVers, afraid of theft, keep valuables in Baggies or empty food containers in cupboards or the freezer. I know of one hapless pair who lost several thousand dollars worth of gold jewelry because the husband, well into his dotage, threw out that box of oatmeal that had been taking up room on the shelf for so long.

Sure enough, in the freezer compartment I found, not bags of peas and frozen pizza, but an old accordion file, bulging with papers and bound with string. The tiny freezer wasn't even cool, let alone cold enough for food. I opened the fridge compartment and discovered that it too was warm.

That a jar of mayo and an unopened package of lunchmeat sat on the rusty shelves led me to believe propane had been in the tanks when the Witherspoon siblings began their journey. I guessed that the tanks had run out of gas somewhere along the route. Odd, since propane is so essential to RVing, especially if one plans to boondock. Propane runs our refrigerators, furnaces, and stoves. Meaning that if we don't refill the propane bottles, we can't store food, cook it, or stay warm while eating it. Someone planning a trip would make certain that the tanks were full before setting out. Unless, of course, they left in a hurry. I let the matter go and turned my attention to the accordion file.

Untying the string, I peered inside at the documents. Sure enough, I found a small address book, assorted other papers in various sizes and colors, credit cards held together with a rubber band and several full-color glossy brochures promoting some animal welfare organization. Between an expired Visa card and one from a gasoline company, I located Janet's Medicare card. I set the little packet containing the card down and again looked around.

Suddenly, I did not want to stay in Janet's rig any longer. For what reason I was not sure, except that it would be a major relief to be out of the smell and the mess. The day had been a difficult one. Right now a glass of chilled wine and a good dinner sounded like just the ticket.

Thanks to the miracle of technology and the expenditure of a few extra dollars, I am able to enjoy all my creature comforts even while boondocking. Equally important, I am never out of touch with the outside world. The first condition is thanks to an expensive generator that keeps me well supplied with sufficient electricity to operate my lights, microwave oven, TV, and even air-conditioning. The communication is possible through my cell phone, laptop computer, and e-mail.

Sudie would not hear of my traveling without a method of daily communication. For this reason almost a bedtime ritual is that I call her from wherever I am to give her a "take on my position," as she calls it. And in truth, I look forward to the evening communiqués as well. Traveling alone, I've recently discovered, is exhilarating and allows me the luxury of going wherever I please, by whatever routes, and arriving on my own schedule. But the trips can get lonely and sometimes I yearn for a familiar voice. These days, Sudie's fills the bill nicely.

Right now, all the responsibility I have patience for is my relationship with my sister. And that goes for demands, too, even though Sudie makes a few. Something curled up inside me and died when Kat departed the premises, declaring eternal love for a twenty-seven-year-old golf pro. That I was diagnosed with breast cancer during that first year of her absence is not lost on me, either as metaphor or as a life-threatening condition. At any rate, I've spent the last twelve months or so traveling, healing my wounded soul, adjusting to my solitude, giving thanks for being alive but keeping myself pretty much to myself.

I turned to give the aging Winnebago one last glance before stepping out into the night, making sure I had doused all the lights, closed the door and cupboards. A thought began to take shape, the kind that makes the tiny hairs on your arm stand up, makes you want to rub your hand across the nape of your neck. I looked around the rig, letting my eyes move slowly, deliberately through the cluttered interior. Something was not right. I couldn't put my finger on it. But something was not as it had been when I was here a few hours before. In some subtle way the Winnebago was altered from the moment I stepped inside and found a deceased man in the bedroom. I gave an involuntary shudder, then stepped outside. The reaction was probably nothing more than exhaustion, or merely a reaction to the grisly events of the day.

At home, I set a package of frozen shrimp in a colander to thaw and arranged oregano, red pepper, Libby flakes and fresh garlic on the counter. I love cooking in my RV, perhaps because I can stand in one spot and reach everything needed to prepare and even eat a full course meal. Special cookbooks are also available for us full-timers, delicious recipes requiring six or fewer ingredients. Tonight's Greek Shrimp Fettuccini came from that book.

While the Greek shrimp baked I sat down at the dinette, and took a sip of good Chardonnay and gazed with satisfaction at my own home on wheels. I am not a neatness freak, far from it. But in these small spaces you must maintain at least a degree of mastery over clutter or it will multiply and bury you. My Corian countertops gleamed. The oak floors spoke of newness and an expensive upgrade from vinyl and carpet. In the bedroom, the drapes and comforter, in muted blues and purples matched the throw pillows—my entire home a study in contrasts to the Witherspoon rig. The bedside table was piled high with mysteries, all of which I intended to read before returning home to Long Beach. I sighed with deep satisfaction, took a sip of wine and opened the address book. Might as well get it over with.

The red, plastic-covered book contained few numbers. A dentist was listed, along with a dry cleaner and the numbers for one or two doctors. I flipped several tattered pages but found very little written there: a convenience store and a pizza delivery service. I was stumped as to how to locate relatives from the smattering of home numbers until on the last page I found what I was looking for.

Two Witherspoons were listed. Sonny Witherspoon was first. No address given but a number had been scrawled next to the name. Could that mean Sonny lived in the same house as his aunt and uncle? Just below his name was the name of Myra Witherspoon-Hampton, listed with a Pasadena address and phone.

I dialed Sonny Witherspoon. No one answered, but after about ten rings, a recorded voice informed me that the mobile phone I had dialed was out of reach. I should leave a message or try my call later, the voice announced. I didn't. Poor Mr. Witherspoon—coming home to find a message about the death of a relative. Leaving the information on voicemail just seemed so cold.

I had much better luck with the second call. A woman with a thick German accent answered on the fourth ring. She informed me that Mrs. Hampton did not wish to be disturbed.

"I see. Well then, is Mr. Hampton available?" I asked

"Nein," the German lady huffed. "Him neither. Out of town." Clearly the lady was of the belief that the less said, the better.

I asked the German lady to convey to Mrs. Hampton that the call was of an urgent nature and suggested she might want to take it. I could almost hear her harrumph as she slammed down the receiver and went to fetch Myra Witherspoon-Hampton.

After several long moments, very long when I considered the per minute charge, Myra picked up the phone. "What urgency? What are you talking about?" She sounded sleepy, or drunk. Or both.

"I'm sorry to have to ask you this," I said with great care, "but are you by any chance related to Janet Witherspoon?"

There followed a prolonged silence. Finally, she said, "Miss Witherspoon is my aunt. Why?" Myra's voice had taken on a noticeable tremor.

"I'm calling with rather bad news," I said as gently as possible. "I'm afraid your uncle has passed away."

"My uncle? But—? What about?—" she yelped, almost causing me to drop the phone. "Who are you? How did you?—" Mrs. Hampton paused and recovered herself, if only slightly. "And what was it you said about dear Aunt Janet?" The word 'dear' was served up colder than my last sip of Chardonnay.

I took instant offense at her rudeness and tone of voice. "Mrs.

Hampton," I said, keeping my voice level. "I'm merely trying to help." I swallowed hard. "In answer to your question, Miss Witherspoon is resting well and listed in stable condition at a local hospital. You see, Miss Witherspoon and I are old college sorority sisters and, as luck would have it, we had pulled into the same café. I recognized her—"

"She's what?" Mrs. Hampton screamed. She cared not a fig who I was. Nor, it would appear, was she in any mood for even a brief recounting of Janet's and my sorority days.

"I suppose I'll have to come," Myra said without a hint of kindness. I heard a man's voice in the background, quizzical, trying to determine what all the fuss was about. It sounded as though Myra turned from the phone and spoke in a hiss over her shoulder. I made out the tones if not the words of a whispered argument, but did distinctly hear Myra call the fellow a stupid ass. She turned her attention back to me. She asked for directions, then instructed me to wait for her, which of course I planned to do anyway. In a clipped tone she added, "Do not allow Aunt Janet to leave the area." Had she not understood when I said Janet was hospitalized? I pressed the END button with relief. Despite her willingness to come for her aunt, I did not detect even a trace of warmth about her.

I enjoyed my dinner despite Myra Witherspoon Hampton, who had the potential to sour anyone's digestion and finished off a second glass of wine. I hit the toggle switch on my generator and soon was pumping homemade electricity through my wiring system to watch a little TV. After about an hour I realized I was bone-tired—so tired that I hadn't registered the mindless made-for-TV drama flickering out of the twenty-seven-inch TV, and I couldn't even remember how we got to the weather report so fast on the evening news. One thing I've noticed in my travels is that if you close your eyes, no matter where you are in this great nation, all television newscasters sound alike—as though they went to the same diction school prior to appearing before the camera to deliver the day's carefully selected, condensed and often sanitized news. I flicked off the TV and the generator and headed for the bedroom.

There I changed into a T-shirt and a pair of boxer shorts, my choice of sleeping apparel and flopped onto the bed. The accordion file of papers winked at me from the bedside table. My earlier perusal of the contents had been limited to finding Janet's insurance card though the file was stuffed with an assortment of papers. Tired as I was, I couldn't resist a bit of snooping. I opened the file and spread the contents over my comforter.

The first item I picked up was a full-color glossy brochure of an animal sanctuary by the name of Friends in Need. I quickly warmed to photographs of cuddly puppies being adopted by smiling families. My faith in the human race came near renewal as I looked at the pictures of Great Danes and German Shepherds wearing leg casts, the stories under the pictures recounting tales of rescue from abuse and of prompt medical attention by Friends staff.

The setting was pure picture postcard. Beautiful white kennel buildings nestled under graceful palm trees. White pickets fenced and cross-fenced grassy fields. A Romanesque fountain splashed sparkling water before a graceful, tile-roofed administration building. Very pastoral. The stray dogs and cats taken in by the Friends in Need Sanctuary were lucky indeed. I perused the obligatory appeal for funds on the last page before setting the pamphlet aside.

I myself am a supporter of animal causes and make donations to a number of worthy organizations. Even though I had never heard of this one, I made a note to myself to try and find out more about the group, maybe even drop in for a visit on my way home. If I liked what I saw I might add this one to the list of places I support.

Before long my eyelids felt droopy and the words on the papers began to swim across the tattered pages. I made my obligatory call to Sudie, wanting the familiar sound of her voice and a chance to unwind a bit, but she was out so I had to be content with leaving a message. Then I replaced the file on my bedside table and slipped under the covers. Numerous papers remained unread, but I was too tired to explore them, at least this evening. I like to do twenty minutes or so of yoga each evening. Same for the mornings. It keeps me young. Tonight I was just plain too tired to function. No downward facing dog or warrior poses for me. I slipped between the cool sheets, but even before my head hit the pillow I remembered I had left Janet's Medicare card somewhere in the Winnebago. Damn!

With a sigh I rose and slipped my toes into fuzzy mukluks and padded outside. Leaving a job unfinished is not in my nature. The damn Medicare card would haunt me throughout the night unless I brought it to its rightful place in my handbag.

I clomped across the parking lot to the Winnebago, flung open the door and peered into the darkness. Now where on earth had I put the thing? I didn't want to use up yet more battery power by turning on the lights, so, flashlight in hand, I aimed the narrow beam, searching for the thin piece of cardboard that would insure Janet got the care she required. A source of pride for me is the nimble quality of my memory. It seldom fails—except for now.

Frustrated, I sat at the grimy dinette and it was then that I heard the sound of a car crunching on the loose gravel of the Knight's Rest parking lot. As a precaution, I reached over and latched the door, then listened as the vehicle approached the Winnebago. I make no claim to expertise in engine repair but I do know a piston from a distributor cap. Anyone planning to travel in an RV as a lifestyle would do well to gain at least a rudimentary knowledge of the machinery involved.

The vehicle in question here was a six-cylinder job, of that much I was sure, but it was firing on only about half of them. The uneven, raggedy noise of the motor gave the distinct impression that the thing would cease running altogether at the slightest provocation. I checked my watch and was surprised to note that the time was just short of eleven. The café was closed and the motel sign turned off. Who on earth could be visiting at this hour?

A car door slammed shut with a resounding thunk. Footsteps, then, moving toward the door. Like the heroine in a B movie, my hand flew to my mouth. Seconds later I watched in horror as the doorknob slowly turned.

"Who's there?" I called with more bravura than I felt.

"Huh?" A startled male voice—the footsteps moved quickly away. Then the ramshackle engine firing up again, the squeal of tires churning asphalt. I pulled the dirty curtains open and peered at the departing automobile. A man, the driver and lone occupant, sat hunched over the wheel, peering down the highway. His profile appeared youngish, but menacing. In a flash the night was silent again, the car with bad timing receding into the inky darkness.

Janet's Medicare card winked at me from the counter by the stove. I grabbed it and raced outside, my legs shaking from the scare the mystery man had provided for my late night amusement.

Curiosity brought me to the road's edge. I stared into the night in the direction of the anonymous car, and then shined my flashlight left, alongside the Winnebago. The stench of burned rubber hung in the air. The beam illuminated a silvery bit of something protruding from the RV. I trained the light on a spot about midway along the length of the aging motor home and moved cautiously closer.

The yellow shaft of light circled a bit of insulation, the kind contractors buy in huge rolls to insulate the walls and attics of houses. An ordinary, unremarkable object, but one made extraordinary by the fact that it was jammed into the heater vent of the aging Winnebago. One corner of the material trembled in a light breeze.

A bird's nest or leaves that had accumulated over the years would explain a clogged heater vent and an accidental death by carbon monoxide poisoning. Tragic, but still an accident. A wadded-up piece of insulation was another matter entirely.

I bent over and peered at my discovery. The opening of a heater vent is round, about eight inches in diameter, and crisscrossed by thin metal strips. The strips are put there to prevent the build-up of leaves or other debris. The strips on the Winnebago had been cut!

Stinging shock was followed quickly by a cold surge of anger. What kind of cold-blooded killer could have done such a deed? And why to such a seemingly harmless pair as the Witherspoon siblings? I continued staring at the offending tatter of insulation. Maybe if I stared long enough the picture would reverse itself, become explicable, like a nest of mice or a wad of dried leaves. Alas, the facts were the facts and no amount of determined staring was destined to alter them. I returned to my rig and carefully locked the door.

Still confused by my find I toyed with the idea of calling 911. Suppose the tatter of insulation was a mere accident, a freakish one to be sure, but an accident. But wasn't it also possible that the fragment represented the work of a killer who might very well return to finish destroying evidence? Shakily I grabbed my cell phone and dialed.

A sleepy dispatcher answered, asking if the call was an emergency. When I responded that I wasn't sure and described what I had found, the dispatcher asked a few questions about the piece of insulation and then, sounding bored, said they would send someone in the morning to check things out.

The incident was upsetting, but I knew from bitter experience that if I let the heater vent tampering and the visage of my scowling late night visitor get the upper hand, I could forget rest for the night. I put my cell phone within easy reach on the bedside table, let my eyes close and sank back onto the mattress. I would dig a bit further the following day. Doubtless there was a rational explanation for all of it—the heater, the unexplained visitor, even the empty propane tanks. Everything would be cleared up tomorrow.

CHAPTER THREE

Barstow, California, as anyone who has ever been there knows, is situated in the exact Middle of Nowhere. The desert city, therefore, qualifies as one of the more frequently mentioned spots on earth. As in: "Where are we, Edith?" "Hell if I know, Jack. You took a wrong turn and now here we are in the Middle of Nowhere."

The town lies along the banks of the Mohave River, but don't expect restaurants and artsy boutiques lined in picturesque rows along a waterway. The Mohave is actually a dry riverbed with sand filling the troughs that once held water. The river is, therefore, best viewed as grains of sand that whistle through town on the wings of one of the dust storms that plague the area. Barstow, doubtless cherished by its residents has the charm and fascination of dryer lint.

But the town claimed the closest hospital, so to Barstow I had to journey the next morning. Janet's insurance card was in my bag. The nice lady in Admitting would be pleased. I started my car and scanned the bank of dark clouds gathering to the east. Rain doesn't fall here often, but when rain does come, the storms can produce havoc—flash flooding and the like. The realization was not pleasant as it raised the possibility of further delays. I had no idea when Myra would arrive to relieve me.

During the drive the image of the deliberately clogged heater vent thrust itself stubbornly into my mind's eye, and with it a disturbing question—if murder was the intent, why had Janet not succumbed to the lethal gases? Could she be a murderer? Such a proposition was too silly even to imagine. Janet Witherspoon a cold-blooded killer? No way. The woman was tottering on the brink of decrepitude. Yet there was that silvery piece of insulation. Someone had stuffed it into the heater vent of her Winnebago, itself marooned in the parking lot of a derelict motel. But who? Why? To the best of my knowledge there was not a soul for miles in any direction with a connection to the Witherspoons— except for last night's visitor perhaps.

Perhaps more than others, I am intrigued by a mystery—by that which is hidden from initial view. No doubt my training in clinical psychology has a great deal to do with it, or maybe this particular penchant is a professional chicken-and-egg story. Whatever. I simply must dig out the truth of a matter. I've certainly sat across from enough clients who delighted in feeding me important information piecemeal, dangling fragments meant to tantalize. I suppose they felt my hourly one-hundred-fifty-dollar fee entitled them to test my mettle, make me figure it all out and feed it back. They were usually in luck. I would mull and ponder and ask and nudge until a clear picture emerged. Sometimes—no, oftentimes, the picture that emerged was much different from the one the client had intended to present.

The fate of Claude Witherspoon and the uncertain future of his ailing sister presented a puzzle of a far different sort, but my yearning to sort out the mystery was no less strong. By this time I had lied to an officer, been impossibly delayed, and was the only person on the scene with the ability and willingness to take responsibility for Janet. Now, a new burden settled itself onto my shoulders—I had to know what happened to Claude. More importantly, I had to see that no harm befell Janet.

Janet had done me a huge favor all those years ago, one that had endeared her to me forevermore. Drenched in nostalgia, I remembered back to that long-ago day, the day of the college President's Ball. Attendance at the most posh function was mandatory. Also mandatory that female students be accompanied by a person of the opposite gender.

The ball was the biggest social event of the year back then; perhaps it still is. I had scrimped and saved to buy a gown for the event and even had a date. A handsome basketball player, Kevin Block, had asked to be my squire for the evening. I had not yet realized my true identity as a lesbian. There existed something about me that was different, I knew that much. I just didn't know what. Maybe a clue could have been that I would have much preferred to squire my lacrosse teammate, Gloria Stevens, that evening. But the basketball player would have to do.

I had dressed carefully and with trembling hands, pouring myself into a slinky little white number with spaghetti straps and a slit to the thigh. As luck would have it, when I reached into my closet for the matching beaded bag, I accidentally knocked over a carelessly placed bottle of shoe polish. The black liquid cascaded down upon my gorgeous dress a mere fifteen minutes before my date was to arrive. I screamed in frustration and anger at ruining something I had scrimped to buy. With that same money I could have bought a telescope.

Janet heard my distress. She rushed to my room and found me collapsed on a pile of stained satin. She understood the problem at once and wasted no time in returning to her own room. She reappeared moments later with the most gorgeous gown—far more expensive than the one I had scrimped for. I did not find out until later that this was the dress she had intended to wear.

Now Janet needed help and no statute of limitations exists on returning good deeds. Someone might have tried to kill her and had succeeded in killing her brother. Or, just as horrifying, she had killed her own brother in a fit of dementia. Without question, Janet Witherspoon needed a friend.

Is anyone left on the planet that doesn't know it's not OK to touch evidence? I had left the piece of insulation stuffed into the vent. The police would arrive, dust it for prints and soon discover the perpetrator of this terrible crime. Once in Barstow, my first order of business would be a visit to Deputy Ramey to make sure he had gotten my message that Claude Witherspoon may not have died of accidental carbon monoxide poisoning. Quite possibly Claude Witherspoon had been murdered.

A more troubling thought collided with the first one. What if Janet was innocent and had somehow managed to escape the deadly fumes? Could that mean the murderer was close by, intent on finishing the job and killing Janet? The thought brought a shiver of gooseflesh. I rubbed my upper arms and pressed the gas pedal. Right now my job was to get to Barstow and check on Janet. And to notify the police of my findings.

Barstow hunkered down against the heat and dust and did nothing to dissuade me from my opinion of the city and its lack of charms. Before going to the hospital, I stopped in at the sheriff's office and asked for Deputy Ramey. I was informed that he was out on patrol. Seems like everyone was combing the mountains for the lost family, including Ramey. I stood there for a moment, fighting off a sense of my own foolishness. The bored-looking young desk clerk probably didn't even know about the death of Claude Witherspoon and would look askance at a strange lady with laugh lines, a buzz cut and three silver studs in each earlobe, gushing about murder. I merely asked that Deputy Ramey call me, as I had information for him regarding the death of Mr. Witherspoon. The clerk nodded and took my card.

At the hospital I took the corridors to Janet's room in long strides. She looked considerably better than she had yesterday. She was propped up in bed, an IV dripping slowly into her thin arm. I stood at her bedside and leaned down, taking her hand.

Janet opened her pale eyes and tried to focus. After a moment, she became aware of my presence. She knew I was there. And not only that, she seemed to recognize me.

She still did not speak, or even smile, but she squeezed my hand. Maybe it was my imagination, but I thought her eyes showed pleasure at my presence, relief even. She opened her mouth in that horrible grimace of a smile and I smiled back, giving her hand a little pat. She gave her good leg a bit of a kick. I reached down to straighten the bed covers and was surprised to discover her ankles were bound to the bed rail by thin strips of sheepskin. Restraints! Why, for heaven's sake?

Just then, I heard a rustle at the door. I turned to find a young doctor standing there studying Janet's chart. He flipped a couple of pages before acknowledging my presence. His brows knitted. "Are you a relative?"

No sense in divulging the falsehood at this juncture. "Yes," I said and pasted a familial smile across my face. The whole reason I had entered willingly into this farce was so that I could take the place of a relative where medical matters were concerned, and this occasion suited the intention. "How is she?"

The doctor frowned. He fixed his dark eyes on me, and instead of answering my question, began a barrage of his own. He began berating me as if I were a wayward child. "As I am sure you are aware, your sister has suffered two serious strokes which have left her with little ability to speak and with a diminished capacity for reason and memory. What in the world were you thinking, Madam? Miss Witherspoon is suffering from exposure and should never have been left alone. Moreover, she should never have been removed against medical advice from the Shady Grove Nursing Home. She was still wearing their identification bracelet. Why on earth was that done?"

The doctor's lips stretched into a thin line of disapproval. "And where are her blood pressure medications? She could have another stroke at any time."

Filling to the brim with guilt, I struggled to find answers to his questions—to provide excuses. In the middle of my tongue-tied response I remembered: Wait a minute! I'm not really her sister. I haven't the faintest notion how all this came to be.

I didn't say this, of course, but knew I had better make something up, and fast. "I'm afraid my sister and brother are nomads, Doctor. They sometimes leap into their RV and disappear for days." Good story, I told myself as I smiled innocently. Perhaps not truthful, but certainly plausible. Lying, after all, is really no more than creating stories that make sense to someone else. Novelists do it all the time. And liars. "It's so difficult for the family," I went on blithely. "We don't live in the same town, you see. And I arrived to take charge of the...situation. As you may be aware, our brother Claude passed away quite tragically."

"Yes. I heard about that," the doctor said, still studying the chart.

By the look on his face I sensed my ploy had worked. The thin line of disapproval had eased. The doctor flipped the chart shut and turned his attention to Janet.

Walking to the bed, he put a stethoscope to her thin chest, listened a moment, then glanced back to me. "I'm sorry for the restraints, but your sister, as I'm sure you know, is a night wanderer. The charge nurse found her roaming the halls at around two this morning, dragging her IV stand, just walking up and down the corridors and babbling to herself. It's not uncommon with older people. It is particularly prevalent in those with some form of dementia. Night wandering can be dangerous. However, in your sister's case, her tendency to roam about is probably what saved her life."

"Excuse me?" I was taken aback.

"If she hadn't gotten up to wander around that night she could have succumbed to the carbon monoxide, just like your brother." The doctor paused for emphasis. He cleared his throat, and then went on. "As to her condition, she is stable now. Much of her confusion on admittance was due to exposure. This is not to say she does not suffer from a mild form of dementia, for she does. But I believe you will find her more responsive in a matter of days. She should be ready to leave the hospital tomorrow."

Wait a minute. Had he said babbling? "Excuse me, Doctor, but did you say she was talking to herself?"

"Yes, so the charge nurse reported. Why?"

Another opportunity for a bravura performance by the legendary Libby Merchant. Perhaps I would do well to practice my Oscar speech. Ladies and gentlemen, members of the Academy— "It's just that, well, she talks so, ah...so seldom," I gushed. "I'm always pleased to find her talking at all." That last part, at least, was true.

"Miss Witherspoon's verbal skills, or lack of them, are not all that uncommon. At times she is quite lucid and responsive, as I'm sure you know. She has suffered a relatively severe stroke. Other times she retreats to a private place in her mind and is unavailable to the rest of us. If you're asking for a prognosis, you'll need to check with her personal physician. But I can tell you her condition is not likely to change, except to grow worse."

"Yes. Thank you, Doctor. Tomorrow it is." The doctor left and I sat for a minute by Janet's side, praying for Myra Witherspoon-Hampton's speedy arrival. Janet had fallen into a light sleep.

So, Janet had a tendency to get out of bed at night and roam around. Yet I could not ignore the possibility she had committed the crime of murder herself, however addle-brained her motive. She could have stuffed the insulation into the vent, turned on the heater and taken her evening stroll.

It made equal sense to think the killing had been the work of a sicko madman, a random killer who went around bumping off old folks in campers for sport. Worse things have happened.

I mulled the sicko madman theory but didn't completely discard it. After all, I had met Otis. Yet, I was still squeamish about Janet's culpability.

For an instant, I considered taking a motel room in Barstow. But I had no idea when Myra might arrive and I wanted to be there when she finally made it. Besides, as we RVers say, home is where you park it. The best thing to do now was return to my Airstream and wait for Myra. I could even try to contact her brother, Sonny Witherspoon again. Perhaps he could get to the Knight's Rest sooner than his cranky sister. And wouldn't it be better, I thought suddenly, if one of her relatives were present when the subject of murder was raised— especially if Janet bore some culpability?

On the drive back I noticed dark thunderclouds forming over the mountains to the north. Not far outside town a driving rain began in earnest. Fat drops splashed heavily on the dusty ground. The purplish sky looked truly menacing. The one good thing about these desert storms is, while they are fierce, they are usually brief. Only about five inches of rain fall in an entire year out this way and I gathered that all five of them intended on coming down today.

My cell phone rang. Deputy Ramey cleared his throat before

speaking. I could almost see him tugging on his mustache. "You wanted to talk to me about something?" I had to think quickly. If Janet had placed the stuffing in the vent, then one of her relatives should be with her when that fact became known. The poor dear could be placed under arrest, for heaven's sake, an investigation ordered. More questions. For me it could only result in more delay and greater opportunity to become involved in something more complicated than I was prepared to handle. Once Myra showed up, she could take over Janet's care and I could give her, or the police, my information about the heater vent stuffing. In a flash I changed my mind about reporting the stuffing in the heater vent. The nasty piece of evidence would still be there when Myra arrived. I'd point out the obvious to her and let the family handle things from there.

"Ah, I wanted to…that is…when can we arrange to have the body sent home for burial?" I am unaccustomed to such constant fibbing and felt my cheeks redden.

Once more, Deputy Ramey sounded less than pleased. Again, I had interrupted his otherwise important schedule for a mundane matter. In a brusque voice he instructed that I phone the coroner's office. I thanked him and hung up. I certainly don't advocate cops being sent to charm school. But really, couldn't something be done about these major attitude problems?

I soon drove out of the rain pocket, though the sky still held the promise of intense storms and the wind had kicked up. At my exit I turned off the Interstate and headed toward the Knight's Rest with increasing unease. All this thinking about death, of course, was having its effect. But something else nagged at me, something I couldn't quite name. Then it hit me. I remembered what had felt so different about the Winnebago last night.

First of all, when I had waited there for the ambulance to take Janet to the hospital, I noticed that while the whole place was a mess, the aisle of the motor home was clean and free of debris. I surmised this was due to Janet's uneven gait. Her stroke had affected the left side of her body as well as her speech. She would have been unable to negotiate the passageway had there been stacks of papers and trash lying about. Upon my return, the aisle was carelessly strewn with paper and assorted odds and ends, the kind of stuff that takes up residence in the backs of closets or the inaccessible netherworld of bottom drawers.

Second, I remembered that when I reentered the RV yesterday, a half-smoked cigarette lay in a dented tin ashtray on the dinette. The crushed cigarette had not been there before. I was sure of it. But who would have entered the Winnebago while I was with Janet at the hospital? And why?

The Knight's Rest loomed into view, and even as I struggled to make sense of these questions I saw that I had a visitor. A car was parked alongside my rig, a dark sedan with more antennas sticking from its roof than a Channel 4 News truck. A man sat in the driver's seat, door ajar, speaking into a cell phone.

I eased my Honda into a space to the right of the sedan. This vantage point provided a head-on view of the Winnebago. Then I noticed something else. The bit of insulation was no longer in the furnace vent. The thin metal strips were still cut, of course, and still bent upward in the middle. At least I hadn't imagined the whole thing. But what could I tell the police? The chrome-plated furnace vent looked truly innocent, virginal even, empty and glinting in the last of the sunshine. The piece of insulation was nowhere in sight.

As I attempted to absorb this latest discovery, I tried to assess the visitor. The man in the dark sedan was half turned away from me, his face hidden by his large fist and the cell phone. I stepped out of my car, still staring at him. His dark hair was pulled back in a short, unkempt ponytail.

He turned slowly toward me, revealing a man nearer forty than thirty, his hair thinning on top. A non-youthful dissipation pulled at his eyes and mouth. Dark circles underscored his eyes. The dissipation told of indulgences, of one who stays up too late and no longer has the collagen to compensate. He slipped the phone into his pocket and scrutinized me with wide eyes that gave no hint of the owner's emotions.

"I'm looking for the occupants of that RV." He jerked his thumb at the Winnebago. The wind picked up a wisp of his thinning hair.

"What for?" I demanded.

He looked me up and down before responding. "They're relatives," he declared flatly. "No one's in there. My aunt and uncle aren't in the best of health. Anything could have happened. I banged on the door but—" He grimaced as his phone rang again. He answered it, turning away from me.

He cupped his free hand around the phone so it was difficult to hear his actual words, but I could tell by the urgency in his tone that the call was a distressing one. He punched the END button, slid the phone into his pocket and stood glowering at me.

One thing was certain—a fitness freak he was not. He was a tall man, maybe nearing six feet. But years of bad posture had given him prematurely stooped shoulders. His rounded belly protruded below a concave chest. His complexion was the pasty hue of one who has taken Kipling's advice and seldom ventured out in the noonday sun. Incredibly, for this day and age, he wore a plastic protector in the breast pocket of his shirt, which I noted was frayed at the collar. The pocket protector was jammed with ballpoint pens and pencils. The strange man stood there in silent confusion, pale and blinking.

"Did you say aunt and uncle?" I managed

He nodded. "I'm Sonny Witherspoon. Who the hell are you?"

My gasp was audible. I hadn't been able to reach Sonny Witherspoon. I hadn't even left a message on his voice mail. What in heaven's name was he doing here? And how did he find out where "here" was?

"You mixed up with those crazy animal people?" Sonny cocked his head, his eyes narrowed to slits. "You look like the type."

He continued staring, sizing me up. "Where are my aunt and uncle?" Without giving me an opportunity to respond he barked, "You think we don't know what's going on, but let me tell you something. We know. I could have you arrested. In fact, I think I'll do just that." He pulled the phone from his pocket, glaring at me. "Isn't there a law against bilking the elderly?" he asked with barely concealed sarcasm.

"Just a minute, please." Fortunately my voice held firm and didn't betray my apprehension. "First, you have nothing to arrest me for, and second, I'm afraid...well, I'm afraid I have some unpleasant news. You see," I said softly, "your Uncle Claude has passed away." It did not seem an opportune time to mention the word murder.

Sonny's eyebrows shot up. "Oh my God," he moaned. The wind whirled around, kicking up little dust devils at our feet. The bravado went out of him with a whoosh. "Janet! What about my aunt?"

"She'll be fine. She's been hospitalized—"

"You sure we're talking about the same people?" Sonny blurted, taking my elbow and dragging me to the open door of his car. He grabbed a battered appointment book from the passenger seat and slid off the rubber band holding it closed. After fiddling with assorted pieces of paper he extracted a photograph. He held the brownish Polaroid up for me to see. "This the guy you're talking about?"

I could not mistake Claude Witherspoon, even from a photograph taken some years back. "I'm afraid so," I said with as much compassion as I could muster under the circumstances.

Sonny stood there, gaping at me as though the news had not quite sunk in. "Dead?" he asked again. Confusion and shock rounded his eyes and pulled his mouth into an unsightly circle. I was still pressed against the car, his meaty hand on my arm. I reached up and removed his fingers from my flesh, then glanced into the car's interior.

Never had I seen such an assortment of gadgets. Dials and screens and little black boxes were affixed to every available surface of the dash as well as the space between the seats. Sonny apparently subscribed to the same school of housekeeping principles as his older relatives. Trash and debris filled the inside of the sedan. Styrofoam burger boxes and soda cans vied for space with a laptop computer and an old daisy-wheel printer. Reams of computer paper streamed over the floor and seat, the perforations along the side still in place. Old flyers for discounts on hotels in Las Vegas took up much of the passenger seat. Several well-read books littered the floor. I thought I recognized one of them from the visible fraction of the title, written on the spine in gold letters,

*Ainsley's Complete….*something…something.

Just then the rain caught up with us. If we stood here a moment longer, we would be soaked. Lightning flashed several miles in the distance and I didn't like the idea of ending up fried to a crisp mere steps from the Knight's Rest Motel and Café. And I still had to enlist Sonny in getting his aunt Janet out of the hospital, thus relieving myself of responsibility for her further care. "Quick, come with me." I made my way to my own rig. He followed me in.

We stood inside the door shaking off water. When I felt he was dry enough I motioned for him to take a seat on my sofa, a plush tuxedo style with marvelous soft cushions one could get lost in. I sat across from him in the swivel rocker. All that was missing from this cozy scene was a box of Kleenex and my discreet little clock. With them, I could have been back in my office, counseling a client.

Sonny did not utter a word. Like an old mainframe computer, he seemed to be sifting through huge volumes of information. His eyes flicked and his mouth worked as he bit and re-bit his lower lip. Any minute I expected to see little cards with square holes punched in them and emblazoned with the words DO NOT FOLD BEND OR MUTI-LATE come flying from his ears.

He sat slumped on my sofa, forehead propped in his hand. I cleared my throat to get his attention. "Your aunt Janet is resting well in the hospital in Barstow. You'll be pleased to know she'll be released tomorrow." I waited for Sonny to offer a word of relief, or, better yet, a promise to take over from here. I waited in vain.

"Good," he said, then veered off onto a subject of seemingly greater concern to him. "You never answered my question. Are you with those animal fanatics?" he demanded again, looking up. "Because if you are, I can tell you right now we won't stand still for this."

"I'm afraid I have no idea what you're taking about," I answered truthfully. "Hard as this is to believe, I'm merely an old school friend of your aunt. I happened upon her yesterday, here at the Knight's Rest Café." I could tell by the scrunched-up look on Sonny's face he found my story highly unlikely. Come to think of it, who wouldn't? "I'm the one who discovered your uncle's body and notified the police. I also tried to notify your family. I found a number for a Myra Witherspoon-Hampton and telephoned her. I found a number for you, too, but only got through to your voice mail. I didn't leave a message." Now for a question of my own—a big one. "How did you know where to find us?"

"I followed them," he admitted in a matter-of-fact tone. "They thought they had given me the slip, but they underestimated me." As an afterthought, he added, "just like everybody else."

"Tell me more about that," I asked, hoping he would expound on following his aunt and uncle. Now I really was feeling like a therapist again.

Sonny eyed me sourly. "Just like everybody else? Nothing. Really. It's not important." He shifted uneasily on the sofa, drawing his knees up and crossing his arms over his chest. Sonny turned away and stared out at the rain. He muttered, "Man. I do not need this right now," very softly but loud enough that I heard.

Need what? I had to wonder. If anything, Sonny seemed more inconvenienced at his uncle's passing than grief-stricken. Plus, after twenty years in private practice you learn to pick up a few clues and whatever Sonny had meant when he said, "Just like everybody else," his emotion over that circumstance was far from nothing. However, delving into the psyche of Sonny Witherspoon was nowhere on my to-do list today. Getting Janet the help she needed topped the list, followed closely by the enigma of the missing tatter of insulation. "But you admit you followed your aunt and uncle. Why?"

After a pause he responded. "Sure, I followed them. If I didn't take the time and trouble, God only knows what they'd get themselves into. Listen, I've pulled the bacon out of the fire on more than one occasion for those two. Not that anybody else notices or gives a hoot."

"So you're feeling unappreciated by your aunt and uncle?" Oh God, I prayed silently, please let me stop this shrink-talk.

"Unappreciated? You bet I am. If it weren't for me..." his gaze drifted. "And, it's like...like I've got my troubles. I can't. I don't..." He stopped and shook his head. After a brief moment he collected himself and went on. "Somebody has to look out for those two. They have zero ability to care for themselves. Hell, just look at that rusty bucket of bolts they travel in." Sonny swept his arm in a wide gesture. "It's a downright embarrassment. But will they spend the cash for a newer, safer rig? No. Meanwhile, they send out fat checks to one whacked out group or another. All you have to do to get money out of them is come tell some sob story about abused chickens or endangered toads, or some damn thing." Sonny was working himself into a first-class snit. He rambled on, his voice rising in pitch, his face darkening. "Hell, after our parents were killed and my sister and I were sent to live with them they made us buy our clothes at the Goodwill store, if you can believe that. And with all the money they had!"

Sonny's face turned wistful. "I mean, they weren't all bad. They took us in, after all. Fed us. Kept a roof over our heads. It's just that they…they were so…off in their own world."

I must say I did not find his revelations about my sorority sister all that surprising. She had always seemed a bit of an eccentric. I doubted she had the slightest ability to care for children. Still, none of this meant she or her brother deserved to be killed. Sonny rambled on. I tried to head him off at the pass. "So, tell me Sonny, what line of work are you in?"

"Line of work? Uh…I work at home. At the computer. Business investments. You know…stuff like that." Having said this, Sonny continued unabated his tale of self-pity and woe, blaming Janet and Claude for everything from his grades in school to the measles he had come down with when he was nine. I found this difficult to listen to and I probably would have tuned out had he not started in on Myra, my last hope for salvation.

"That bitch," he spat. "If she hadn't started the damn mess, Uncle Claude might—" Sonny stopped in mid-sentence and pressed his lips tightly together as though to prevent further slippage of words. He then looked straight at me. "But, I never answered your question, did I?"

By now, I had forgotten what question I had asked.

"How I found them. Don't you want to know?" Sonny's look changed again, this time to one of pride. "I always find them. No matter where they go in that beat-up old Winnebago, I always know where they are." He smirked, put his hands behind his head and leaned back in a gesture of confidence and relaxation. "There's not an electronic device made I can't build, take apart and operate. Ever hear of an automotive trailing device?" He assessed my face for a response. "I guess not. It's a radio transmitter hidden under the dash of that over-the-hill Winnebago. I have the receiver in my car. I can tell from the signal where they are and how close I am to them. I've come to their rescue more times than I can count. Old fools have no business out on the loose."

"But if that is the case, why weren't you here when...when Claude died?" No sooner was the question out of my mouth than I wished I had not asked it.

Sonny's face closed. He regarded me for a moment without responding. "I followed them to this dump, then left before they could spot me." He experienced a sea change, his face tensed. "I had business to take care of." Suddenly agitated, he drummed his fingers on his thigh and looked toward the door. He was almost on his feet when he blurted, "By the way, how did Uncle Claude die? You never did say."

I explained about the carbon monoxide, leaving out the part about the insulation in the vent.

"Too bad," Sonny said and shook his head. I detected genuine sadness in his eyes. "Though there's worse ways to go, I guess," he added softly.

Nervously, he fished in his shirt pocket, extracted a crumpled pack of cigarettes and stuck one into his mouth. "Got an ashtray?" he asked as he flicked a lighter.

"I don't allow smoking in here," I said, making my voice as pleasant as possible. I'm not one of those tedious reformed smokers who act as though cigarette smoke is an evil on par with the Ebola virus. I merely wish to resist the temptation. Certain activities, once accomplished, need never be repeated. Riding the Superman ride at Magic Mountain comes to mind. Cigarette smoking, unlike amusement park rides, presents the constant threat of another sampling.

Sonny frowned and returned the pack to his pocket. He cocked his head toward the door and listened for a moment. The steady thrum of rain on the fiberglass roof of the RV had quieted to a patter. Suddenly he stood and stretched his arms, wiggling his fingers and shaking them as if shaking off water. He jammed his hands into his pockets, hiking his shoulders in a show of nonchalance. "You find a wallet or anything?"

What a dilemma. Should I tell him about finding the wallet? After all, he was a relative. I decided to go for the stall. "Was Claude carrying a large amount of cash?"

"I don't know for sure. Probably. They stopped at an ATM on the way out of town. I figure he'd have had several hundred on him."

"Well, no," I said slowly, "I didn't find anything like that. Sorry." The wallet I had found was empty. But if the Witherspoons had been traveling with several hundred in cash, what had happened to the money?

Sonny looked dejected, then agitated. "Listen," he said, his eyes darting about. "I gotta go. I've got business." His mind seemed to be spinning, considering options. "What about Aunt Janet?" he blurted suddenly.

At last. The much needed offer of help. I smiled, feeling gracious and glad to have been of assistance. I anticipated the heady rush of tires pulling onto pavement, wheels rolling...on the road again.

"She have any cash on her?" Sonny directed his nervous stare at me. Though startled, I recovered my smile, along with my composure. "Janet took her purse with her to the hospital. I don't think she carried any cash. We searched her bag for her medical identification card."

He wiped his palms on his trousers. After a pause he looked directly at me and said, "Well...what about...ah..." He didn't finish the sentence and after a tense pause he whirled around, opened the door and stepped into the wet night.

I fumbled for a business card from my purse and thrust it toward him.

Without looking, he stuffed the card into his plastic-coated shirt pocket and bounded for his car. "By the way, if anybody comes asking for me," he called over his shoulder, "tell them I'll be back later." He gunned the engine and sped off, sending sprays of gravel flying in his wake.

I stared after him in open-mouthed shock. Had he been about to ask to borrow money from me? And even more deplorable, Sonny Witherspoon had not offered to take over the many details that now required a relative's care. I shook my head at the contradictions. First he follows his aging relatives from Pasadena to the middle of the Mohave, supposedly out of concern for their welfare. Yet now his concern seems focused exclusively on the contents of his deceased uncle's wallet. What a fine mess.

Turning away from the door I spied Otis, his face intent, peddling his bike along the highway. He passed quickly without looking at me but as he passed he raised a fist and shook it threateningly. I hoped Hazel was right. He certainly didn't look or act harmless. I closed the door and locked it after me.

After I recovered from Sonny's visit, I was actually glad he had left. He was hardly my idea of an enjoyable dinner companion. Anyway, I really needed time to think. I also needed time to poke around again in the Winnebago. I was eager to see what else I might find that would shed light on this most peculiar situation. But before I could accomplish either of these my cell phone rang.

Noting the Caller ID, my heart skipped a beat, a tiny one, but a beat nonetheless. "Hi, Ellen," I said warmly, careful to keep my voice even. No sense in spreading false hopes. Or should I say, no sense in encouraging my own feelings toward this petite redhead with the most amazing green eyes. Ellen Littlefield had careened into my life a few short weeks ago and already I was starting to feel my iron resolve melt a tad at the edges.

It had all started out innocently enough. We had both signed up for a watercolor class at the local city recreation program. Turns out we had met a year or two earlier at the home of a mutual friend. I had liked her then, her sense of humor and self-possession. We clicked at once. At that time I was living with Kat, in ignorance to be sure, and Ellen was with someone else. But both our spouses had deserted us—hers for the bar and mine to flirt with a woman golf pro, who appeared to hang on every utterance from Kat's shapely lips. We latched onto each other. As I recall we spent the next three hours virtually glued to each other, laughing and talking just like old friends. This was back in the days when I remained blissfully unaware that Kat was developing quite a reputation as a gigolo, or in this case would it be gigala?

"You in Albuquerque yet?"

"Well, actually I've been detained for a short while." I plunged into the tale of the body in the Winnebago and my involvement. I rattled off the story in great detail, one because I love telling a good tale but also to keep the conversation headed away from the romantic.

Ellen, bless her, stayed right with me. "I'm really sorry about your school chum and her brother. But really Libby, you must be having one amazing adventure—murder, of all things."

"Yes, I'm afraid so. And it looks like I may get stuck here for a while. At least until the family arrives to take charge of matters."

"I don't like the sound of this one bit. I'd be happy to jump in the car and meet you. Sometimes adventures are more…ah…adventuresome when shared. Besides, capable as I know you to be, this situation could prove dangerous. I could be there in a couple of hours."

Ellen's proposal was not an unpleasant one. She was quick and energetic with a seemingly inexhaustible supply of energy. She might be invaluable in sorting out all the pieces to the puzzle here at the Knight's Rest. But beyond that she was also someone I was starting to care for and caring for someone—anyone—was not in my Day Planner. Nope. Not just yet. Truth to tell, I was running away from involvement just as surely as I had run smack into a murder mystery at this derelict, near-deserted motel.

"That's very thoughtful of you, Ellen. But no. Don't come. I doubt I'm in any danger. I'm sure one of the relatives will arrive before you could get here. And I really do want to travel on to Albuquerque." I heard her sigh of disappointment. "And remember the real reason for this trip. I need to sort out my feelings. I care about you, Ellen. Really I do. It's just that—"

"Just that the ghost of the ever-fabulous Kat still hangs around you like a mantle."

"If that's how you want to put it. But fifteen years of living with someone, trusting them—it isn't easy to pick up and go on from there. Particularly for the leavee."

"It's OK, Libby. I know what you're feeling and what you're going to say. So save it and just know that I think you are the most wonderful woman to have entered my life in…let's see now…how about ever. I'll be here when you get back. We'll have dinner and talk. No pressure, OK? Meanwhile, for your own sake, I'd really feel better if you weren't stranded out there in the middle of the Mohave desert with a killer on the loose."

"It'll only be for a while. Like I said, just until someone else shows up to take over Janet's care. I'm sure I'm perfectly safe. And, about that dinner. I'd love it," I said evenly, for it was the truth. And if things proceeded as before I knew the dinner and talk would lead to more, and that thought sent a frisson of pleasure shooting through my body. I hung up after promising to call and let her know how my investigation turned out. I held the tiny phone to my ear long after the connection went dead, imagining I heard her musical voice with the slight Southern accent still echoing inside the phone. I lay the phone down and thought for a moment. Maybe Ellen was right. I should just pack it in and get out of here.

I got up and paced the length of the coach. Stay? Go? What to do? Finally I squared my shoulders and with all my might directed my attention back to the problems at hand.

Nothing like the open road, a little time to oneself and a good mystery to solve to get one's head straightened out about one's love life.

CHAPTER FOUR

I heard a story once about an entire family killed when lightning struck their travel trailer. An urban legend? Probably. Surely the tires would have provided protection. The family was asleep at the time, or so the story goes. At least there's that. Still, lightning storms—and this one was turning out to be a doozy—give me the jitters.

When I stepped out to go next door to the Winnebago, I noticed the worst of one storm had passed, but another front was gathering strength in the western sky.

Before beginning a further look around, I wanted to stop by the motel office and inquire about a room. The Knight's Rest was hardly my idea of cozy quarters, but neither was I foolish enough to risk high winds, a possible madman on the loose and certainly not the threat of electrocution. I could put up with a lumpy mattress and a thin chenille bedspread for a night or two, just until the storm was over. Or until Myra arrived to take charge of Janet, whichever came first.

Later I could phone Sudie and fill her in on my adventure. I realized, with no small amount of disappointment, that I might miss the Balloon Festival and a fun time with my chums altogether this year. This turn of events created a big problem in regard to an article I had promised to write for *RV Travel* magazine. One of my justifications, as if I needed one, for all this freewheeling is that I'm a travel writer wanna-be. I have contracted with a monthly magazine devoted to RV travel to produce a series of articles for them, little tales of the places I visit in my Airstream. My piece on the Balloon Festival was due by November first. What could I possibly find to write about out here on the remains of old Route 66?

I stepped into the motel office and rang the bell at the desk. After a moment, Hazel Tutt surged into the doorway separating the office from the living quarters. "You're just the gal I want to talk to," she huffed before I had a chance to utter a word. "You got to move them rigs. I don't allow no boondocking here. Might give the place a bad name." She did not so much as crack a smile as she said this. She looked at me, her hands on her hips. "And just what the hell is goin' on out there in my parking lot? Cars are wheelin' in and out at all hours of the day and night. You folks havin' a party? And as if that ain't bad enough, I must'a had fifty people out here gawking and asking questions 'cause they saw the ambulance and the sheriff at my place. Guess you could say there ain't a hell of a lot to do out here." Hazel almost smiled.

But how many cars constitute a party? I counted my car, the sheriff's. And Sonny's, of course. Perhaps Hazel was counting the six-cylinder job, the driver of which remained a mystery. "I...uh—"

Hazel cut me off in mid-stammer. "And, one of you people stiffed me for pie and coffee. That ain't right. So, like I said, either pay for a room and move them rigs up to the motel or move 'em out. Pronto."

"Actually, the reason I'm here is I'd like a room." Sonny Witherspoon took another dive in my estimation. How much could a cup of coffee and a slab of pie have cost him? "I assume you take cash."

Hazel grabbed a ledger book from under the counter and pretended to study the pages. "You're in luck. I happen to have a room. How long are you stayin'?"

"Only a night or two." I prayed this information would prove correct. What possible method of transportation was Myra using? A camel? The image of Myra Witherspoon-Hampton sashaying into town on the back of a camel brought forth a giggle.

But my mirth was quickly dissipated by Hazel's gravelly voice. "That'll be eighty dollars. Paid in advance."

Eighty dollars! Highway robbery took on a new and much deeper meaning than ever before. I've stayed in four-star Hilton's for less. And at least they have decent restaurants, or most of them. Of course, no Hilton's were situated in the area; no Motel 6s either. In fact, even a good RV resort probably couldn't be found within fifty miles. So the Knight's Rest it was, whatever the cost. I fished the bills from my wallet and handed them over. Hazel might as well have been standing there in a black mask holding a gun to my head.

She accepted the cash, then leaned toward me over the counter. She had been eating onions. "The old guy croaked, eh? I hope to hell there wasn't no foul play. Thing like that gets around and it's bad for business. But we see everything out here, believe you me." Hazel sucked her lips together and nodded gravely. "What happened?"

"Unfortunately, Mr. Witherspoon succumbed to carbon monoxide poisoning in his rig yesterday. The family is on their way to take care of the details. I'm only here until they arrive. Janet is in the hospital. Oh, did I tell you it turns out we are old college chums?"

Just then I heard a wet, snuffling, half-growling sound, much like the soggy gurgling emitted by someone with an extreme case of sinusitis. In another instant, the source of the sound ambled through the door from the living quarters and plopped herself down right at my feet. The dog, all fifty or so pounds of her, leaned against my leg and peered up at me. I was convinced the creature was something dreamed up by Maurice Sendak for his flamboyant fantasy Where the Wild Things Are. When she yawned and smacked her considerable chops, I was sure of it. I laughed out loud. "Is this a bulldog?" I asked.

"Yep. Her name is Sugar. You want her?"

Want her? Heavens no. I grinned down on her. She was cute, in a bulldoggy kind of way. I couldn't help but smile on looking into that pushed-in face. Sugar was solid white but for a dark brindle ring around her right eye. But I'm not really ready to accept that much responsibility...or even let myself care that much about something. Not right now. I reached down and petted her massive head. I could have sworn she grinned up at me. "Why are you giving her away?"

"Oh, she's not mine. Some trucker left her here over a month ago.

Just checked out and was gone. Poor Sugar. She's been lookin' out my front window ever since, especially when an eighteen wheeler pulls up out there."

"Well, thanks, but no thanks. A dog is the last thing I need, believe me. I'm just not ready..." I was on the verge of explaining all about how I had lost track of my heart back when Kat took off for parts too well known, at least by her. I stopped myself just in time. "I'm sure you'll find someone to take good care of her. She's very cute in an 'only a face a mother could love' kind of way."

"Suit yourself," Hazel said. "But I think you're missin' a good thing." She shrugged and turned her attention back to the business at hand. "The guy died of carbon monoxide, eh? Gotta watch them geezers. See it all the time. Shouldn't let 'em on the road, you ask me. Menace to transportation." Despite the callousness of her remark, I had to admit that in the case of Janet and Claude Witherspoon she probably had a point.

I signed the register and turned to leave. "Hazel," I said after a pause, "one more thing. Are you sure that Otis character is harmless? Has he actually gotten aggressive with anyone? He seems very hostile. Each time I see him he gets angry and shakes his fist at me. Not an altogether reassuring gesture, I must admit."

"I know. He's a bit much, isn't he? Sorry he scared you. I'll try and have a talk with him. Don't know how much good it'll do, though. Not a lot gets through to him, if you know what I mean." Hazel shook her head. After a pause she said, "He's not really mad at you. He's got the notion that them big rigs, eighteen wheelers and big RVs like yours, interfere with his reception. You know, from the space aliens. It gets him upset."

"Oh I see. Then there's not much that can be done, is there? Poor fellow. How does he live? Who supports him?"

"He gets a government check, I think. He's a vet. Came back from 'Nam all messed up. To make ends meet he sets up a little stand down the road a ways. He sells rocks he claims the aliens have written on. Crazy designs—that kinda thing. Once in a while a gullible tourist buys one. Can't imagine he makes very much. I feed him sometimes, give him pocket change to sweep up. Stuff like that. Don't worry. He wouldn't hurt a fly." Hazel signaled an end to this conversation by turning back toward the living quarters, Sugar on her heels. "And remember, no wild parties. It a rule."

I'll try and restrain myself, I muttered as I turned to go, still thinking about Otis. At the hospital where I interned we saw many cases of Post Traumatic Stress Disorder, though this diagnosis failed to calm me. Moving the rigs proved no problem. The key was still in the ignition of the Winnebago and it started right up, which was a mercy. My Airstream and the ancient Winnebago now sat side by side in front of cabin number four, my temporary home.

The room was everything I had dreaded, and more. The blond veneer on the dresser had cigarette burns along the edge and had peeled off in big patches on the top. The bed was, indeed, covered by a thin chenille spread, dusty pink when new, now faded to dull beige. One chair, of a style popular in the fifties, sat beside a round table, its lime green cover dotted with cigarette burns. Needless to say, no miniature bottles of shampoo, no in-room coffee service and no TV were in evidence. The place smelled of decades of smoke and mildew.

I don't care much for motels and stay at them infrequently. They seem so universally utilitarian and impersonal. And the breakfast bars! I could lapse into a sugar-induced coma just thinking of those trays of gooey pastries. I sighed and transferred a few necessities to my room. I always keep a smallish shoulder bag packed for just such an emergency. It contains the usual toiletries, a change of clothes and a toothbrush. I also stock a battery-powered hairdryer in there, which I have been meaning to remove. My hair, unlike the wig I had worn for several months, doesn't require styling. But I had paid a lot of money for the contraption and, after buying it from a specialty catalog, have never seen another like it. Maybe one day I'll feel in the mood for longer hair.

I liked the bag so much; I bought two of them when I found them on sale one day at Macy's. The bags are about eighteen by twenty inches in size with zipper pockets on each side and a choice of shoulder strap or carrying handles, making it more of a brief case. I use one for emergency motel stopovers and the other as my everyday handbag. The only way I can tell them apart is that the everyday one has a little scratch on the imitation alligator covering and the one I use for emergencies is still in pristine condition.

I still thought it a good idea to conduct a renewed search of the Winnebago, having doubtless overlooked something important the first time. The accordion case containing the jumble of Janet's and Claude's papers was still in my Airstream. I planned to rummage around in hope of finding other clues, then take whatever I found to my room along with the file and give the whole shebang a good going-over.

Janet and her recently deceased brother must have had a reason for traveling along this deserted stretch of highway—perhaps not a very good one, but a reason nonetheless. And why were Sonny and Myra so upset about a group of animal lovers? Those who gave succor to pets and wildlife in need were the most harmless, gentle people you could find, at least those I knew anything about. The biggest question, of course, was why Claude Witherspoon lay cooling on a slab in the Barstow coroner's office, his poor sister hospitalized and no one around to help.

The Winnebago batteries were holding up nicely—better than I, truth be told. The task of searching the rig was daunting, though. I was surprised afresh at how much junk two people could cram into such a limited space. I stood in the middle and looked around, then lifted a corner of a magazine stack here, brushed aside a pile of debris there.

After several minutes I had turned up nothing of importance, but had realized something new about myself. I found creeping about where I didn't exactly belong—on a mission, as it were, searching for important information—oddly satisfying. Perhaps I should have considered a career with the CIA. Or, even better, maybe I'm another Mata Hari, just now realizing espionage, not travel writing, is my true second-wind career. Perhaps I could hire myself out to foreign governments, preferably those with tropical climates, beautiful seashores and miles of bougainvillaea dripping from quaint balconies. A beautiful blonde knocks on my tropical motel room…a fan turns slowly overhead. I see her silhouette through the slatted blinds. "Stop, stop," I said aloud to myself. "Enough of this."

As if on cue there came a mighty knock at the door. "Open this door," commanded a female voice.

I obliged instantly, flung open the door and stood gaping at the slim figure of a heavily made-up woman, dressed to the nines in safari clothing. Abercrombie and Fitch would be my guess, or maybe Banana Republic. A canteen hung from the webbed belt at her waist. The only accessory not in evidence was a pith helmet. And the camel, of course.

"I'm Myra Witherspoon-Hampton," the voice announced through lips painted a violent red. "Who the hell are you?"

I knew, beyond all doubt, that the clothing was brand new and the only safari the wearer had ever undertaken was to the furthest reaches of some remote discount mall. Myra Witherspoon-Hampton's arrival had obviously been delayed by the need to purchase proper attire for her trek into the Mohave.

While just who the hell I was should have been obvious, I nonetheless answered politely and moved aside, allowing Myra to enter. Despite her jarring first impression, I was more than relieved to see her.

She swept past me in a cloud of leather lace-up boots polished to a gleaming sheen and clothing with enough pockets to hold provisions for a family of four. I took a closer look at my visitor as she surveyed the motor home. Even through the thick make-up, and despite it, she was pretty in the classical sense. Of course, she was Janet's niece and Janet, in her day, had possessed that same regal beauty. Myra's face was still beautiful but was marred both by the pounds of pancake and the hardened lines around her mouth. She wore her mink brown hair in a pageboy, the ends of which danced merrily at her shoulders when she moved, a sight entirely inconsistent with the rest of her.

"My God," she muttered. "How can anyone live like this? Old fools." She spun around to face me, her voice marinated in vinegar. "Just why the hell are you interfering in affairs that don't concern you? And where the hell is Aunt Janet?" Myra spat these questions while her eyes wildly searched the musky interior. She brought her gaze back and focused on me. "You'd better pray she is unharmed."

"What?" I practically staggered away from her. "I really don't—"

"Oh don't pull that innocent routine on me, my girl. How can you expect me to believe some cockamamie story about sorority sisters and chance meeting in the middle of the Mohave? Please! I know you are connected to those animal fanatics somehow."

Clearly I was failing miserably at establishing credibility with Myra, a situation that held scant promise of improvement. Not the best moment to bring up my suspicions of murder. "I'm sorry. I really don't know what you're talking about. Both you and your brother have mentioned an animal rights group. Believe me—"

"Brother! Brother? Sonny was here?" Myra's eyes narrowed to dangerous slits and her breath began coming in short inhalations.

"Why, yes. Not for very long. But he was here. He didn't say when, or if, he would be returning."

Myra held her gaze on me for a long moment before asking, "Did he take anything from this repugnant contraption they call a recreational vehicle?" Myra never took her eyes from mine. She fairly glittered from all the steel in her eyes.

"I really couldn't say," I explained. "He spent most of his time with me in my motor home. I guess he could have though I'm fairly sure he left empty-handed."

Myra allowed her face to relax just the tiniest bit. "My dear brother is a—a screw-up—as you doubtless noticed. Him and his big mouth." Myra said this last more to herself than to me. "How I would love to get my hands around his geeky neck."

"What do you mean?" I hoped my voice conveyed only wide-eyed innocence.

Myra opened her mouth to answer, and then slammed it shut. She stood glaring at me. "Hah! As if you didn't know."

"I don't. Honestly. Clearly you don't believe me, but I really am a sorority sister of Janet's. It's sheer luck I happened to stop here—"

"Whatever." Myra dismissed my explanation with a shrug. "In any case, what happened back home, what Sonny did, is none of your god-damned business."

She contorted her face in what she must have thought was an appeasing smile. "Have you come across a file of documents?"

I shook my head vigorously. I intended to pore over the accordion file of papers myself—without Myra. So far, no one in Janet's family struck me as trustworthy. And, as little as I knew of Myra, I felt I was still the person with the most objectivity about Janet's situation. Plus, and this was a big one, I had the least to gain or lose from whatever the papers might reveal. I'd just keep my mouth shut. Keeping my mouth shut has never been my strong suit, of course. But in my current predicament, keeping mum was getting easier and easier as time progressed.

"My driver is waiting and I have to find a folder of important documents."

I peered out the door. The rain was coming down again. Sure enough, a battered taxi sat outside, engine running, belching exhaust. The driver sat scrunched down in the seat, a bottle of cheap tequila tilted toward his lips. He grinned at me and raised his fingers in a V for Victory sign. I could make out the name of the cab company written in badly faded letters on the door panel, Friendly Cab, though not their place of business. If Myra had engaged the cab in Pasadena, the driver had no doubt scored the biggest fare of his career. I doubted, however, that he could count on a substantial tip.

Just at that moment, the taxi's engine emitted a low coughing sound, shuddered twice then sputtered to a standstill.

The driver got out and flipped the hood, only to stand there scratching his head of curly black hair and peering into the nether reaches of the taxi's engine compartment. At length, he aimed a kick at the nearest tire and wobbled unsteadily toward the Knight's Rest Café.

"You're driver isn't going anywhere." I announced. "—for some time."

"Good. Then you'll help me? I must find that file of papers. If I find what I am looking for I'll give you a tip for your...ah...your services. I'll start in the kitchen. You take the bedroom."

Myra must have forgiven my supposed association with the animal rights group—forgetting I'm neither her servant nor her housekeeper. But since a search of the rig had been my intention in the first place, I decided to let her bad manners go without remark. "No problem," I sang out and headed for the cramped and dingy bedroom, thinking of Myra's offer of a tip. My emotions swung between anger and amusement and finally stuck on the latter. Myra was merely a product of her class, carrying her *noblesse oblige* around with her like an extra suit of clothing.

Myra scuffled about the other room, emitting occasional grunts of distaste. The lack of cleanliness and the disarray clearly presented problems for her. Understandable. I poked about, pulling out drawers from the built-in bureau to find nothing but old underwear, T-shirts and socks. On the top stretched a veritable mini-Walgreen's of half-squeezed tubes, pills, salves and assorted balms so indicative of the elderly or infirm.

I was thoroughly caught up in the search when a bloodcurdling scream reverberated through the Winnebago.

In a heartbeat, I was standing in the small, untidy kitchen where Myra, lace-up boots beating a tattoo on the seat of the dinette, her hands fluttering beside her ruby red face, screamed, "Oh my God. Please, somebody help me."

I looked around for the cause of such profound discomfort but could see nothing amiss.

"There!" Myra managed between choking sobs. She aimed one well-manicured finger at the floor. "Don't you see it?" Her pageboy fell across her face in the style of a '40s movie star. "Quick. Do something!"

I looked harder and at last saw the cause of the fuss. A dead roach lay sprawled on the dirty linoleum. No surprise, except that I hadn't stumbled across one sooner. The Winnebago was surely a veritable beacon for hungry vermin of all kinds.

I grabbed a paper towel from the roll above the sink, knelt down and gathered up the deceased insect. Then, and only then, did Myra cease her wailing.

Myra extended her hand, indicating she wished help in stepping down from the dinette's bench seat. She stepped onto the floor gingerly, a look of disgust still plastered on her face. "I simply cannot go through with this. It's too…too distasteful. My nerves are a wreck. You may continue. I'll send my driver in to assist you. When you find something, let me know. I'll be waiting in the car."

At the door Myra looked in astonishment at the empty cab, then snapped, "I thought I told you to have my driver wait."

"I did. I believe you'll find him in the café."

Without a word, but with a scornful look over her shoulder, Myra stepped into the drizzle and headed for the eatery.

I was eager to be gone from the messy RV. I could think of no other place where something of interest could hide. My head ached, probably from all that I didn't yet understand. I felt sure the papers in the accordion file would tell an interesting tale and I relished the notion of further snooping.

CHAPTER FIVE

"Are you out of your mind?" Sudie has never been known to mince words and didn't bother to do so now. Okay, for one thing, I hadn't called as scheduled. Secondly, the path I trod diverged radically, yet again, from that which Sudie considered acceptable. "You're where?" Her voice rose in tone with each succeeding question.

I explained about finding a college sorority sister out on old Route 66. I then told her of Claude's unfortunate demise, and about the weird cast of characters that had pranced onto the stage in the last few hours. Oddballs, the lot of them.

To her credit, Sudie listened to the entire tale, right up to the point where I explained my suspicion about Claude's death. At that revelation, she let fly with, "I shudder inwardly...thinking of you there...vulnerable. A girl, really, facing the reality of her aloneness..."

Right away I knew that Sudie was working on a new romance novel. I cut her off mid-gush. "Sudie. Stop it. I can hardly be called a girl these days. Besides, I can take care of myself. Really I can. It's just that I needed to vent. Can't you give me some feedback that isn't tinged purple?"

Sudie laughed, her throaty rich laugh born of decades of cigarette smoking. "Sorry, Sis. Got carried away. My best advice is to flee. Leave the detective work to those who are paid for such tasks. Speaking of detectives, is there one on this case? Is she cute?"

"Sudie! Really!" Even when Sudie isn't talking like a romance writer, she's thinking like one. "I refuse to turn into the plot of your next book. I can do without the complications of love, believe me."

"Bah! That blonde bitch has been gone for over a year now. You have got to wake up and smell the—"

"Thanks for listening, Sudie. Gotta go." I hung up before she could finish her sentence. My sister has made no secret of her feelings for my former domestic partner. Even with the attempted matchmaking, though, I was glad I had called. I felt better having unburdened myself. The last twenty-four hours had been more trying than I'd realized.

Now I stared at the accordion file that sat on my bed and then eased down alongside that much-traveled folder. I rotated my rump on the mattress, positioning myself between several large lumps. As soon as I was moderately comfortable, I opened the case to the As and began to sort through a jumble of papers. I would have enjoyed having a radio, or even a TV, to give some background noise. As it was, only the sound of the rain on the roof and the occasional boom of distant thunder disturbed the silence.

The moment I found a recipe for German chocolate cake filed in the As, along with a set of instructions for playing the harmonica, I realized that Janet and Claude made use of a filing system understood only to them. Not surprisingly, given the givens, the task of snooping through the file of papers might take longer than I had first imagined. What I really wanted to discover was anything related to animal rights groups, and any organization Janet and Claude might have supported or belonged to. I remembered the brochure describing the Friends in Need Sanctuary and wondered if that was the group the younger Witherspoon family members had taken a lunatic stance against.

I didn't have to wait long for my answer. Filed neatly in the Ds was a folded newspaper article from the *Los Angeles Times,* dated just two months earlier. WITHERSPOON FORTUNE GOING TO THE DOGS, the article's headline announced. The news story went on to report that Janet and Claude Witherspoon, heirs to the Witherspoon lumber fortune, planned to bequeath a sizeable portion of their estate to the Friends in Need Animal Sanctuary. The article explained that the Witherspoons, brother and sister, had been supporters of the sanctuary for a number of years and had recently changed their wills in order to provide ongoing support for their favorite charity after their demise.

The next to last paragraph of the article was most enlightening.

The reporter stated that over the years the Witherspoon fortune had dwindled, due in large measure to inattention toward financial matters. What had once been an estate counted in the tens of millions was now worth only a fraction of that amount, possibly as little as five to six million.

The last paragraph stated that the heirs had taken the news of the bequest badly and vowed a court battle to protect their interests in the remaining estate.

I folded the newspaper on my lap. The article certainly explained the anger Sonny and Myra had displayed toward the animal rights cause. While the sum might be paltry compared to the earlier amount, still five million dollars was hardly to be viewed as petty cash. Murders have been committed for far less.

My suspicion of the younger Witherspoons started to grow with each passing moment. But why would they have to resort to murder? Wills, by all accounts, had already been changed, and so killing them would hardly alter the consequent beneficiaries. Maybe Sonny was just angry. Maybe Myra needed her share of the estate in a hurry. Maybe, maybe, maybe.

Much as I dreaded doing it, I knew I must notify Ramey. This time I would not chicken out with some lame excuse like concern for shipping the body home. This time I would simply bite the bullet and explain, clearly and in a rational voice, that I was calling to report a murder.

I picked up my cell phone and dialed the number on the card that he had given me. When he answered, I willed my emotions to remain calm. No one likes to do or say something that will make her look foolish, but the time had come. "I believe Claude Witherspoon may have been murdered," I blurted out, fully expecting a hearty male guffaw from the other end of the line.

Instead, my remark was greeted with silence. I bit my lip and refused to say another word until Ramey acknowledged my allegation. I knew I would be able to tell by the tone of his voice whether I was to be an object of ridicule or taken seriously. To my everlasting relief, he merely asked, in a businesslike tone, "Tell me why you believe he was murdered."

I explained about the heater vent and about the little protective strips over the opening that had been cut.

Ramey said he would drive out shortly and have a look. "And don't touch anything," he admonished. "Leave the insulation just where you found it."

"Oh dear, well, you see...that's the problem—the piece of insulation is missing." I swallowed and plunged ahead. "Someone removed it while I was visiting Janet at the hospital."

"Who?"

"Janet Witherspoon. You remember, my...uh...sister."

"No, I mean who removed the insulation?"

"Well, I haven't the faintest idea. It was there when I left and gone when I got back."

Ramey sighed. "Just leave everything as it is and I'll come out there as soon as I can." He hung up and I plopped back on the bed, immeasurably relieved to have made the call and to have had my information taken seriously.

Now that I had made the call to the sheriff, the time was right to confront Myra. She was doubtless waiting for me over at the café. She of all people should be aware of the possibility of foul play in her uncle's death. Sonny might have provided a more sympathetic ear, but he was nowhere in sight. Myra would have to do. Surely the sheriff would want to interview her. And I had a personal agenda operating here as well. Myra had another important role to fill and fill quickly. Janet was due to be checked out of the hospital tomorrow. Thus far, not one member of her family had so much as mentioned what to do about her.

The rain had turned the parking lot into a muddy lake. I hopped and sidestepped the deeper puddles on my way over to the café. I had last seen Myra as she splashed across the lot in search of her erstwhile cabbie.

Dark clouds still roiled overhead, though the rain had stopped for the moment. The leaden sky blotted out sunlight and bestowed upon the afternoon the look and feel of evening. Doubtless to combat the early darkness, the neon sign over the café was already lit, a tacky pink glow projected onto the afternoon gloom.

As I entered the café I saw at once that the sign was not the only thing lit. Myra sat at the counter with the cabbie, glasses of cola in front of them, soda generously spiked, I feared, with tequila. Myra leaned into her driver, one arm resting across his shoulder. Her mascara had run. Her violent red lipstick was more in evidence on his shirt and neck than on her lips. She was in the throes of a drunken ramble about the difficulty of finding people one could trust.

An Elvis Presley tune floated out of the jukebox as Hazel Tutt stood glowering behind the counter. What a tableau. If only Edward Hopper could have wandered in at just that moment we might all have become famous.

I remained in the doorway for a second, not sure exactly how to proceed. It was painfully obvious that Myra was in no condition to have a conversation, let alone figure out what to do with her aunt. And given Myra's state of insobriety, the subject of murder seemed a less than prudent topic for discussion.

When I plopped onto the vinyl stool at the end of the counter, Hazel strode over and I ordered coffee. Myra had hardly noticed me, engrossed as she was in the curly-headed cab driver and her running commentary on trustworthiness.

After Hazel brought my coffee, she stood towering over me, her arms crossed in front of her chest. Finally she nodded in the direction of the lovebirds. "They with you?"

"Not really. You see, the woman, Myra, is the niece of the dead man. She's the one I've been waiting for. She's here to help with all the, um, you know, details."

"Yeah, I can see that." Hazel frowned. "Well, detail this. I ain't servin' no more cokes to them two. I seen 'em pouring booze into them drinks. You gotta get 'em outta here."

"Me? I hardly know the woman."

"She's with your group, ain't she?"

"We're not exactly a group, as you call it."

"Call it whatever you please. Just tell your friend and her friend they can't stay in here no more. Fact is, I'm closing up. Weather like this, won't get no business anyhow."

I looked again at Myra and her paramour. They were deep into a boozy, half-slurred conversation on the virtues of truth and the importance of total honesty in human relationships. Myra was clearly a woman with a raging alcohol problem and the acting-out manners of an alley cat. A not uncommon problem, especially among adults who, as children, weren't given enough nurturing. Now that made sense.

"Myra," I said loudly and leaned forward over the counter.

Myra lifted her eyes and attempted to focus them. "Well, well. Look what we have here." Her mouth opened in a big red slash; lipstick had found its way on to her front teeth. "If it ishn't little Mish Busybody." She listed dangerously on the stool. "Or is it Mish SPCA." She leveled her gaze. "You know what I think, Miss SPCA. Screw Bambi. And screw Flipper. In fact, screw all the furry little creatures. There are legitimate uses for money and saving the whales is not among them."

Myra's comment proved irresistibly funny to her. She slapped the cabbie on the back until he, too, found the comment amusing.

Hazel interrupted their merriment. "The two of you gotta get outta here. Now. You owe me five dollars and fifty cents for the cokes. Pay up and scram."

The cabbie stood, Myra still wound around him like a kudzu vine. He paid Hazel and staggered in the direction of the exit. With one hand on the doorknob, he paused and peered out at the gathering darkness. He then grinned and murmured into Myra's neck, "Oops, I forgot. My cab's not running. Think it might be the distributor cap. Can't get it fixed now. Guess we'll have to take a room." He winked and turned to Hazel. Myra, still clinging to the cabbie for support, said unevenly, "I'll remove my aunt from these disgusting premises...uh...tomorrow."

Despite Myra's epithet, not one to spurn a business opportunity when she saw one, Hazel quoted a price for the room. Another eighty dollars in the till. Business was looking up at the Knight's Rest.

I realized with dismay that with the café closing, getting a meal would not be easy, and I was hungry. I could have prepared something in my RV, as a supply of propane kept my refrigerator good and cold. But Hazel had said no boondocking and I had no question but that she meant what she said.

I searched the food cases behind the counter for something I could possibly take to my room. A lone piece of rubbery lemon meringue pie leaked a thin yellowish liquid onto its saucer. Beside the pie stood a few small cans of grapefruit juice. Neither looked appetizing—certainly not in combination.

Hazel was giving the counter a vigorous wiping. I took a sip of the coffee. "I know you are about to close, but I wondered if I could order something here for supper. Something quick."

Hazel gave me one of her now famous glares. "I just wanted those two drunks out of here. The way they carried on made me sick to my stomach."

"It was a bit much," I agreed. "Could I see a menu?"

"That ain't the way it works around here. You eat what I got the fixin's for. And today I got the fixin's for osso buco and a salad of baby greens with a mustard vinaigrette dressing."

But for good manners, my jaw would have dropped straight to the floor. Hazel a gourmet cook? "That will be just fine," I said, and covered a smile by wiping my lips with a paper napkin. Hazel's menu sounded luscious and I quickly realized I was not just hungry, but utterly famished.

Hazel topped off my coffee and disappeared into the tiny kitchen. Soon the sound of banging pans and rattling cutlery, interspersed with Hazel's epithets, came from the chef's workroom. The delicious aroma of sautéed garlic and a bouquet of good cooking smells followed.

When dinner preparation was well under way, Hazel reappeared, red-faced and sweating. She took a seat at the little counter two stools down from me and mopped her brow. "Whew. Hotter 'n Hades in there."

"Hmmmm. Dinner smells wonderful," I offered. For the first time in my experience Hazel actually smiled. "I don't mean to pry, Hazel, but I confess I'm a little surprised to find such epicurean fare in, well...such an out-of-the-way place."

Hazel's smile widened. "I reckon you would be. Hell, when I think about it, so am I." She actually allowed herself a little laugh. She hitched her thumb at the chalkboard with the day's menu scrawled on it in pink chalk—chili with beans, burgers and fries, and the special of the day, lemon meringue pie.

"Right after me and the old man bought this place, I figured out that there ain't much to do around here. One day I saw an ad for a gourmet cookin' class. You could take it by correspondence. Signed myself right up. At least learnin' about veal marsala and crème brûlée would give me somethin' to do."

I was charmed by Hazel's ingenuity. "How do you come by your ingredients? I doubt you have a Dean and DeLucca anywhere near here."

"Mail order, some of 'em. I drive to L.A. once a month or so and buy stuff, too. Thank God for my big ole' freezer." Hazel grinned again. "Not that I have to buy that much. Seems I'm the only one who likes to eat my cookin'. I tried fixin' fancy food for the customers. But wouldn't nobody around here eat any of it."

Hazel snorted and shook her head sadly. "Would you believe I made steak tartar the very first night I opened and a couple of diners sent it back to the kitchen sayin' I forgot to cook the special of the day. One other guy asked where was the tartar sauce and made me bring him some, then slathered it over the entrée before eating it. I pretty much gave up."

I thought I saw a touch of sadness around Hazel's dark eyes as she cast her glance around the dim café. "I'm cookin' tonight because cookin' gives me somethin' to do besides stare up and down this empty old road." No question about it. Her voice sounded melancholy. "And there's another reason, too," Hazel said but did not elaborate.

"Do you feel like talking about it?" I asked automatically. You can take the girl out of the profession—

Hazel bit her lower lip and twisted a paper napkin around her fingers. "Man trouble," she said, finally.

Uh oh. Now I had asked for it. Hazel's trouble could be unrequited love, a two-timing lover or an abusive relationship. Any decent psychologist worth her hourly fee of one-hundred and fifty dollars an hour would realize that the forthcoming tale could easily consume months of fifty-minute appointments. I only had till dinner was over. "What sort of man trouble?" I supposed it would take longer than a few months, however, to shed my own conditioned responses. Oh well, I was getting tired of dwelling on the fate of the Witherspoons. And dinner smelled wonderful.

"It's Billy Ray." Hazel dabbed at an offending tear with her napkin. "I love that man like a twister loves a trailer park." She smiled a wry smile. "I just can't stay away from him. Trouble is, he seems to be able to stay away from me just fine. This here," she swept her arm toward the simmering osso buco, "this here dinner was all for him. But do you see him anywhere? Not a chance. He just glides in when he feels like it. And if he don't, well, I've had to eat a pretty fair number of nice meals alone. He just ain't trustworthy."

"I'm sorry," I said lamely. Several shrink-type questions begged to be asked, but I quickly discarded them. After all, she was only giving me dinner.

"And it'd be hard to miss him if he was here," Hazel went on as if I had not spoken. "He weighs over three hundred pounds." She giggled like a schoolgirl. "Lots of man to love, I say."

"So, do you and Billy Ray own this place together?"

"Oh, hell no. I just met him a couple of months ago. He owns a mechanic shop over in Ludlow."

It seemed a perfect time to ask a question of Hazel, something I had wondered about. Besides, I wanted to change the subject. "So, Hazel, how did you come to operate the Knight's Rest? This life must be fairly lonely for you."

"Oh, it's a long story," she answered with a sigh, rising from her perch on the stool. "Fell in love with an old rounder and got talked into buyin' this dump. They were sellin' it dirt cheap, too, believe you me. The old bastard said we would get rich. Ha. That's a laugh and a half." She started off for the kitchen. "Anyways, he up and died and here I am, still trying to make a buck offa' the place."

Hazel disappeared into the kitchen and reappeared moments later bearing a bottle of good Merlot, two glasses and a gorgeous salad of baby greens, radicchio and tangerine segments. Now I was truly amazed, but sad for Hazel and her solitary cuisine.

"Somethin' I been meanin' to ask you," Hazel said and poured two glasses of the dark wine. She put one hand to her unruly hair and peered at me. "How did you decide to cut your hair that short? Like a boy's. Looks good, mind you. It's just I been thinking of cuttin' mine off, too. Can't quite get up the nerve though."

"Simple, really. Nothing like a little chemotherapy to take the decision out of your hands."

"Oh, God. I'm sorry." Hazel looked stricken. "You gonna be all right?"

People have the oddest reactions to the discovery that a person has had cancer. Some melt into the woodwork and disappear as soon as the dreaded word is uttered. Others act as though they want to wrap you head to toe in bunting cloth to prevent so much as a jostle or a scratch. "So far so good. I was very lucky. The tumor was discovered quite early and it's been over a year since my mastectomy. As for the hair, I cut it off myself before the chemo started. Didn't relish the idea of seeing big clumps of my salt and pepper tresses on the shower floor." I smiled to assure Hazel that I was quite all right discussing the subject at hand. "I found myself in possession of a very nicely formed head, so I've kept it in a buzz cut ever since. With all the traveling I do, I can't imagine going back to the days of hairdos. But whatever you decide to do with your hair, just make yourself a promise to have a mammogram once a year."

Dinner was soon ready and over the best osso buco I have ever tasted, Hazel regaled me with tales of the Mother Road and the characters who lived along its faded lengths. A memorable one, Bob Waldmire, was an old hobo who erected a twelve foot-high metal cutout of a hula dancer along the route. He collected odds and ends, scraps, mementos and oddities and charged tourists to view his Hula Girl Museum, all dedicated to the memory of his deceased hobo friends. Bob lived to be a hundred years old, but by the time he died most of his treasures had been stolen. The hula girl sign remains though, a shadow of her former self, gathering dust in a museum in Barstow.

"Museums are the way to go out here, I reckon. We had a burlesque museum for a long time, till the old lady died. We got snake museums and railroad museums and even a Harvey Girls Museum over to Barstow. Harvey Girls were hostesses for the railroad hotels. All proper and first-class-like, though. Judy Garland was in a movie about the Harvey Girls."

Hazel warmed to her tales, so much so that by the end of the meal she had transformed herself into an almost enjoyable dinner companion. Since she knew the area to such an extent, I thought to ask her about the animal sanctuary with which Janet obviously had a connection. Someone there should be notified of the fate of a major benefactor, I decided. Surely they would want to pay their respects.

And dare I also hope that someone at the sanctuary might have the ability to help with Janet? Sonny had proven totally useless, while Myra seemed bent upon doing her interpretation of the female lead in *Days of Wine and Roses*.

Hazel took a sip of her wine and set the glass down heavily. "I think I heard somethin' about a place like that. But a long time ago. Where's it at?"

"I'm not sure, exactly. Somewhere near Baghdad, according to the brochure I saw."

"There ain't nothin' in Baghdad anymore. Not even Baghdad." Hazel threw back her head and laughed at her own joke. "Whole town is gone. Just a few old abandoned buildings and such. Nobody lives there. Course, it would be a good place to put an animal kennel, or whatever you call it. Nobody to complain about all the barkin'.Seems like some bunch of whackos did try and start up a place like that a while back. Don't think they lasted long, though. Maybe the new owners changed the name."

Though Hazel did not seem to know much about the Friends in Need Sanctuary, I was nevertheless glad I had thought to inquire. It had given me an idea. I would try and reach someone at the Friends in

Need organization. The brochure was out in my Airstream. Desperation was setting in. I needed help.

We finished our meal in relative silence. While I ate my fill of the delicious meat, I marveled again at the surprises life springs on us, especially when we aren't expecting anything but the same old thing. Happiness often slips through doors we don't remember leaving open.

Hazel forked in her last bite of osso buco "So. Where's your husband at?"

"Don't have one."

"Sorry," she said.

"I had a partner for quite a few years, but, ah..." I quickly sized Hazel up. "But she left me for someone else."

"Whatever," Hazel said and began clearing dishes.

I was grateful but not really surprised at Hazel's nonchalance. And the more I thought about the term 'whatever' the more I was delighted that it had been applied to my now defunct relationship with Kat. The use of the word denotes, to me at least, that the utterer finds nothing of consequence in the revelation in question. The fact was that there was really nothing of consequence left of our fifteen years together, despite our starstruck beginning. Ah, dear Kat, she of the golden hair and the high-flung ideals and the ability to charm just about anybody into or out of anything. And, oh yes, she of the vast emptiness inside that nothing could really fill, certainly not me.

"Yes, whatever," I agreed amiably.

The meal had been so outstanding that I asked Hazel for her recipe. Though the entrée violates my six-ingredient rule, I will nevertheless try it one day when in need of a fabulous party dish.

After finishing off the last of my wine I bid Hazel a good night, thanked her for the great meal. I would have hugged her but for the fact that she didn't appear to be the hugging type.

The night was inky black as I stepped into the parking lot and headed for my little cabin. Behind me, Hazel turned off the lights. Just as I reached the door, I heard a sound and froze with my hand poised over the knob. The sound, a soft rustling, seemed to be coming from the darkness to my left. Cabin four is the last in the row and the sound seemed to emanate from around the corner. Slowly, I rotated my head and allowed my eyes to follow the noise.

At first I saw nothing. After a moment, I convinced myself that I had imagined the sound and began turning the doorknob. Then I heard it again. This time the rustling noise was louder. And closer. "Get inside and lock the door," my mind commanded, but not before Otis stepped out from the corner of the building and stood glaring at me.

He reeked of stale clothes and sweat. If anything, his eyes seemed even more menacing than on our previous meetings. "Get out of here if you know what's good for you," he rasped. "You're causin' trouble."

I didn't hesitate. With one push the door to my cabin flew open and I fell inside. Quickly, I turned the deadbolt and drew the chain lock into place. From the peephole in the door I watched until Otis climbed aboard his battered bicycle and disappeared slowly into the night. What a disturbing man. And what a disturbing thought—that he had been lurking out there in the darkness. Had he been waiting for me?

Just on cue my cell phone rang. Ellen wasted no time in stating her opinion. "I just think you should leave all this to the authorities and hot-foot it on to Albuquerque. I'm worried about you. I have perfectly self-ish reasons, if you must know. I'm only just getting to know you and I want you back here in one piece."

"Really, Ellen," I said slowly, even though my cheeks glowed a deep pink. "I'm OK. I've made a call to the local law enforcement to tell them my suspicions. The officer should arrive any minute. After that, maybe I'll take your advice. We'll see. Someone has to care for Janet, even though her niece is here, I don't think she is in any condition to help much. Maybe by morning she will have pulled herself together and I can hit the road."

After the call from Ellen I did my best to relax. Actually, truth be told, I would very much have liked to leave here and head for home. After all. I would have done my duty by pointing out my reasons for thinking Claude had been murdered. Really, it was up to law enforcement now.

CHAPTER SIX

Otis's appearance at my cabin had been unsettling. For a time I watched the deserted parking lot uneasily thinking of Ellen and her admonition. I would feel so much better about leaving if only there were someone to help with Janet, someone to look after her.

Soon enough however, Hazel's osso buco, assisted by the wine, lulled me into a pleasant stupor. I lay on the lumpy mattress waiting for Deputy Ramey, experiencing inspired reveries about food. Hazel had offered a slice of luscious looking pear torte to complete the meal, but I had declined. Now, with dinner settled comfortably, I found myself fantasizing about that dessert.

Just nodding off into a light sleep, I heard a car pull into the parking lot. It slowed, then came to a stop beside the parked motor homes. I ran to the bathroom and splashed water on my face. The conversation with Deputy Ramey would require my full concentration. When, after several moments, I heard no knock on my door, I opened it and peered outside.

The night was dark. The café sign had been turned off. I assumed Hazel had gone to bed. I was so certain my late night visitor was Ramey that for a time I didn't see the well-dressed man standing at the door of the Winnebago. One hand was closed over the door handle, the other cupped his forehead as he pressed his face to the grimy window. He was so intent upon his task that he didn't notice me standing in the lighted doorway of my cabin. "May I help you?" I called.

He spun around at the sound of my voice. "What th—"

He didn't finish his sentence, but stood staring at me, his head cocked to one side, his mouth open. He wore nicely tailored slacks in a buttery cream color and a silk shirt open at the neck. Even in the darkness, I could see that his shoes, tassel loafers worn without socks, boasted a spit and polish shine. He took a couple of steps in my direction. "I...uh...I heard about the accident."

He rearranged the surprised look on his face to one of sadness and after a long, awkward moment, extended his hand. "I'm David DiMarco, the Director of Friends in Need Sanctuary. Who—?"

Relieved, I stepped out onto the narrow step. "I'm Libby Merchant, an old school friend of Janet Witherspoon." I offered my hand to him in return.

"Such a tragedy," he murmured. "Both of them at once. Tsk, tsk." He shook his head slowly.

Withdrawing my hand, I stared at him. "Both of them? Oh no. You're mistaken," I said at last. "Only Claude succumbed to the carbon monoxide. Janet is alive and resting in a hospital in Barstow." I watched his face as he absorbed this news. "What made you think both were dead?"

"I...I uh heard about the accident from an associate of mine. He saw the ambulance...the squad car. He thought, he said—" DiMarco's face registered a wild display of emotion ranging from confusion, to shock, to relief, then back to confusion again.

At last, he recovered himself enough to speak. "Just one death? Forgive me. This is just so...out of the blue." DiMarco smiled weakly, laced his fingers together and cracked his knuckles. "You see," he went on, "Claude and Janet Witherspoon are, that is...were friends of mine. Janet! Will she be all right?"

"We can certainly hope. She's recuperating nicely, I believe."

For the longest time, DiMarco didn't speak. "How did it happen?" he finally stammered.

A light sprinkle began falling just then. "I can fill you in on what little I know. Why don't we step into my RV?" I indicated the Airstream. "I'll make us a cup of tea."

DiMarco followed me inside my home on wheels. I quickly put on a kettle, overjoyed to be back in my own surroundings. I fervently hoped Hazel had gone to bed and would not notice. If she saw lights on and people about, she might very well send us back into my cramped and dingy motel room.

As I put tea bags into mugs, DiMarco paced, not an easy task in so confined a space. Finally, he slumped onto the couch and I took the swivel rocker across from him. In the light, David DiMarco, probably in his mid-forties, looked like a cross between a movie star and a pitchman for a corporate-sponsored success seminar. He wore his dark hair a little longer than is currently stylish, combed back with just a bit of curl over his shirt collar. He leaned forward, his hands clasped together as I related the story, which by now was becoming rote.

"So. Let me get this straight," he said after I finished. "You and Janet were in school together, and you just happened upon her in this...this...place?" His eyebrows shot skyward. He opened his mouth again, but quickly clamped it shut. He stared at me for a confrontive moment, every flicker of his eyes warning he found my story barely credible.

I can't say I blamed him. Even telling the tale as often as I now had, I felt as if I were relating a fairy tale. "I know it's strange. But life is often stranger than fiction." I smiled brightly. "And it's a good thing, too. If I hadn't come along, I don't know what would have become of Janet."

DiMarco cracked his knuckles once more, then jammed his hands into the pockets of his expensive slacks and began prowling the cramped space of my living room/kitchen area. "It was so ill-advised," he almost screeched, "for those two to have been traveling alone." He calmed down for a moment and returned to the sofa. "Call me David," he said, smiling, as I handed him a mug of chamomile tea. I figured we could both use something to steady the nerves.

"Now I'll always wonder if I could have saved him."

I must have given him a questioning look, because he went on almost without pause. "You see, Claude called me from the road. He and Janet had left home rather suddenly." DiMarco watched me with narrowed eyes. "He told me they had tried to reach me but had gotten lost. I insisted they wait here, at the Knight's Rest. At least here they would have access to a restaurant and phone. I promised to drive out and meet them as soon as I could get away." David paused and looked into the middle distance. "Unfortunately, I was delayed."

"They called from here?" So, this DiMarco was the one Hazel mentioned when she related that Claude and Janet Witherspoon had said a friend was coming to pick them up.

"Yes. They wanted to journey on and meet me at Friends in Need right then, but I explained the place was difficult to find. I suggested they wait for me so I could guide them in; the poor souls had already gotten lost once. I'm afraid Claude's eyesight wasn't the best."

At last, the saga of Janet and Claude's trek across the Mohave started to make sense. "Janet was wearing an identification bracelet from a nursing home when I found her. If they left suddenly, was she taken against medical advice?"

"I wouldn't be at all surprised. Claude was very angry and when he got angry his emotions sometimes got the better of him." David eyed me cautiously. "You see," he said after clearing his throat, "the Witherspoons have been donors to my organization for some time now. Generous ones, I might add." DiMarco straightened a faultless crease in his trousers. "They were the primary benefactors of our new Planned Giving program. That's a program wherein donors leave funds to an organization in their will." He looked directly at me.

"Yes," I said. "I know what a Planned Giving campaign is. Go on."

"Well, Claude and Janet signed up and before long the newspapers got wind of it. The niece and nephew became absolutely enraged when the local paper published the article about the bequest. Otherwise, no one would have known of the proposed change. The family wasn't close," David said by way of an unnecessary explanation. "However, as soon as the newspaper let the cat out of the bag, so to speak, the niece and nephew initiated court proceedings, intending to declare Janet and Claude incompetent."

"How sad," I offered. "For everyone."

"Yes." David leaned back on the couch. "They were such kind-hearted souls. Animal lovers to the core. Such a shame. He spoke to the ceiling. "And so sad, too, that...well,.now that Claude has passed away...what will become of their wishes in this matter?" David heaved a huge sigh.

"Yes. I can certainly see your dilemma." A warning light began flickering in my brain. The man seated on my sofa clearly stood to lose out on a substantial gift. In his place, I'd sigh too. "What will you do?"

David paused for a very long moment. He cracked his knuckles and stood, stretching his frame onto tiptoes. He brought his arms back to his sides and stared at me. "I don't really know, at this point. I only know that neither of the senior Witherspoons wanted to remain in Pasadena and that they felt no trust whatsoever in their kin to look after them or their interests."

David gave another huge sigh that came out almost a groan. "Sonny lives with them and I hear he is something of a loose cannon. Seems he was never able to make it on his own. And Myra. Well, let's just say she is rather a bitch." David immediately apologized for his language slip, looking chagrined.

"It's OK. I've heard the word before. Maybe even used it a few times." I smiled and winked.

"Anyway, they practically begged me to allow them to come live with me at the sanctuary. I couldn't refuse—knowing what I did about the lack of care at home."

"So, they were on their way to take up residence with you when they got marooned here?"

"That's about the size of it. And Claude promised that, once he and his sister arrived, he would extract revenge on his relatives."

"How so?"

"Actually, he told me as soon as he and Janet got to Friends in Need they intended to make new wills, this time leaving everything to my organization, cutting his niece and nephew out altogether." David's face turned red, but I couldn't read whether from anger or embarrassment.

Well, that certainly gave Sonny a solid motive for wanting the aging relatives dead and Sonny was a man with financial troubles. But what kind? And how serious? He had seemed desperate somehow, yet but one could use that term to describe lots of people. Suddenly I remembered the book I had seen in Sonny's car and realized with a shock that it might well hold a clue to his money problems. I'd need to give this new thought a bit more consideration and perhaps do a bit of snooping the next time he showed up.

"Claude and Janet must have very strong feelings for the work you do at the sanctuary," I went on, picking up my conversation with David. Later, when I was alone in the cabin, I could contemplate this last little wrinkle about the proposed accommodations for the Witherspoons and the resultant effect on their heirs. "Have you been associated with them for long?"

"Oh yes. I've known Janet and Claude for some time." David was up and pacing once again. His was a restless energy, befitting someone not used to sitting still for long. "In truth, I became like a son to them. In fact, I'd say the treatment Janet and Claude received at the hands of their kin was nothing short of neglectful elder abuse."

I felt a hot surge of anger. That type of behavior is a sore spot with me—probably with all of us in the age group that remembers Elvis Presley and gasoline for twenty-five cents per gallon. The entire Witherspoon mess was becoming more and more infuriating and not just because Janet was my college friend, either. The siblings were doubtless the soul of gentleness. So what if they cared more for animals than for people? I know lots of folks who feel the same way. The Witherspoons were in ill-health. Janet and Claude Witherspoon were old, expendable, frail and rich—all told, a bad combination.

"Did Sonny or Myra physically abuse them, anything like that?" I held my breath, dreading the answer.

"No, I don't think so. It was more a case of benign neglect, though I can't swear to the benign part. Myra never lifted a finger to help, according to Claude. Sonny lived with them, but he was useless. Always locked up in his room playing with electronic gadgets or on the computer. They could have been a big help after Janet suffered her stroke, for example. But it was as if they either didn't care or, in Sonny's case, just didn't have a clue." David sank back on the settee, his brow dropped into his hand.

We sipped our tea for a moment in silence. I peered over the rim of my cup at the man on the settee. His face, tanned and angular, was softened by concern. "You know, David," I blurted out. "I hardly know you, but I feel I must confide in someone. I certainly didn't feel I could trust Sonny or Myra."

"Are they here?" he asked, abruptly sitting forward on the sofa, his eyes intent on me.

"Oh yes. Indeed, they are. Actually Myra is here. Sonny has left for parts unknown. And the worst of it is, Janet is due to be released from the hospital tomorrow morning and I have no one to help me. I had been counting on one of them to take some responsibility."

David didn't say a word, but I could tell my news concerning Myra and Sonny's whereabouts did not make him happy. Probably the less interference from them, the better. "Sorry," he said, "I interrupted you. Go on."

"Well, the fact is, I am beginning to wonder if Claude's death was really an accident." There. I'd said it and the world didn't end nor did the sky fall to earth.

David sat back with something akin to a gasp. "What makes you say a thing like that? Do you have any proof?"

I explained about the heater vent. David's eyes narrowed, his jaw clamped tight. "I know," I said quickly. "It makes me very angry, too. Those poor, defenseless—"

"Right. Defenseless. And alone."

I watched the muscles of his jaw ripple with tension. "Actually, when you arrived, I thought perhaps you were the sheriff. I called him to report my suspicions. The officer said he would drive out here and take my statement. Maybe it would be a good idea for you to talk with him also…" Intimidated by David DiMarco as he strode to the door, glowering, I felt my voice trail off into a thin whisper, "Tell him what you know of the Witherspoons and the wills and everything."

"Look," he said, his hand on the knob. "I didn't kill anybody, if that's what you're thinking."

"I wasn't thinking anything of the sort. I just wanted to—"

"In fact, I was in Temecula that evening. Delivering a gift basket to a benefactor. You can check it out if you want. The donor is Frank Gemilli, of Gemilli Vineyards fame. You know, the wine guy. His wife is a big animal lover. He makes generous contributions to keep her happy, if you know what I mean. I was there all evening."

"Mr. DiMarco...David...please. Don't get me wrong. I wasn't accusing you. I'm sorry I said anything." I stood, followed him to the door and gently placed my hand on his arm.

He removed his hand from the knob. His body eased, some of the tension let go. "Sorry. I guess this has affected me more deeply than I thought. I overreacted. Please forgive me." He hesitated for only a fraction of a second. "Look, I had no motive for murder. I stood to gain everything if they arrived safely at Friends in Need." A look flitted across his face, unreadable. After a pause he went on, "In the morning I'll be more than happy to assist in any way I can. I could go with you to pick up Janet at the hospital, if you'd like."

I could have wept with relief. At last, someone who cared about something other than booze, sex or money. "I'd appreciate that more than you know," I responded. "You're the first and only person who has acted in the least concerned about Janet. I can see why she and her brother came to rely on you. I'm so relieved you're here." I smiled and patted his arm.

David returned my smile and took my hand in his. "There is a small favor you could do for me. I hope you won't find this crass, but I would really like to look around their Winnebago. I'm looking for anything that might strengthen my case regarding the Witherspoon bequest. I don't know if Claude and Janet actually changed their wills, or even if he brought them with him. But it means so much to my group—to the animals. Would you mind if I...er, looked around in there?"

"That is not for me to say," I responded. "It's not locked. The

Winnebago doesn't belong to me. I have no right to—"

"Yes, yes, of course. Well then. I'll just have a quick look and be on my way. I still have an appointment to keep tonight." David stood.

"I am a supporter of the SPCA, and a few local animal welfare groups. I'd love to tour your facility. Perhaps—"

"Uh, sure," he said with a wave of his hand. "Later, OK?" With that, he stepped outside and toward the Winnebago. I watched from the door as he strode across the macadam in the direction of the battered motor home.

"See you in the morning," I called after him. I noticed his car, a shiny Toyota station wagon. His bumper sticker read: "THERE AREN'T ENOUGH HOMES FOR THEM ALL—SPAY/NEUTER YOUR PET." —a sentiment with which I heartily agreed.

I gulped the last of my now-cold tea and slumped onto the sofa. What a bizarre evening. More than anything, I wanted to go to bed for a good night's sleep. Instead, I was waiting for yet another visitor and had no idea when the officer might finally arrive. I yawned and thought of making a cup of coffee, but that would guarantee a night of restless tossing and turning. At least I now had someone to help with Janet. With that in place I could stay a little longer and pitch in to assist Janet till suitable arrangements could be made. Ellen would be disappointed but with a grin I thought about all the ways I could make it up to her once I returned home.

David had been gone for nearly an hour when I heard a car pull into the parking lot. I looked out the window. Deputy Ramey had come to a stop in front of the office. By my watch, the time was a little after ten pm— well past my bedtime. I experienced a surge of irritation. What had taken him so long to get here? But at least he had finally arrived and we could get to the bottom of this horrid business.

A little bell over the door jangled to announce my entry into the now crowded office. Hazel stood behind the counter, wearing her robe and an expression that spoke volumes about being awakened in the middle of the night. Sugar, the bulldog, lumbered over as soon as I came through the door. I was glad to see a friendly face, even hers. I reached down and petted her massive head to Sugar's intense pleasure, which she promptly demonstrated by wiggling her behind and leaving a little puddle of pee on the floor. I was getting a sense of just how Sugar felt being marooned at the Knight's Rest and I sympathized with her.

The earlier camaraderie between Hazel and me, spurred on by the wine and good food, had vanished. She turned her steely gaze toward my face. She was clearly disturbed by Ramey's presence and the implication that something was amiss at her place of business. Though, for the life of me, I failed to see who would notice here on this deserted stretch of road.

Sugar had parked herself at the door, so that Deputy Ramey almost stumbled over her as he followed me back into the parking lot. The sheriff and I walked out into the inky night and strolled over to the two parked rigs. My irritation returned. "I was expecting you earlier," I said testily.

Ramey looked me over, from head to toe. "Sorry I'm so late. I've got a sick kid. We had to take him to the ER just after dinner."

I was chagrined at the tone I had used. "I'm so sorry. I hope he'll be all right."

Deputy Ramey smiled weakly. "We hope so. There's a new drug they're trying on leukemia patients now. It's been very effective for the kind Timmy has."

I watched the big officer's face as he struggled with his emotions. Part of him wanted to tell me more, another part wanted to cry and another just wanted to get this heater vent thing over with and get home.

I touched his sleeve gently. "If you need to talk, I'm a good listener." I wanted to make up for my earlier rudeness. "Besides, I've been down that road myself. I know how scary it can be."

"Thanks, Miz...ah Miz...?"

"Merchant," I finished for him, having decided against using the title Doctor, or letting on that listening to people had been my life's work. The officer hitched himself to his full official height. "I can take your statement now."

For the hundredth time, it seemed, I related the story of the heater, pointing out the obvious tampering. He bent down, shining his flashlight on the vent. "Not much to go on," he said slowly, still staring at the fresh cut in the protective strip over the opening. He straightened, took a pen from his pocket, flipped open a notebook and made a few notes. "What else have you got?"

The trouble with subjective information is just that. I related the business about my suspicions. Someone else had entered the Winnebago after Janet had been taken away. Then I told the officer about Sonny Witherspoon and how he had tracked his aunt and uncle into this remote corner of the desert. Deputy Ramey never even batted an eye.

I asked him to follow me to my room, where I showed him the newspaper article. He scanned it quickly, and then turned to me. "So, you think Claude Witherspoon was murdered and that the culprit wanted to stop Mr. Witherspoon from giving away his fortune. That would make the motive money."

My theory sounded so simplistic when he said it like that. I gulped and came within a hair of retreat. "Yes," I said, "I most certainly do think Claude was murdered over money." I could hear my voice rising in a plea to be heard. If Deputy Ramey didn't believe me, then where was I to turn? Should I also mention this DiMarco fellow? I decided against it. David, of the lot of them, had seemed genuinely concerned and I really needed his help tomorrow.

Ramey flipped his notebook closed and slipped the pen back into his pocket. "Tell you what. I'll dust for prints and have the boys run 'em. Like I said, we don't have much to go on. That heater vent thing could have been an accident, you know."

"But the piece of insulation—remember, I told you, I saw the fragment that had been stuffed into the vent. Now it's missing. I think someone removed it."

"Why didn't you call me right away? Before it could be removed?"

85

"I tried. Really, I did. But no one seemed interested."

"Well, like I said, I'll look into it." He paused and stared at me for a long moment. "I get the feeling you know more than you're telling. Am I right?" He cocked his head toward me coolly, waiting.

I pressed my lips tightly together and gazed at the stars just over his left shoulder. He was dead-on right. I knew something, all right. But what? All I could manage was to shake my head in vigorous denial.

"OK, have it your way," he said at length. "But I'm going to ask you to remain here for another day or so, in case I need to question you again. Might need your fingerprints, too. For elimination. Oh, and just for the record, where were you the night Claude was murdered, if he was murdered?"

CHAPTER SEVEN

It takes several days for the hours between midnight and four am to pass, as anyone who has lain awake during that particular time span knows all too well. It is also during this time that even the stable mind is willing, even eager, to dwell in the darker recesses and fetch up perfectly good reasons for worry, depression and despair. My own mind was no exception. Time and again, I willed myself to remain calm. The question was logical, right? Deputy Ramey would be expected to ask the exact same thing of everyone after a murder had been committed, wouldn't he? And as far as Ellen's request that I get the hell out of Dodge...well, as of a couple of hours ago, it was out of the question.

I sighed, wrestling my pillow, searching for the cool spot. A mere two days ago, I had been happily on my way to the Balloon Festival in Albuquerque with no thought other than having a good time, perhaps seeing a few friends, who, like myself, travel from place to place just for the fun of it. Tonight, as I tossed and turned in a motel room that could only be called sleazy, my visions of bright-colored balloons, majestically rising into an azure sky, were obliterated by the image of Claude's corpse. His insensitive relatives and that last question Deputy Ramey had asked before wheeling out of the parking lot didn't help much, either. Plus, I would now have to call Ellen and tell her I'd be staying on a few days more...and why. I prayed Ellen was as level-headed as she has always seemed to be.

Was I a suspect? Surely not. "Where were you at the time of the murder?" is just a routine question, one that policing textbooks, no doubt, school officers to ask of anyone in the least connected to a crime scene. And why did he suspect I knew more than I let on?

Well, so what if he did think me a suspect? I knew I was only playing the Good Samaritan, and that I had nothing to do with the crime. The fingerprint test would reveal the culprit. I had nothing to fear. Of course, I had heard those stories about innocent people, just like me, who have been falsely accused and sent to prison, victims of mistaken identity or foul-ups in the forensics lab. But then there were my fingerprints all over the Winnebago, the papers...God knew where else.

And so it went, into the predawn hours.

At great length, morning arrived. I had managed a few hours of light sleep, but not nearly enough for what lay ahead. Getting Janet checked out of the hospital and settled at the Friends in Need Sanctuary promised to take up most of the morning, if not the day. David DiMarco had mentioned that the sanctuary was close by, but I realized I had no idea how to find it. The brochure had listed only a post office box as a mailing address. Frankly, my lack of sleep and the stress of these last couple of days had left me feeling less than my usual cheerful best and I didn't want to spend precious time driving to remote, out-of-the-way locations. Sorority sister bonds notwithstanding, I wanted the whole disturbing business over and done with. I wished I had never borrowed the damn dress from Janet in the first place. Look where it had got me. And the basketball player? Well, let's just say I wish I hadn't borrowed the dress, all right?

The rain had finally run its course. The sun was already hot in a blue-white sky when I opened the dusty Venetian blinds and peeked outside. DiMarco had not said what time he planned to pick me up to journey on to the hospital. I hoped he would come early.

The parking lot was empty, save for one rusted pickup parked in front of the café. Coffee sounded like a good idea. I threw on jeans and a T-shirt to make my way over and was greeted by the aroma of frying bacon and burned toast even before I was halfway across the parking lot.

Judging by the girth of the lone patron at the counter, I guessed I was about to make the acquaintance of the fabled Billy Ray. I slid onto the seat next to him and studied the man out of the corner of my eye. Hazel had been right about the three hundred pounds. He was all of that and maybe more. But a more forlorn three hundred pounds of man I would have been hard put to find. He sat with his head propped up on thick fists, gazing straight down into a cold cup of coffee. The man's hair was so blond it was almost white and cut so short you could see the pink scalp peeking through beneath. He wore gray mechanic's overalls with darker gray stripes, causing him to resemble the Michelin Tire man not just a little. He moved neither right nor left as I took a seat beside him. Out of nowhere, his massive shoulders heaved and a sigh escaped his lips.

Hazel stomped out of the kitchen just then and placed a cup of hot coffee in front of me, pointedly ignoring Billy Ray's cold cup. Decades of practice in clinical psychology weren't needed to sense the icy daggers she shot at Billy Ray. Without a word, Hazel stalked past us to return to her small kitchen retreat. Billy Ray emitted an audible groan, then said into his coffee cup, "Awww, woman. Can't you give a guy a break?"

The coffee was good and nicely strong. I took several sips before smiling and saying to my less-than-chipper breakfast companion, "Unless I miss my guess, you're Billy Ray. Hazel has mentioned you."

"She has!" Billy Ray exclaimed, his features illuminated by the singular light of hope renewed. He turned his head so that he faced me squarely. "What did she say, exactly?"

I couldn't remember the last time I saw so much eagerness for good news, from whatever the source. Was this the same man who had brazenly stood Hazel up and missed a great osso buco into the bargain? Something more had to be going on than met the eye.

"Hazel thinks very highly of you," I ventured. "I just happened to be here last evening, and, well...let's simply say you missed a great meal."

Billy shook his head slowly. "I forgot," he said apologetically. "I get to tinkering, messing around with cars and...I don't know, time just gets by me. Hazel thinks I got another girlfriend, that I've taken up with someone else. But I don't have any other girl than her. I love Hazel. I wish she wouldn't get so fired up."

"It's hard to go to all the trouble she did for a special meal. Why don't you just say you're sorry? She'll forgive you." Even as the words left my mouth, I doubted them.

"No she won't," Billy Ray refuted, confirming what I already thought. He returned his gaze to his cup of cold coffee. I noticed his wrists. No watch was in evidence, no white skin that told of a previous watch, either. "Maybe you should buy a watch," I said brightly. "With an alarm. That way you would be on time for your dates with Hazel."

"Yeah," said Billy Ray with a new bounce in his tone. "I got a friend over to Vegas. He has the same problem. But he's a security guard so when his lady friend gets suspicious all he has to do is show her his time card. He works lots of overtime...stuff like that."

A blaze of inspiration, powerful and delicious, almost knocked me from my perch on the red vinyl stool. I congratulated myself for giving birth to it even before finishing my first cup of coffee.

The book I had seen in Sonny's car had suddenly thrust itself into my consciousness, complete with associated details. During my psychology internship with a mental health agency, the social worker and I had shared a desk. In a top drawer, ready at a moment's notice, he kept a dog-eared copy of *Ainsley's Complete Guide to Thoroughbred Handicapping*. He studied the book when he thought no one was looking. He then placed his bets with the man who drove the catering truck, who was, conveniently, a runner for a local bookie. All in all, the social worker did pretty well for himself, and I must admit, upon a closer study of the volume I too made a few judicious wagers. The supervising social worker never found out. At least I don't think she did.

"Billy Ray," I said, leaning closer to him, my whisper conspiratorial, "do you think your friend might do me a small favor?"

The question drew a blank stare from Billy Ray. "What kinda favor?"

"Well, I know insiders in Las Vegas keep lists, deadbeat lists, names of card cheats, be-on-the-lookout-for lists. Would your friend have access to such lists? More importantly, would he be willing to look up a name for me?" Visions of the Las Vegas hotel flyers from Sonny's car danced before my eyes.

"He might be. All I can do is ask. What's the name?"

Just then a Toyota station wagon pulled into the lot at the front of the café. David DiMarco stepped out of the car into the sunlight and grinned on seeing me through the window. "Sonny Witherspoon," I said with a surge of excitement. "Could your friend check to see if he has lost a lot of money lately...anything like that?" If Sonny was a gambler, as I now suspected, and a bad one, his name might appear on one of those lists. Gambling debts surely constitute a motive for murder. At last! My first real lead.

David sauntered in, took a seat at the counter and asked Hazel for coffee, picking up three plastic containers of cream before he spoke. "Have you had breakfast?"

"Just coffee." I peered at David over the rim of my cup. He seemed to crackle with the same energy as last evening, but this morning wore a look of faint unease. Hazel set a steaming mug of coffee on the counter and David dumped in all three of the containers of cream before blowing over the cup and taking a sip.

"Was your mission successful last night? Did you locate anything in the Winnebago that might be of help?"

"No, actually I couldn't find the light switch and hadn't brought a flashlight. Plus..." David screwed up his face, "whew, what a mess in there. I'd like to try later. Maybe when we return from Barstow." He took another sip of his coffee. "Let's go. We can get breakfast in Barstow. You ready?" He slapped a few bills down on the countertop, cracked his knuckles and started for the door.

We were almost to his car when I turned around and walked back to the café. Hazel stood behind the counter glaring after us. "Don't forget what I said about the watch," I whispered to Billy Ray, "and the question for your security guard friend."

Within moments, I was seated comfortably beside David and we were headed toward Barstow. I noticed that the rear seats were folded down and the back converted to a carrying space. Stacks and stacks of folded brochures filled the area. I reached back and grabbed one.

"My main job is raising funds," David said with an easy smile. "The day-to-day management of the sanctuary is left to others. I do have an—well, sort of an assistant who accompanies me from time to time. Perhaps you will meet him. He actually went with me on several of my visits to the Witherspoon residence." David eased the car a notch faster then indicated the brochure I still held in my hand. "You have no idea how hard it is to meet our expenses."

"Actually, I do have an idea. In my work as a clinical psychologist I've had close ties to several nonprofit organizations. I remember all those fund-raising banquets, those endless meals of rubbery chicken and peas."

David laughed. "So you do know how it is. And that's how you know about planned giving appeals."

I turned my attention back to the brochure. Sure enough, a return envelope was tucked inside, with the usual plea for money. I noticed a box the donor could check if he or she wished to be contacted about planned giving.

We passed the time amiably on our way to the hospital. David filled me in on many details of the sanctuary. He glanced quickly between me and the road, his fingers drumming on the steering wheel. Once again, his energy seemed barely contained.

Friends in Need, he explained, specialized in sheltering animals that had been abused or abandoned—sometimes both. They provided vet care and resocialization before giving the charges over to carefully selected adoptive families. I was ready to take out my checkbook. "You must have a good deal of admiration for Roger Caras," I said lightly. I had read of Mr. Caras and applauded his efforts in founding the ASPCA and bringing the plight of neglected animals to the fore.

We turned into the visitor's lot at the hospital in Barstow and David found a parking space. As we got out of the car and he said, "Caras. Oh, yes. Indeed I do. But I sometimes shudder at the huge sums of money those big guys raise. The administrative costs must be off the scale. My belief is that the smaller organizations, like mine, can do much more good on the local level."

Janet grinned at us from her wheelchair. Her hair was immaculately clean and brushed. She wore the aqua polyester pantsuit that she'd worn on the day I found her. Her yellow scarf was draped over her thin shoulders. I walked over and put my arms around her, giving her a hug. I supposed she still either did not know, or had not been able to grasp, that her brother was dead. For the zillionth time, I thanked whatever gods there be that David was now by my side.

He stepped out in front and when he did I saw the tiniest spark of light flit in Janet's eyes. She attempted to smile and then leaned forward, her arms spread open. David walked into them, as though he had been befriending spinster little old ladies forever.

Soon the nurse arrived, bearing a sheaf of papers. "Here are her discharge instructions. Who's going to be responsible? Where is she going?"

I took the clipboard. "I suppose I'll sign her out, though she's going with my friend here. To his place." I jerked my head in David's direction.

"No, she isn't." David put his hand on my arm. "I assumed you were going to take her back to the Knight's Rest today." He laced his fingers and cracked his knuckles—his signature gesture, it would appear.

"Why ever would I? I thought she was going with you to the sanctuary. It's the only solution." My panic began to rise again. I simply could not be responsible for Janet's care. I tried to remember if David had actually said he was taking her to the sanctuary. Maybe I had just assumed he would.

"I should have been more clear when we spoke yesterday," he apologized. "You see, that rainstorm washed out our road. Can't you keep Janet with you until the access is fixed? A day or two, tops."

His smile appealed. "We've been making all kinds of preparations for Janet's and Claude's arrival. I'm thrilled with how well it's going. It's just that...well, that we need more time. We've already rehabbed a lovely old home on the property with its own garage for the Winnebago. The crew is adding wheelchair ramps today. They'll...that is, Janet, will have everything she could want. If only the road hadn't washed out." He opened his hands in a gesture of helplessness.

What could I do? There sat Janet, my old college chum, grinning her lopsided smile, looking as vacant as a strip mall in the rust belt. No one else appeared ready to step into the breach.

"You're a wonderful woman," David crooned just beside me. "Not everyone would have shown the kindness you have, or the consideration. I'll help all I can. We'll get her settled in your room. I really don't think she should be alone." He didn't wait for an answer, but charged right ahead, grabbing the wheelchair and giving it a shove. Unfortunately, I was caught off guard and almost lost my balance. The hospital floors were waxed to a sheen, and as I struggled for purchase I dropped my handbag. The contents skittered onto the floor—maps, lipstick, comb, Swiss Army knife, tire pressure gauge. The usual.

David knelt and tucked everything carefully back inside. He handed me the bag and began pushing Janet toward the door. "My staff informs me the road crew was out there this morning. The road could even be fixed as early as tomorrow."

If I had learned anything from my experiences of late, it should have been that planning is a futile exercise, employed mainly to waste time and raise false hopes. That was how, about an hour later, I came to be sitting in my wretched little cabin at the Knight's Rest, feeding a cup of instant soup to Janet Witherspoon. David had dropped us off, then, instead of searching the Winnebago, had driven away. Rather quickly, too it seemed.

The doctor had been right. Janet could talk, though not much and not always clearly. She slurred her words and had difficulty pronouncing syllables starting with 'th' or 'st'. She smiled and nodded to indicate her pleasure with the soup, leaving me to wonder about her taste buds and dietary habits. Now and then, as she sipped, she uttered snippets of conversation, mostly limited to responses to "How do you feel?" or,

"Would you like a cracker?"

I was suddenly struck with the thought that Janet herself had more information than anyone else about the night Claude was murdered. After all, she had been there and had herself been a target. If I could get her to talk about that night, even a teensy bit, perhaps Ramey could be persuaded to listen and lead to an arrest in the case.

"Janet," I said, getting her attention by looking directly into her face and patting her knee. "Do you remember the night you came here the first time?" I waved my arm in an expansive gesture, taking in the motel and café, as well as our rigs parked out front. "You and Claude were in your Winnebago. Remember?"

Janet smiled. I took that as a good sign and waded in. "You had a visitor, right? Do you remember who it was?" I held my breath waiting for her reply.

I had turned a touch bluish by the time she responded. "I remember."

My heart skipped a beat. Here it came—the real story. Janet might not necessarily know that her visitor had intended to kill her. But I knew that someone might have had to go inside the Winnebago and turn the heater on, probably using the pretext of a friendly visit. I was furious with the murderous lout. "Who was it, Janet? Do you remember?"

"He came in the early evening. The sun was not yet down." Janet spoke hesitantly. She gazed out the window, as if the remaining information were a bird perched there and she wished to catch it before it flew away.

"Yes, dear. That's right. Perhaps you and Claude had just settled in for supper. Someone came to the door that night. Do you remember who?"

Janet nodded in the affirmative, but kept her lips pressed tightly together. She motioned that she'd like another drink of the soup. I steadied her hand as she lifted the cup. After drinking, she smacked her lips and gazed again out the window. I was afraid I was losing her. Her attention span was shorter than a puppy's. I pasted on a huge happy-face and nudged her again. "Tell me about your visitor, Janet. Was it a man? What did he look like?"

"He was tall. Dressed in a movie suit."

"A movie suit?"

Janet nodded agreeably. "You know, like John Wayne."

I smiled, though my hopes were sinking fast. "Did you recognize him?"

"Oh yes. He is a nice man."

"What is the nice man's name?"

"Don't know. He never told me that. Myra might know."

Janet looked into the middle distance and smiled. "But I remember what he wanted."

At last we were getting somewhere. Any minute now, I could place a call to Deputy Ramey. Justice would be served. I rather enjoyed the role of avenger and basked in the warm glow of self-congratulation. I had been clever, indeed, to question Janet herself.

She peered out the grimy window as though it was an opening to the past, her voice growing weaker. "He wanted to borrow something."

"What, Janet? What did he want to borrow?" My heart began beating faster.

"Silly. My dress. You remember. You had spilled the ink all over yours. You had a date with that basketball player."

Janet rambled on, describing the long-ago evening, though she got most of the details wrong. It's one of the odd quirks of a mind no longer firing on all cylinders. Dementia victims can't remember what they ate for breakfast, but can recall the distant past quite easily. Unfortunately Janet's memory was like a plate of scrambled eggs.

My spirits sagged, my ego deflated like a punctured balloon. Janet, tired from recounting the tale, nodded off while I sat in the lime green chair and wondered what the hell a movie suit might be.

Fresh out of bright ideas, I made my obligatory call to Sudie early, thankfully just leaving a message on her machine. "All's well here. Not to worry. Talk with you soon." With nothing better to do, I made my way over to the café, still trying to sort out Janet's revelations. Maybe Hazel would be in the mood to whip up a delicious luncheon for the two of us.

Sonny's car sat parked at the café, the antennas and doodads poking from it like pins from a cushion. Wherever he had been since our first meeting, he was now back. Hoping no one in the café would notice, I stooped and peered into Sonny's car as I passed. The interior was cluttered, as before, and the flyers still rested on the passenger seat. My eye went to the windshield wiper and I noticed a parking stub impaled there. I bent down and peered at the piece of cardboard— Acme Parking Company, Las Vegas, Nevada. The stub was dated yesterday. Ainsley's book still rested on the floorboard. Sonny had left me sitting in my Airstream and had flitted off to Vegas. Worse, he had done so with the full knowledge that his aunt lay in a hospital and needed his care. Any shrink worth her salt could diagnose his raging problem with compulsive gambling.

In the café, Myra sat at one of the cracked red vinyl booths, facing me as I entered. Sonny sat with his legs stretched along the opposite seat, his back against the grimy window. Myra shot me a look full of daggers, but, undaunted, I slid into the booth just behind them and opened a grease-splattered menu.

Perhaps my imagination was at work, but I thought I could smell the stale alcohol seeping out of Myra's pores. And what a fright the woman looked. Dark bags drooped under her red-rimmed eyes and her whole face appeared as if it had melted and slid down toward her chin. Sonny didn't look much better. His skin seemed oily and he, too, sported dark circles under his eyes. A light sheen of sweat stood out on his pale brow.

I decided against the chili fries. Ditto the burgers. I yearned for a chef's salad, but the closest I could find on the menu was tuna on white toast. Hazel finally arrived. I placed my order and asked for a Coke.

I don't particularly like to eavesdrop, yet when an argument is in progress one can't help but overhear. The combatants hissed at each other in stage whispers, each attempting to keep his anger from bubbling up into the vocal chords.

"You ass," Myra spat. I could almost see the venom squirting from her fangs. "How could you be so stupid?"

"I'm not stupid," Sonny retorted, sounding like a defensive teenager. "The whole court thing was your big idea. Or maybe it was that worthless husband of yours. By the way, how is the dear boy?"

"My husband is indisposed."

"In jail is more like it." Sonny guffawed. "Or maybe you meant indicted."

"He hasn't been indicted," Myra said archly.

"Not yet, anyway," Sonny snickered. "Say, that gives me a thought. Maybe you bumped off Uncle Claude yourself. Out of curiosity, where were you the night he bit the big one?"

"Don't say another word, you ass. And you are an ass, Sonny. A complete and total ass. It could just as easily have been you. Where were you on that fateful night, my dear brother?"

"Ha! Gotcha. I was in Vegas and I can prove it."

"Oh right, like anyone would believe the cast of lowlifes you associate with— Please. I'll believe that when pigs take wings and fly." Myra winced and called over to Hazel for an Alka Seltzer.

"No Alka-Seltzer. No Tums. You eat the food, you take your chances. Though it ain't the food got you down, missy." Hazel actually chuckled. "Your friend the cabbie crawled out of here earlier, lookin' like death itself. An' you don't look too much better."

"Cabbie?" Sonny's voice recoiled in mock horror. "Oh, Sis."

"Just shut up, creep. I've got troubles of my own. I don't need your sarcasm." Myra winced and placed her palm on her forehead. "Christ, what a mess," she muttered.

"Oh, I'm sure you do." Sonny's tone changed to anger. "But I got problems, too, you can bet on that. Hell, I don't even see how I can get past some of this shit. Man, this sucks." Sonny banged his fist on the table.

"You jerk. Betting is the problem. But you already know that, don't you?"

Hazel appeared with my sandwich on a plate. She shoved it toward me. "You got an extra person in your room. That's another forty dollars a night."

Hazel's announcement brought the conversation in the next booth to an abrupt halt. I scarcely had time to take a bite of my sandwich before Myra loomed at my table. "You've taken my aunt hostage. I demand you return her. Immediately," she said, then hiccuped. "This is a family matter. Butt out."

Family matter, indeed. "Actually, it's a good thing I'm here. If not for David DiMarco and me, your Aunt Janet would be stranded in a hospital in Barstow with no one to care for her. I expect no gratitude from you, but I'll thank you to keep a civil tongue in your head." I wanted to add a line about how, if Sonny and Myra were the family in question, Janet was better off without one. But I didn't want to create a bigger scene than was already in progress.

"Janet will be my guest for the evening. Tomorrow, Mr. DiMarco will take over her care, mercifully for her."

"Hold on just one minute. I knew you were lying. You are in cahoots with those bleeding heart animal freaks." Myra stood over me, exhaling yesterday's tequila, "I'm thinking of suing you and your entire organization for bilking my relatives."

Myra's voice rose to a feverish pitch. "I'm calling my husband. He will rescue us from this...this dreadful place. As soon as he arrives, he and I'll take Aunt Janet back home with us..." She hiccuped again, "where she belongs." Her eyes rolled and I thought for a terrible moment she was about to faint or throw up. "You can inform the rest of your Lassie-loving group that the jig is up, as they say." Sonny took her by the arm and steered her back to their booth.

"Forgive my sister," he said. "She's just upset. This DiMarco fellow. Where is he?"

"I'm afraid you'll have to ask him that yourself. I've merely provided a room for the night for your aunt." And a costly one, I said to myself. Warning bells were going off all over the place. The less these two knew about plans for Janet, the better. Just as soon as I could slip away, I intended to phone David and suggest he get here as quickly as possible. I prayed the road would be fixed in time.

Just then, Ramey pulled to a stop in front of the café. He eased himself out of his patrol car and strode inside. He wore an especially glum expression and I felt a moment's apprehension for his ill child. He pulled on his mustache, looked back and forth between Sonny and me. "Miz Merchant," he said, taking off his hat, "I've got some information for you. You want to walk with me to my car?"

What perfect timing. I wanted the officer to meet the culprits and here they were in the same room. "Deputy Ramey," I said, "this is Sonny Witherspoon. He is Claude's nephew. And the lady in the booth is Myra, Mr. Witherspoon's niece." I watched Ramey's face as he shook hands with Sonny. Had his years of training and experience given him a sixth sense about matters involving murder?

Apparently not. His face remained impassive as he nodded at Myra. "Since Miz Merchant here talked to me, the chief wants to look a little further into Mr. Witherspoon's death."

"Talked to you! What the hell did she say?" Myra was on her feet. "She knows nothing and has no right—"

"Please, ma'am. Sit down and keep quiet." Deputy Ramey cleared his throat. "Miz Merchant here stated she suspects Mr. Witherspoon's death might not have been an accident. To back that up, she showed me a couple of things. Things that didn't add up."

Myra's face instantly drained of what color remained after her date with José Cuervo. Her hand flew to her face.

Sonny sank back into the vinyl booth, his eyes round, his mouth agape, staring at his sister.

"I'm afraid I'm going to have to ask all of you to remain in the area for a short time," the officer said. "Just until the investigators have had a chance to take your statements and ask a few questions."

"What questions?" Myra's voice had lost its brassy ring. She sounded angry.

"Like where each of you was on the night Mr. Witherspoon died."

"Surely you can't believe one of us, his own family, would have

100

done such a thing."

"Look, Miss. I don't believe anything at this point. But I can tell you this much. In most homicides, it's the family we suspect first. Now, I'm not saying that anyone in this room is guilty. I just want you all to be available for questioning, that's all."

"I'll have you know I was home with my husband. He'll vouch for me." Myra's strident tone returned.

Deputy Ramey took out his notebook again. "Who is your husband and how can I contact him?"

"Well!" Myra huffed. "The nerve. I don't see how any of this concerns him. He's a very busy man."

"Busy dodging the summons server is what she means," Sonny mumbled uneasily.

"Shut up, Sonny!" Myra turned again to the officer. "My husband, Mr. Hampton, is a respected businessman." She extracted a card from her purse. "Here's his number. Feel free to contact him anytime you like. He'll verify that we were enjoying a quiet night together at home."

Deputy Ramey stuffed the card into his shirt pocket and turned to Sonny. "What about you, sir? Where were you Thursday night?"

"Me? I dun'no. I was—ah, let me see. Oh yeah, I was with my pal Lonnie Street. All night. We had some business to take care of."

"What kind of business?"

"Investments. Stuff like that."

"What my dear brother means, Deputy," Myra offered in a clipped voice, "is that he and this Lonnie character are gambling buddies."

"Anyone see you together?" Deputy Ramey continued writing.

"Sure, lots of folks. Everybody in the, ah, the Lucky Dog Casino, I guess."

"I'll check that out. Give me Mr. Street's phone and address. And Mrs. Hampton, please give me your home address and phone number. Like I said, everybody just stay put for a while."

"How is your son today?" I asked quietly as he moved to leave.

Ramey's face opened in a wide smile. "Much better, thanks. Fact is, I'm headed home right now to read him a story before lunch. You mind stepping outside with me, Miz Merchant? I'll just take a moment."

No one moved a muscle as the officer and I exited the café. "I still got a funny feeling about you," Ramey said as we neared his cruiser. "Anything else you'd like to tell me?"

"No," I said without hesitation. I still had no proof...of anything. Only wild speculations. And to add to my mounting frustration I had now witnessed Myra in a bald-faced lie. "Well, maybe just one small thing," I offered. "I'm pretty sure the Hamptons' housekeeper stated that Mr. Hampton was out of town on business that night, the night I called, the night after Claude died. Maybe you could check that out.

"Oh. And one more thing," I said. "The night the piece of insulation disappeared I heard a car."

"What kind of car?"

"Older. Sedan type—I got a glimpse of it. It was badly in need of a tune-up."

"Great," Ramey muttered. "I'll check that out." I could see him mentally tallying up the number of automobiles in this area that would fit that general description. The officer paused and stared at me. "I could run you in, you know, till you remember whatever it is you don't know." He squinted at me and tugged his mustache. "But I won't. Just stay here and keep out of trouble. Got it?"

Back in the café I slid gratefully into my booth, but had lost my appetite for the tuna sandwich. Why couldn't Deputy Ramey accept my intuition about this crime without suspecting me of something awful?

The high-pitched, tinny tones of the William Tell Overture rang in the air, announcing someone's cell phone. Myra fumbled in her purse, extracted the phone and jammed it to her ear, turning away from the rest of us.

After a moment and with a pointed look in my direction, Myra stood and said, "I'm going to lie down. The news about Uncle Claude is devastating. It's given me a terrible headache." As she strode past, she asked her brother, "Did you bring me what I asked?"

Sonny pulled a fifth of cheap vodka from a shopping bag at his side and handed it to her. Myra grabbed the bottle, then strode to the counter. "Give me a large tomato juice. To go."

Sonny lifted his hands in a gesture of helplessness and walked toward the door.

"Where are you going?" Myra demanded.

"Don't worry about it, OK?" Sonny narrowed his eyes and glared at his sister. "If the cop wants me, he's got my phone number."

I was frankly relieved he wouldn't be hanging around the Knight's Rest. And from all appearances, Myra intended to sequester herself with that bottle of vodka and indulge in a bit of hair of the dog, as the saying goes, at least until she telephoned her husband to come and fetch her.

Hopefully, David would be here in the morning to take Janet to the sanctuary well before Mr. Hampton's arrival—whereupon I would then myself be free to leave when cleared to do so by the sheriff. How long did it take to run fingerprints, anyway?

CHAPTER EIGHT

They don't call Long Beach, California 'Iowa by the Sea' for nothing. Oh, the town has a beach all right, but a breakwater installed years ago reduces the surf from a mighty curl of water-bearing surfers, to a meek ripple suitable for plastic-shovel-wielding toddlers and straw-hat-wearing grannies. The red 'Beamer' convertibles that flood other California coastal towns are few and far between in Long Beach, and scarcely a sun-kissed starlet of the type crowding the beaches in Malibu can be found. All of which is why I chose Long Beach as my home. That and to be nearer to my sister, Sudie. Getting back to Long Beach was looking better every minute.

With Ramey gone, Janet resting in the room and the rest of us admonished to stay where we were, I decided upon a drive out along Route 66, as there was precious little with which to while away the hours at the Knight's Rest. But before setting off, I put in a call to David DiMarco. I wanted to alert him that Myra intended to spirit Janet back home. David wasn't in, so I left a message on his voice mail, suggesting he arrive as quickly as possible in the morning. Myra didn't strike me as an early riser, especially given the fifth of vodka she had taken with her to her cabin. We could get the jump on her. I hung up, hoping David checked his messages often and squinted out at the highway.

I felt as lonesome as the old road looked. In fact, I had begun to feel like Dorothy in *The Wizard of Oz*, the part where Glinda the good witch tells Dorothy to click her heels and repeat, "There's no place like home." Oh, where were the ruby slippers when you really needed them?

It occurred to me that if I drove around a bit I might come up with another inspiration for the article I had promised to write for *RV Life*. I'd cruise through the ghost towns of Amboy and Ludlow, reflecting on the past glories of these Mohave stop-offs, long-faded respites along a mean stretch of desert road.

I remembered traveling Route 66 with my family as a child. We were headed from St. Louis to California, a big vacation in those days. The desert presented a formidable challenge to motorists of that time, as few cars had air conditioning. Therefore, the trek across the baking wasteland was best undertaken during the night.

My most vivid memory was the excitement of stopping in Arizona and attempting to put my twelve-year-old self to sleep in broad daylight. The grown-ups lolled in coffee shops or in metal lawn chairs on small grassy spots in front of our tourists cabins waiting for the evening and the start of our voyage. I remember the canvas bag of water hung from the car's grille, a hedge against an overheated radiator.

But mostly I remember the heady adventure of rising at six pm and setting out down the two-lane road for a long drive under a star-filled sky, the promise of California glittering just as brightly as any constellation out there.

Now I made my way back to my Airstream, staring at it and thinking that even the motor home looked desolate and anxious to be on the road again. I went in and snatched a cold bottle of water from the fridge and grabbed a bag of chips. With these provisions and my cell phone stowed neatly on the passenger seat of the Honda, I set happily out in search of something to write about. As I pulled the car parallel with the motel, I noticed a decrepit car parked in front of Myra's cabin, but since her room was the nearest to the café, the car could have belonged to a customer. Or maybe Myra had company. I was convinced that if this was so, her visitor was doubtless male and probably young. Where on earth did she find them all?

I turned the wheel to ease the Honda onto the pavement and slammed on the brakes. Otis whizzed by me, shaking his fist as usual. Just past my car, Otis skidded to a stop, whirled around and started toward me again. I couldn't help but notice, even as I drew a quick breath of apprehension, that Otis rode what appeared to be a brand new bike. And the cycle was no ordinary one, either. Puzzled, I watched as Otis made his way toward me on a motorized bicycle, the kind that allows the rider the choice of pedaling or using a small battery-powered motor for propulsion. Lots of RVers have bikes of this type for getting around in the campgrounds and resorts. I knew the thing had cost Otis several hundred dollars.

Instead of passing me, Otis stopped his new ride directly in front of my car, thus making it necessary for me to back up in order to leave. I threw the car into reverse, but not before Otis dismounted and stood peering through the driver's side window. He grinned, showing badly rotted teeth. He pointed at his new bike and grinned all the wider. I knew instantly that he wanted praise.

"How nice," I said with a smile through the partially-opened window. "Where'd you get it?"

"Bought it," he exclaimed. "Sold all my rocks to this fella..."

Otis seemed in a rare mood to talk, but I was not. Who knew when he might next shake his fist and threaten me? I smiled and slid into reverse. "Very nice, Otis. I'm thrilled for you. Now, if you'll excuse me?..."

I was soon onto the highway, leaving Otis standing on the shoulder, scratching his disheveled hair and adjusting the direction of the eggbeater.

It amazed me still just how isolated this part of the world can be. I headed east and didn't spot a sign of life as far as my eye could see. I wasn't more than a few miles from the Knight's Rest when I noticed a slight vibration in the steering wheel. "God, not a flat," I muttered to myself. Maybe the problem was merely the road surface. I held my breath and kept on going. A road sign informed me the next town was twenty-three miles ahead. For all I knew, the town could be just as washed up as the ghost town of Bagdad, the remnants of which I had just passed.

Less than a mile later, the steering wheel began to vibrate more violently. I grasped the darn thing tightly with both hands, but still had trouble keeping the little Honda on the road. I fought hard, braking gently and attempting to ease the car onto the shoulder.

Suddenly a loud clanging, scraping noise bellowed from some-where near my right front tire. Then the car lurched to the right, at an angle that made me feel as if I were tacking in a small sailboat. I invol-untarily let out a shriek and immediately careened into a small sand hill at the side of the road. "I've had a blowout," I announced to no one after a stunned moment. My hands moved carefully over my face, arms, and torso. No blood. Everything seemed in good working order. Everything but my tire, apparently.

The driver's side door opened with great difficulty, owing to the angle of the car in the ditch. With great effort I finally got it open and crawled out into the glare of the sun. The air was still, not even a hint of a breeze. Heat rose from the asphalt in shimmering waves. It didn't take long for a river of sweat to make the trek from the middle of my back down to my legs.

I stooped to examine the offending tire. I shook my head and stared again. Could this be a mirage? My eyes could scarcely take in what I thought I saw. I had no tire. No wheel, either. Instead, half buried in the sand, lay the axle and drum, but no tire and no wheel. I looked behind me and there, about twenty feet back, lay the right front tire, alloy wheel glinting in the sun.

A flat tire I could have fixed. A car down in a sand hill on its axle was a horse of a very different color. I went back and stared again at the front axle until I realized I was thirsty. My water bottle, the bag of chips and the cell phone were in the front seat of the Honda. Ah, cell phone. My salvation. I could just call a tow service. They would have me out in no time. Unfortunately, my auto club card was back in the Airstream. I made a mental note to make a duplicate so that I could have one in each of my vehicles in the future. Live and learn.

After a long swig of water, I punched in the number for local and national information. "What city and state, please?" a disembodied voice inquired.

The state part I knew cold. The city part threw me. "Bagdad,

California," I said tentatively. I heard a series of clicks and a bit of static and took another wet gulp. A voice came on the line, this one a real person. "Did you say Bagdad? Is that with an 'h' or without? I responded that I thought it was without. Soon the voice was back. "Sorry, I'm not showing a Bagdad, California."

A vision of death by dehydration filled my gritty eyes. "Well then, may I please have the number for AAA in Barstow?" Surely they could send a tow truck. They would just have to trust me until I could get back to the Knight's Rest and retrieve my membership card. The operator gave me the number, which I dialed immediately.

The Barstow dispatcher wasn't thrilled that I could not pinpoint my exact location and wasn't impressed when I described my surroundings as a vast expanse of sand and lava rock. "That could be just about anywhere!" she said in exasperation. I didn't go on to explain that I had only one small bottle of water to my name and that the heat was fierce out here. I could see the headlines in tomorrow's paper: "Crazy Old Lady With No Business Being Out on Such a Hot Day Dies of Thirst. Buzzards Lead Police to Body."

"I'm headed east on Route 66, just a few miles outside what used to be Bagdad. Oh, and one more thing. I don't have my card with me. But please come. I'll die of thirst—"

"We'll have a truck there when we can," the dispatcher shot back grumpily and disconnected the line. I was left holding my phone, staring at it—my last connection to the world as I knew it.

Mouth parched, I leaned against the car and peered down the ribbon of road. I was afraid to drink more of the water. What if the tow truck took hours to reach me? How long did one take to die of dehydration?

On feeling the first nettles of panic at my temples, I reasoned that this line of thought could serve no useful purpose. Best think pleasant thoughts, I reminded myself gently, and allowed myself one small swig of precious water. Now, what to ponder? I searched for likely subjects to distract my mind. I tried to remember my life before setting out on this ill-fated trip. Oddly, I felt as if I had not had a prior life, or perhaps the one I remembered actually belonged to someone else. I scarcely remembered Sudie's face. But I remembered Janet's quite well, thank you very much.

The heat pressed down on me like a blanket. If only I could find a piece of shade, however small. The top of my head was practically on fire. Heat stroke was a real danger in such an environment as this. But crawling back into the Honda struck me as akin to plunging headfirst into Hades. As a last-ditch effort, I removed my T-shirt and placed it over my head.

I squatted next to the Honda, leaning against it, my mind filled with images from cowboy films of yore—especially the part where the old prospector stumbles out of the desert talking nonsense, then falls to the ground, dead.

Now and then, I got up and peered down the road in both directions, aching for the sight of another car. Time and again I returned to my perch at the side of the road. About two small swigs of water remained. I took one of them, and then paced to the side of the road for my regular sighting.

Ahoy! I could have shouted for joy, but for the parched condition of my vocal chords. The light bars of a distant tow truck glinted in the sunlight.

I jumped up and began waving my arms over my head as if the driver couldn't plainly see me and my car in all this nothingness, forgetting that I wore my shirt on my head and only my bra from the waist up.

As the truck slowed to a stop, I got another happy surprise. The driver was none other than Billy Ray. I grinned foolishly up at him as he swung his girth out of the cab and ambled over to the disabled Honda. He took off his greasy baseball cap and shuffled his feet. "Uh, Miz Merchant." He swallowed hard and cast his eyes to the ground, his cheeks flaming. Quickly he reached behind him and extracted a blue chambray work shirt from the seat of his truck. He thrust it at me. "Here. Put this on."

Only then did I remember I was shirtless, but was just too hot and too relieved to see a human form to be embarrassed. I donned the shirt Billy offered as if wearing my T-shirt on my head was something I engaged in regularly.

Recovered, Billy Ray scratched at his pink scalp. He walked over to the half-buried axle. "Looks like you lost your wheel there, Miz Merchant," he announced thoughtfully. "When's the last time you checked your lug nuts?"

"Never, I guess." And here I had prided myself on being such an experienced traveler.

Within minutes, Billy Ray had the Honda hauled onto the tow arm and me giving thanks for the mercy of air-conditioning. I lay my head back on the vinyl seat of the tow truck and let the cold air spill over me.

"I was hopin' to get a chance to thank you, Miz Merchant. Sorry it had to be like this. But what you said about the watch. Well...lookee." Billy extended his meaty arm for me to see and, sure enough, affixed to his left wrist was a shiny new watch. "It's got an alarm, too, just like you said." Billy Ray beamed. "Now me and Hazel are gettin' along much better. Thanks to you."

I smiled weakly. If only all troubled relationships were as easy to fix.

"And one more thing. You know that thing you asked...about that guy? Well, my friend in Vegas says he might have something for me. He's still checking. In Vegas they got so many lists they got lists of their lists. It's a big job but he said the name did sound familiar. Can't be that many folks name of Witherspoon, right? I'll keep you posted."

We soon reached Billy Ray's garage in Ludlow, where I gratefully accepted a Coke from the machine and plopped down on a filthy settee in the office to wait for the car to be fixed. The place smelled of grease and oil and old cheeseburgers. The obligatory mechanic shop posters were pasted on the wall—scantily clad girls smiling lasciviously at an oil filter while draped suggestively on the fender of a car. I reflected on Billy Ray's news...that Sonny Witherspoon might be a familiar name around the casinos in Vegas. Good, I thought, then groggily nodded off to the sound of the pneumatic drill.

A moment later, Billy Ray stood in the doorway, scratching his white head. "Miz Merchant. I think you better come here a minute."

My Honda had been hoisted onto the rack and the wheel that had come off replaced. All the other tires looked in good condition. "What Billy?"

"Well, Ma'am. The thing is. Lookee here at these wheels." He raised a grease-stained thumb to a lug nut on the left front tire and spun it around. I stepped closer and peered where his finger pointed. Then he walked to the rear tire and did the same. "Looks like to me somebody tampered with your tires, Miz Merchant. Somebody loosed these here lug nuts."

"Why on earth?" I stared open mouthed at the evidence before me. "Who on earth..."

"Couldn't say. 'Course, lug nuts can come a-loose by themselves once in a while. Maybe one or two. But you got two whole sets of 'em loose here. No way could that be an accident. You're just lucky both wheels didn't fly off and that you weren't going all that fast. Otherwise...." He raised his eyebrows and looked skyward.

Billy Ray's pronouncements echoed in my mind all the way back to the Knight's Rest. Who on earth would want to kill me? Or, in defiance of all odds, were the loosened lug nuts a fluke? I much preferred the latter explanation.

The neon sign had been extinguished and the place was dark when I turned into the Knight's Rest. I would have to content myself with whatever I could scrounge from my larder in the rig for supper, not that food had any great appeal just at the moment. That someone had possibly tried to do me harm was a surefire appetite suppressant. I vowed to keep my eyes and ears on alert and to lock my door at night.

Janet was awake when I came in. She seemed pleased to see me, but I couldn't be sure her smile was one of recognition or if she would have reacted the same way to a stranger. I dreaded the day, should it arrive, when my mental faculties would be in similar tatters. I resolved then and there to begin taking gingko biloba the day I arrived back home.

Janet and I shared a sandwich and a bag of chips from my rig. Since we had no TV, I attempted to converse with my dinner companion. I certainly couldn't talk with her about my recent brush with death.

She was sometimes lucid, commenting on the sandwich, or the amazing array of stars in the desert sky. Other times, she just went away, replaced by a Janet doll that smiled but did not speak.

The doctor at the hospital had prescribed several medications for Janet, and I attempted to administer them after our meal. She willingly took each pill as I proffered it, put it into her mouth, drank some water, then, politely as you please, removed the pill and tossed it onto the floor. It was like a game played between an adult and a recalcitrant child. We repeated this exercise four times before I gave up. Perhaps David would have better luck with her. I was just wasting both my time and what I was sure was costly medication.

I tidied up the room after our supper and thought of David DiMarco and his revelations. He had said Sonny and Myra had filed papers for conservatorship of Janet and I had no doubt, especially with Claude dead, that the request would be granted by any court in the land. Janet was clearly in no position to look after her own bath, let alone her finances. More's the pity. If I understood guardianship, the court could rule that Janet Witherspoon was incapable of caring for herself and her fortune. Sonny and/or Myra would be named as conservators until her death. My guess was such a court order would signal open season on the Witherspoon bank account by either or both of those obvious scoundrels.

But David had also said that in their wills Janet and Claude had left him a sizeable portion of the estate. The threat to leave everything to David had been made by Claude just before he and Janet left home. It had been made with the understanding that the elder Witherspoons would come and live at Friends in Need in return for changing their wills. The implications were chillingly clear. If Janet and Claude were to die before getting to Friends in Need, Sonny and Myra would benefit. If Janet got to the sanctuary, David and his attorneys might be able to assist her with her problems, and perhaps even file a countersuit of some kind. So much for Myra's love of money and Sonny's unpaid gambling debts.

It was none of my business, really, who inherited what, or how much. I just felt so sorry for Janet now that Claude was gone and wanted to see her receive proper loving care somewhere. I wanted nothing so much as to see Janet off safely in the morning.

Tomorrow, in fact, would be the dawn of a new and much better day for all of us—Janet, David and me. I felt my spirits lift to the point of giddiness. Everything would work out for the best. Deputy Ramey's fingerprint reports should be back from San Bernardino with the culprit named therein. The washed-out road to Friends in Need would be repaired and Janet could proceed to her new home with David. Calmed by such agreeable thoughts, I helped Janet to bed, then slipped in beside her and was asleep in moments.

I was awakened sometime during the night by the most awful caterwauling. It sounded like the train that ran beside Interstate 40 had derailed and had run smack into my cabin at the Knight's Rest. Startled, I sat up in bed and looked around. Just then, Janet took another deep breath and let it out in the most thunderous snore I have ever heard. Kat, too had snored, but hers was more of a steady stream of sound, like a cat's purr, only louder. It got so I couldn't sleep without hearing that resonating hum. Janet, on the other hand, could have brought down mountains with her bellowing.

Annoyed, I shook her shoulder, which only served to exacerbate the problem. She gulped and snorted and snored right on. At this rate I would get no more sleep for the remainder of the night. I tried to think of the tricks I knew for stopping a snoring bedmate. I recalled something about dipping the sleeper's fingers into a bowl of water, but I couldn't remember if finger-dipping caused a cessation of snoring or induced bedwetting. It seemed prudent to forgo finding out.

I could think of only one solution to my problem. Obvious. Simple. I knew of a perfectly good, serenely quiet bed—the one in my Airstream. Hazel would just have to overlook one night of boondocking. For eighty dollars, plus the additional forty dollars for Janet, I figured I deserved at least a good night's sleep. I grabbed my robe from the back of a chair and headed out.

Some minutes later, comfortably snuggled in my own bed, I fell into a light sleep, disturbed by the oddest dreams. We were back in college, Janet and I. And my date, the basketball player, was there, too. The three of us rode endlessly in a dark sedan with a bad engine. All night long, we roared around, never stopping, never getting anywhere. The car's engine was missing on at least one cylinder. I was exhausted but powerless to stop the endless roaming. Worse, the basketball player had failed to improve with time and was as boring in the dream as he had been in real life. Janet grinned her enigmatic smile, Mona Lisa in the back seat of a '66 Chevy.

The next thing I was aware of was a loud commotion. Red and blue lights flashed just outside my window, while male voices barked orders and called loudly to one another. From far in the distance, I heard a gruff voice demand, "Open up in there," followed by banging on the door of my rig. The clock on my bedside table registered nine am. I couldn't remember when I had slept this late. Still wiping sleep from my eyes, I peered out my door.

Two police cars sat outside my cabin, lights flashing. The door to the room stood completely open and a stream of light poured onto the pavement. Several officers milled about in the doorway.

I threw on my robe and rushed outside. "What's the matter?" I asked as I tried to peer into the room. A burly officer with a camera held to his face blocked my view.

Deputy Ramey emerged looking stern. "Janet Witherspoon has been murdered," he stated flatly, staring at me with a curious, half-accusatory look. "Please get dressed. We'd like to ask you a few questions. At the station."

The next several minutes flew by in a haze. My hands shook. I tasted the acrid tang of bile at the back of my throat. Somehow I managed to throw on a pair of jeans and a blouse. "My wallet is in the room. May I get it?" I asked the officers.

Deputy Ramey followed me into what was now a crime scene. Instinctively my hand flew to my mouth. Everything was in disarray. Drawers were pulled open and their contents strewn across the room. My bag had been searched; my toilet articles were spread over the dingy floor of the bathroom.

Janet lay on the bed, her throat sliced neatly from ear to ear. Blood covered the faded chenille spread and pillows and was splattered on the wall behind the bed. Spotting the murder weapon wasn't hard. My Swiss Army knife lay on the floor. I nearly fainted, both from the sight of the knife, and also from the sudden realization that had I remained in that room I too might be lying there dead.

Officers milled about, dusting for prints, taking photographs. From behind me, Ramey said, "She was pretty frail. Couldn't have put up much of a struggle." He placed his hand on my arm and steered me toward the door. "A kid, or a woman, could have done her." He sneered.

I followed Ramey out, my stomach lurching, my mind hazy from the horror of the scene inside the cabin. I would have to tell him that the knife was mine. Dear Lord. What a nightmare! He escorted me to his car and assisted me into the back seat.

"Who found her?" I managed to ask.

"The owner...when she came to clean the room. According to Mrs. Tutt, you and Miss Witherspoon were sharing that room. When was the last time you saw her alive? What were you doing out in your rig?"

I explained about the snoring. "I don't really know what time it was. Very late, I suppose. Or very early this morning. Look, officer, I could have been killed as well."

"Did you lock the door behind you?"

Did I lock the door? I couldn't remember with all these disturbing thoughts. I might have been an intended victim, Deputy Ramey seemed less than impressed. "I think I just pulled it shut behind me. Believe me. I had nothing to do with this. I—"

"Nobody said otherwise, Miz. Merchant. We just need to clear up a few things."

"It could have been a robbery. Did you see how thoroughly someone trashed the room?" Even as I said this, I knew my words sounded false. Robbery implied that someone had been lurking outside the Knight's Rest, just waiting for an opportunity to break into a room where two older women were staying.

"Might be. We'll look into it."

"And," I proceeded gamely, "there are others you should be questioning. Like Sonny Witherspoon. I'm sure neither he nor his sister wanted Janet to arrive at her destination. Actually, Myra Witherspoon is staying right here at the Knight's Rest. Why don't you question her?" Suddenly I remembered that Ramey had taken possession of my knife...that it was the murder weapon. "Deputy," I continued, my voice trembling, "The weapon lying on the floor, the red knife? Well, it is mine." I choked back a sob. "Please don't think—I had no reason kill Janet Witherspoon—Nor Claude."

"Don't know what I think. Yet."

He sped out of the parking lot, leaving me alone in the backseat with my thoughts. Tears welled up behind my eyelids—for me, my situation, and, of course, for Janet too. What an inglorious end for anyone, especially someone I knew. I remembered Janet in her younger days, quirky yes, but bright and committed to her causes. The tears streamed down in earnest. I buried my forehead in my clasped hands and wept without shame.

CHAPTER NINE

I had never been deep in the bowels of a police station before, though I had seen my share of them on television programs. They were usually depicted as dreary and utilitarian. This one was no exception. If I had not already had a headache from stress and lack of sleep and lack of coffee, I would have developed a doozy from the flickering fluorescent lights alone.

At a scarred table in a narrow conference room, I recounted my movements over the last several days while a detective took notes. After each answer, he would ask the question in a different way and off we would go again. I was getting dizzy from all the back and forth. Finally, another officer brought a Styrofoam cup full of acidic coffee and a stale donut—the Barstow equivalent, I supposed, of good cop, bad cop.

The coffee, though bitter, did help my pounding head and allowed me to gain a measure of self-possession over the course of the questioning. The notion that I had murdered Claude and Janet Witherspoon was simply too preposterous. No one could be dense enough to suspect me, at least not for long. Forensic evidence had to reveal the real killer in due course.

"You are pursuing other suspects, I presume," I said.

"Everybody is a suspect until we make an arrest." Deputy Ramey tilted back in his chair and crossed his arms over his head. "But I gotta be honest with you." He let the chair's front legs fall back to the floor, then leaned toward me over the table. "You had access to the room. It was your knife. And another question I got is why you were so conveniently elsewhere. What I can't figure out is why. Far as I can tell, you don't have a motive. You got the other two though—opportunity and means—in spades. Does that answer your question?"

The stale donut briefly threatened to reappear. I swallowed hard. "May I go now? I've answered all your questions. I've told you everything I know."

"Well, not quite. You told me you and the deceased were sisters. That's not true, is it?"

He must have talked to Sonny or Myra. I gulped. "Actually, we were sisters. In a way."

"Yeah? What way is that?"

"We were sorority sisters, from our days at college. I'm sorry I led you to believe otherwise. I was afraid...you know, the hospital and all...any decisions regarding her care. No one else was there for her. I believe Janet wanted it too. So against my better judgment, I led you to believe we were related. End of story."

"So you lied."

If only I had remembered to tell him myself. But with all the confusion, my little fib had simply fallen through the cracks. Now things looked even worse for me. "As you wish. But I meant no harm to anyone. May I go?"

Deputy Ramey stared at me a long moment before answering. "OK. I'll get one of the boys to drive you back. I've always had this suspicion you knew more than you let on. I don't want you leaving the area right now. Understand?"

I nodded and was out the door before he had a chance to change his mind.

When I returned to the motel, the office was closed. Hazel Tutt was nowhere to be found. My only option was to go to my RV. No one could be expected to stay in a room bloodied by a vicious murder. Besides, yellow police tape was placed over the entrance. A quick peek inside told me Janet's body had been removed but everything else was as it had been when I had first seen the room in the morning.

This time, yellow police tape surrounded the Winnebago as well as cabin number four.

I sank onto my sofa and let out my breath in one long whoosh. I craved sleep. More than anything else I wanted long, deep and uninterrupted slumber. However, under the circumstances, sleep was not on my short list of have-tos. Unbelievably, I was a suspect in a murder, possibly two. Worse, no one but me seemed inclined to step forward to prove my innocence. The way things were shaping up, I would need to do that job myself.

"Fine," I said out loud with emphasis. "Very well, then. I shall!" When next I spoke to Deputy Ramey, I intended to present him with evidence and facts, not suspicion and conjecture.

I'm a great believer in lists. Without list-makers, I daresay the world would not be so far along its evolutionary path. I applaud the first Cro-Magnon who placed a pebble alongside a symbol scratched on a rock and removed it when the task was complete. Whoever she was, and I'm sure it was a she, I am forever in her debt. I took a pen and a pad to list every fact I knew about the Witherspoons and their murders.

They had recently threatened to change their wills in order to leave a rather large estate to David DiMarco's Friends in Need Animal Sanctuary, with the understanding they could come and reside there whenever they chose.

Sonny and Myra Witherspoon, the heirs, upon learning of the change via a newspaper article, filed a petition for conservatorship over Janet and Claude, intending to declare them incompetent.

Angered by the court filing, Claude fetched Janet from a local nursing home, and together they set out for the Friends in Need Sanctuary in an aging Winnebago.

According to David, Claude was so infuriated at the attempt to declare him and his sister incompetent, he threatened to draw up new wills upon arrival at the sanctuary, leaving everything to DiMarco and nothing to either Sonny or Myra.

Claude and Janet got lost and phoned DiMarco, who told them to stay put. He offered to drive out and escort them to Friends in Need the following day.

Sometime during the evening of October fourth, an unknown person visited the Winnebago. The murderer somehow induced Claude Witherspoon to consume an overabundance of sleeping medication, turned the furnace to high and stuffed a piece of insulation into the heater vent, intending that both occupants of the motor home would die from carbon monoxide poisoning.

Janet Witherspoon seemed to have been spared because she was a night wanderer. She apparently rose soon after the murderer left and went for a moonlit stroll in the parking lot.

I had found Janet, dazed and in shock, standing in front of the Knight's Rest Motel and Café on the morning of October fifth. Within a short time, I discovered Claude's body and notified the sheriff.

I tapped my pen against the pad of paper. At least one conclusion was possible. Someone had not wanted the senior Witherspoons to reach the Friends in Need Sanctuary and that someone had wanted to prevent this arrival badly enough to commit a murder.

That left the question of Janet's murder two nights later. Without question, that same someone felt Janet, however diminished her capacities, could not be allowed to journey on to the sanctuary. But why?

I was glad I had taken the time to construct my list, but no new insights leapt from the page. Sonny Witherspoon, either acting alone or in cahoots with his sister, had the world's oldest motive to kill—greed. With their aunt and uncle dead, they would stand to inherit their part of the estate. If either Claude or Janet Witherspoon reached the sanctuary, chances were good the younger generation might be cut out of the estate, altogether.

The only person not on my list was David DiMarco, for the very reason that he, of all of them, stood only to gain by welcoming the Witherspoons to his organization's sanctuary. On the other hand, was his story about a washed-out road true? Had he been hedging, unwilling to bring Janet to the sanctuary for some reason?

I pondered this for a moment or so, then plunged ahead. This was murder and I was a suspect. I should at least verify his alibi. If it turned out that David indeed was at the Gemilli Winery the night of Claude's murder, then I could scratch him off the list entirely.

As long as I was stuck with little to do but worry, I thought I should give the Winnebago one last going over even though the crime scene people had been there and it was restricted with tape. Something could have been missed. But, first, I called information for the number of the winery and scribbled it on a piece of paper.

I stood and stretched and was just about to dial the number when a knock sounded. I opened the door to see Hazel Tutt standing there, her face lit by a wide grin. She looked positively girlish.

Actually, I had been dreading a confrontation with Hazel. In my mind, she was likely to be unpleasant about the state of affairs in cabin four. It wouldn't have surprise me if, after the police left, she tried to force me to clean up the place. Therefore, I was mightily astonished to stare out the door at her open and beaming countenance. I hoped she wouldn't make a fuss about my boondocking.

"Hazel, " I said pleasantly, "I hope you understand. I've been asked to stay in the area, but I can't stay in the room. You know—"

"Hell, I wouldn't let you stay there. Not even if the police would." Hazel grinned wider. So she did have a heart underneath that brusque exterior.

"That's so kind of you. I'll be happy to compensate you for the use of your parking lot."

"No need. I'm about to make all the money offa' this dump I could possibly want. And it's about time, too."

My confused stare must have tickled her.

Hazel threw back her head and laughed. "I'm a businesswoman. I see opportunity where some others, like yourself, just see a big mess."

"I'm afraid I'm not following you."

"'Course not. I'm the one with a head for business. I'm gonna turn this old heap of a place into one of the finest tourist attractions to be seen along Route 66 since the old road's heyday, that's what I'm gonna do."

"Really?"

"Yep. I can see it now. Hazel Tutt's Murder Museum. If that old hobo Bob Waldmire could do it with his stupid Hula Girl's Museum, which was nothing but a bunch of junk, I can do this. See, I'll give tours—maybe have actors do a reenactment. I'll charge extra for tourists to stay in the room where the murder actually happened. People will pay good money for the experience." Her teeth showed themselves in a wide grin, as Hazel calculated her profits.

Appalling as the plan was, I had no doubt she was right. People would pay money for a tour through Hazel Tutt's Murder Museum. Stranger things had happened on this famous road. Hazel was about to take her place in the fabled highway's history.

"My, aren't you the creative one?" I smiled. "But Hazel, if you have a moment, I'd like to ask you a few questions about all this hubbub."

"I already told the police everything I know. Which is exactly noth-in'."

She was adamant. But she could have forgotten something. Even a little thing. Anything. "Do you remember the day the Winnebago pulled into your lot? Did you see anything out of the ordinary? Anything that didn't fit, somehow?"

"Nope. Just the two folks in the Winnebago. Told 'em the same as I told you. No boondocking. You wanna boondock, go into town. Go to the Wal-Mart, someplace like that."

"But they didn't leave. Did you talk to them again that night?"

"Naw. Not really. They was waiting for this friend to take 'em someplace. Said the friend would be here soon to get them. I kinda looked out there from time to time just to make sure they were OK. Felt sorry for 'em." She wrinkled her nose, as if trying to understand her own compassion.

Now, the key question. "Did you see anyone near their rig that evening? Or hear any cars pull in or out?"

Hazel cocked her head and thought. "I told the detective there coulda' been a car," she said at length. "Yeah. There coulda' been a car that night."

As the gold miners used to say just a few hundred miles northwest of where we now stood…Eureka! "What time?"

"Not sure. Maybe just after dark. I was in the kitchen cleaning up. But I like to know what's going on around here. I peeked out when I thought I heard a car drive up, but didn't see nothin'. The way the rig was parked, the car could have been on the far side and I wouldn't have seen it."

"Anything else? Anything at all?" My heart thumped with excitement. Any little observation and I could wrap this thing up and get out of here, finally.

"Nothin'." Hazel paused. "Well, there is one more thing. Billy Ray said to tell you he found what you wanted. That guy you asked about. He's on every be-on-the-lookout list in town. Every deadbeat list, too. Looks like he ran up a bunch of debt and split. He's toast, if I know Vegas." She grinned. "Oh, And one more thing. I owe you one. For what you said to Billy Ray."

For a moment, I couldn't remember what she was talking about.

"You know. The thing about the watch. He hasn't been late a single time since he bought it. Fact is, he ain't really left here. Made me realize he really did care for me. Anyway, thanks."

Hazel promised to let me know if she remembered anything else, then went back to the office, leaving me to contemplate my good fortune. It had been clever indeed to ask about Sonny and gambling debts. His motive was now indisputable.

I dialed the Gemilli Winery and an operator answered on the second ring. "May I speak to Mr. Frank Gemilli," I asked politely.

"May I say who is calling?"

"This is Libby Merchant. I'm the administrative assistant at the Friends in Need Sanctuary." Belatedly, I realized I should not have used my real name. What if the receptionist called Friends in Need? Ah, well, too late now.

"I'm sorry, Miss Merchant. Mr. Gemilli isn't in. Can I help you with something?"

I cleared my throat and tried to sound both officious and harried.

"Oh, I certainly hope so. You see, I've lost track of my boss's schedule for October fourth. I know he planned to visit Mr. Gemilli and present him with a gift basket in thanks for his yearly donation. But the problem is...I have an extra basket and can't reach Mr. DiMarco. I'd be so grateful if you could check to see that Mr. Gemilli received his gift basket from us. We are so appreciative."

"I'd really like to help you but my computer is down at the moment. I keep all Mr. Gemilli's appointments there," she apologized.

"I see. Well then, perhaps you might recall if my boss, David DiMarco, visited Mr. Gemilli on the fourth of this month. It would really help me. I'm preparing a report for our board of directors and I don't want to get into trouble."

"I know what you mean," she said sympathetically. "I keep Mr. Gemilli's schedule. Let me think...actually I do remember something about that visit. I believe Mr. DiMarco arrived just before supper. He and Mr. Gemilli had dinner al fresco on the patio. And he brought a gorgeous gift basket with him. Really lovely."

"Oh, I'm so relieved. Oh, and by the way, do you happen to remember what time Mr. DiMarco left that evening?"

"What has that got to do with anything?"

I giggled and attempted to sound girlish. "Oh, I just happen to know a certain lady wanted to see Mr. DiMarco that night. I just wonder if she got the chance."

"I'm afraid your friend was disappointed. Mr. DiMarco spent the night. I served him coffee the next morning, just before he drove away."

"Oh, I see. Well then, would you mind giving me a ring once your computer is back up and running and you can verify the date? My boss reviews all my paperwork at the end of each month. If my schedule isn't right, I could get fired." I gave her my number and sank back in my chair relieved. David had been in Temecula during the time the first murder was committed. I was silly to have even suspected him, especially since he had no motive.

That left me with my original suspects, the younger Witherspoons.

And to that elite list I now intended to add Otis. I had thought of him and his new bike several times over the last few hours. Sonny had said Claude and Janet stopped at a cash machine before leaving home. Claude's wallet was empty when I found it, and Otis was the proud owner of a new bike. I didn't believe that he made that much money selling rocks to strangers, not for an instant. Maybe he dispatched Janet in hopes of finding another cache of bills. Nothing was out of the question at this point.

Nowhere to go. Nothing to do. Best use my leisure wisely, and another search of the Winnebago seemed the perfect way to pass a little time. Besides, who knew? I might just turn up something useful yet.

I trekked over to the Winnebago and then hesitated, trying to figure out what might be the punishment for crossing the yellow police tape. Did one go to jail? If not, and one is already a suspect, then one at least digs oneself deeper into trouble. But only if caught, right? Besides, how much more buried in difficulties could I get?

Inside, everything was just as it had been the last time I searched. Papers and debris reigned throughout. I scrutinized the small space again for anything that might give me some idea who had visited Janet and her brother that fateful night. I wracked my brain, but just like all the other times, I came up empty-handed. Defeated, I turned to go. Just then I heard the doorknob turning, the sound of the weather stripping as it scraped across the linoleum floor. My heart skipped. I felt a sudden chill course down my spine. I stood slowly, holding my breath. The door between the sleeping area and the rest of the Winnebago was really just an accordion fold that closes across the opening. I pushed the flimsy door a quarter of the way open and looked out at David DiMarco. "My God," I said, "you startled me."

Apparently I was not the only one susceptible to a case of nerves. David whirled around, his face a mask of surprise and a further emotion, harder to read.

Then I realized that David was not alone. Another man pushed into the rig behind him, a youthful fellow dressed in jeans and boots. He

125

swept a battered straw cowboy hat from his head, letting loose a mass of tangled blonde hair. He had the look and the swagger of a ladies man. After his startled look dissolved, he regaled me with a quick toothy smile. He looked just like Brad Pitt in his *Thelma and Louise* role, down to the cowboy hat and tight jeans. I stepped aside to give them room in the tiny space, experiencing an uneasy awareness that he looked distantly familiar.

David recovered himself. "This is the assistant I mentioned, Mr. Rocket. Johnny, this is the lady I was telling you about."

The young man peered at me. "Pleased ta meetcha," he said and stuffed his hands into the pockets of his jeans. His eyes were the most startling shade of blue. Was something about him familiar or was I just thinking back on the movie?

"You've heard about Janet, I suppose," I said, turning to David.

"Yes," David said. "I'm...we're devastated. The motel owner informed us when we came by to...to uhh...to pick her up. So horrible. I hope they catch the guy and fry him."

There was a look on David's face. Could it be relief? I studied him a moment. David righted his features and the peculiar expression vanished.

Johnny Rocket plopped onto the sofa and fumbled in his shirt pocket, extracting a pack of cigarettes. He fished one from the pack, stuck it between his lips then again went fishing for his lighter. I almost asked him to refrain but stopped myself. This wasn't my rig. Not finding the lighter in his shirt, he stood abruptly and patted each of his pants pockets. When that failed to produce results he walked to the kitchen area and opened one of the drawers, extracting a butane barbeque lighting tool I'm sure the senior Witherspoons used to light their propane stove.

This time I got my courage together while marveling that he could find the mundane implement in all the clutter. "I'd prefer you didn't light up in here. You see, I quit and am still a bit vulnerable."

Johnny glared at me, but replaced the cigarette and put the pack back in his pocket. He looked directly at David and cleared his throat pointedly.

"Ah…I hope you'll understand…that you won't find this insensitive," David began, "but with Janet dead…it's just that…I must try and locate…. It is so important…to the sanctuary…to the animals." He began rifling through a stack of yellowed papers on the counter.

"What is it? Perhaps I can help." I had seen nothing here that might relate to the sanctuary. And God knew I had searched the Winnebago thoroughly.

"Actually, I'm looking for their wills"

"You and everyone else," I said. "Sorry to disappoint you but I don't think they're here. I've looked."

"You see, Claude didn't believe in attorneys. He and Janet had only handwritten wills. They kept them somewhere among their papers. Claude told me that he and Janet had decided to leave a good portion of their estate to my organization. What I don't know is whether they actually made the changes to their wills." David seemed uneasy talking about the subject of money. "Now, with Janet gone too…well, I just feel I must find out for myself. I know how this must appear, believe me. But I'm afraid if I don't find the wills, the relatives will…well…you know…try to keep them from surfacing…especially if they actually made the changes Claude promised." David had begun wringing his hands. A line of perspiration glistened on his brow. He stopped speaking and smiled. "I know this is an awkward time…with all that has happened." David looked at me, then away, cracking his knuckles. "But so much is at stake. Perhaps even the very survival of the sanctuary."

"Of course. But I've already looked through much of this stuff. All I found were assorted papers, a few bank statements and the phone numbers I needed to contact the niece and nephew. I don't think the wills are here."

"You won't mind if I just look again?" He began opening drawers.

"Not at all." I took a seat at the dinette. I considered talking to him about my difficulties, the questioning by the police. But at the moment he was totally preoccupied with the search. And who could blame him?

Unless he could produce the handwritten wills, Sonny and Myra could easily claim none had been drawn up. That would mean Claude and Janet died intestate. The estate would go into probate and David and the sanctuary would lose out altogether. Little wonder Myra had been so anxious to locate a file of papers. "I feel so badly about this," I said in understanding. "Perhaps Claude and Janet intended to make new wills once they relocated to Friends in Need. Perhaps they didn't bring a copy of the old one."

"Ummm. Perhaps. They did leave in rather a hurry." He stopped scrabbling around in cabinets and leaned against the counter. "I suppose they might have left it back in Pasadena." This thought, instead of cheering him, appeared to plunge him into an abyss. His face darkened. His brows knit together and his lips pressed into a thin line.

I raised my hands in a matching gesture of helplessness and frustration. "I'm so sorry, David. I know how much this means to you...to the sanctuary. If I turn up anything, I'll call you first."

Johnny appeared in the narrow doorway separating the bedroom from the rest of the motor home. "Nothin' here. Let's go."

"Yes. Please call. I'd appreciate that more than you know."

CHAPTER TEN

Sonny Witherspoon remained my prime suspect. He'd had the opportunity. He had the motive. And anyone could have had the means. Even Otis. Blocking a heater vent doesn't take genius. Even slitting someone's throat doesn't require the skills of a master criminal.

The next time I saw Otis about the place, I fully intended to question him about the new bike—as in, where on earth did he acquire the funds to buy it. Right now, however, the question of the hour was really Sonny's alibi. He'd told Deputy Ramey he had been gambling at the Lucky Dog Casino the night Claude was murdered. Somehow I doubted that. The logical place to begin was at the casino he favored.

I packed a lunch, threw my bag into the car and took off, feeling free as a bird for the first time since the day—sometime during the last century—I had set out from Long Beach. I whistled along with the radio and kept time to the beat of the music by tapping my fingers on the steering wheel.

I knew I was approaching Vegas when the barren landscape began to sport the occasional gas station or small motel. These nondescript buildings became more and more frequent, and some had begun to advertise SLOTS and CARDS on the kind of cheap, lighted signs that can be towed from place to place.

Just on the outskirts of Las Vegas, I spotted the Lucky Dog Casino, Sonny's designated gambling parlor. The place was hardly your opulent gaming establishment, not by a long shot. I doubted the cocktails were complimentary, and if a lounge act was employed here at all, it probably ran to the kind contingent upon the female form, sans clothes.

The squarish concrete building was painted red, but the desert heat had faded the color to a dull pinkish brown. A sign painted on the building depicted a scruffy mongrel dog sitting at a card table. In the pooch's hand—or, should I say, paw—were spread four aces. The dog sported a wide grin and a cigar stuck out from his smiling muzzle. COME ON IN, the sign read, BIG WINNERS. BE A LUCKY DOG.

Only a few cars sat baking in the gravel lot. I parked and stepped out into the heat. I removed my sunglasses as I entered the cavernous gloom of the casino, which was one large room, really, with a bar across the rear and gaming tables crowded into the middle of the floor. Slot machines stood like sentinels along the other three walls. The smells of cigarette smoke and stale beer almost knocked me over.

Most of the action was at the slots, the movers and shakers being a motley group of determined regulars pulling the cranks while clutching large plastic cups of nickels. At the long bar, several patrons stared at a wrestling match on a TV mounted over long rows of bottles. The bartender wiped glasses with a none-too-clean towel. This looked like exactly the kind of place a man like Sonny would choose to frequent.

I had no trouble picturing him here. His pocket protector, gambling systems and unkempt ponytail didn't speak of the lush casinos down on the Strip. The joint was sleazy and wore like a banner an air of barely concealed danger. The patrons looked as though they all had been sent from central casting, extras in a '40s style gangster film. I pranced up to the bar, pulled out a mock-leather stool and sat.

One or two of the customers looked up, but went immediately back to nursing their drinks. The bartender ambled over to take my order. "Give me a screwdriver," I said pleasantly. "Make it a double." I unsnapped my purse, pulled out a twenty and lay it on the bar. I don't know why I added that last part. Maybe I wanted to give the impression that I belonged here or at least in a place just like this. I would have to sip slowly. I still had the trip back to think about.

Now what was the name of the man Sonny said he gambled with? Lonnie something or other. The bartender returned with my drink, placed it on a cocktail napkin decorated with playing cards and left with the twenty. I took a sip of the screwdriver. Then another. The task before me demanded an acting ability I was not sure I possessed, though I had been doing rather well in that department lately, if I do say so myself.

"Excuse me," I called to the bartender.

He walked toward me down the length of the bar. "Something wrong with the drink?" It was not so much a question as a challenge.

"Oh no. The drink is fine. I was just wondering if you could help me." The barman tensed. He probably guessed I had lost at the tables and was about to ask for busfare home. By the look on his face I surmised he had been approached with such a request more than once or twice before. "Actually, I'm trying to locate someone. Do you know a Lonnie?" Just at that moment, Lonnie's last name burst from my memory bank. "Lonnie Street. Do you know him?"

The bartender was practiced at keeping his emotions to himself, but I saw an eyebrow rise and a guarded look flit across his face. "Why?"

"Actually, I'm an old family friend of a buddy of his. His buddy said I should look up Lonnie if I was ever out this way." I smiled as sweetly as I knew how.

"Yeah? You sure you got the right Lonnie?"

"I'm positive he said the Lucky Dog. Is there another gambling establishment with the same name?" Perhaps the barman was just surprised that Lonnie had any friends at all.

"Nope. You're in the right place. So what's the buddy's name? And what did he want you to look up Lonnie for?"

"It's rather complicated. You see, my friend is in a bit of a pickle at the moment. Actually, I shouldn't be telling you this." I hunched over the bar and spoke in a stage whisper. "But he is from a prominent family. You'd recognize the name in an instant." I folded my cocktail napkin in half and smoothed it out on the bar. "They want to keep this little, shall we say incident, out of the papers for now. The family has requested I talk with Lonnie about his association with ah...my friend."

"Yeah? Well, Lonnie's a busy man. Who's your friend?"

Another patron signaled the bartender and he moved away to refill a beer glass from the tap. When he didn't show any indication that he planned to return to me or our conversation, I waved my fingers at him, smiling. "Yoo-hoo. As I was saying..."

He gave the counter in front of me a vigorous wipe. "Look, lady. Like I said, Lonnie doesn't see just anybody. He's busy. Maybe if you tell me who this friend is..."

"Oh, very well. He's Sonny Witherspoon," I said in an exaggerated whisper.

I had expected some acknowledgement, but instead, the bartender spun around and picked up a phone. Then he punched in a row of numbers, his back still turned. As he spoke, he cupped his hand over the receiver. After a moment, he turned back to me. "Wait right here."

I sipped my drink, confident that Lonnie would appear within moments. I'd ask him about the evening and night of October fourth. Dutifully, Lonnie would admit that Sonny had been nowhere near the Lucky Dog on the evening in question. I could be on my way back to the Knight's Rest, my caper undetected. A call to Deputy Ramey would be my first order of business as soon as I returned. I was so engrossed in the apparent success of my mission that I failed to see the two men until they stood beside me, one on either side. They were so close, I smelled aftershave on one of them and a hint of cigar smoke on the other.

"You wanna come with us,"said the darker man, the one smelling like cigar smoke, placing his hand firmly on my elbow.

The slightest shiver of apprehension trickled along my spine, but I was so near to my goal. I rose. The man gripped my arm and steered me between them toward the rear of the casino.

We threaded our way around the various gaming tables toward the bank of slots along the far wall. Just as we approached one of them, the red lights on top began to blink. A cacophony of sirens blared from the machine. A woman, about my age, stooped and cupped her hands under the chute. Quarters came flying out, hundreds of them. The look on her face was one of rapture. I wondered how many days on end she had sat at that very machine, feeding quarters into the slot, dreaming of exactly this event. Actually, I was quite happy for her.

The entire spectacle reminded me of a family trip years ago. Sudie and I had been young, maybe seven and eight. When we came through Nevada, slot machines began to turn up, even in gas stations and cafés. Sudie and I were thrilled and irresistibly drawn to the one-armed bandits. We pestered our parents mercilessly while having lunch in a roadside café. "Please, oh please, let us play the slots," we whined. Finally, our father, a stern and conservative man and a churchgoer, dug into his pocket. "Now, girls, I'm going to teach you a lesson on the perils of gambling. You can each have a nickel for candy. Or you can throw your money away in one of those slot machines. What will it be?"

"The slots," we cried happily and in unison.

He marched us over to the machine, handed us our nickel, then stood aside as I slid mine into the slot and pulled the handle. My machine had given out a high, siren-like sound, and nickels came gushing forth, spilling onto the floor in a heap. So much for object lessons.

The man steering me veered sharply to the left and soon we were standing before a door marked PRIVATE. The one not holding my elbow knocked. We waited a moment.

Finally, the door opened. A man wearing dark glasses and a darker suit stood just inside. He stepped away so that we could enter. The room was tiny and all three of the men large. I experienced another moment of tension. I told myself the tightening in my chest was only due to the smallness of the room and the number of large men squeezed into it.

A door opened at the far end of the room and yet another man entered. He, too, was large, with a protruding belly. His face displayed a neatly trimmed goatee. I was starting to feel like a sardine. "You looking for Lonnie?" he asked, his eyes never leaving my face.

I glanced at my watch. Good heavens, it was after three in the afternoon. I would have to get a move on to get back to the motel before I was missed. I indicated that yes, I was interested in speaking with Mr. Street, but that I was in a bit of a rush.

"Hand me your pocketbook," the man with the goatee said.

"I beg your pardon?"

"I said, hand over your pocketbook."

Was I being robbed? Instinctively I clutched my purse closer. "I'm afraid I don't understand. I only wanted—"

My sentence was brought to a halt by the pressure of a hand tightening on my arm. "Like the gentleman said, hand over your purse."

I quickly delivered my bag to the man standing next to me. He opened it and walked over to a small table where he upended the bag, dumping out my belongings. "She's clean," the man said at length and scraped my possessions back where they had come from. I felt oddly violated by the sight of my personal items displayed for all to see.

"So, what do you know about Sonny Witherspoon?" asked the man with the goatee.

I returned my attention to the business at hand. "I want to speak to Lonnie. I'll explain everything to him." I said this gamely. Actually, my knees had not stopped knocking since I entered the room.

The thug with the goatee looked to the others. They all nodded in agreement. "All right," goatee said, at last. "But Lonnie isn't here. We'll take you to him. Follow me."

With that, the same man took my elbow and aimed me toward the door at the rear. We went through a small office, then, all of a sudden, we were through another door and standing in an alley behind the building. The sun was blinding, but I could make out a dark sedan parked at the curb. "Get in," the goatee ordered.

Perhaps my mission wasn't turning out as successfully as I had first thought. I did not want to get into that car with those men. "Oh dear," I exclaimed. "I hadn't realized the time, I'm afraid—"

"Get in." This time, a hand pressed against the small of my back, propelling me toward the car. A door swung open and I was pushed roughly into the backseat. The windows had been darkened like a celebrity limo; those inside the car could see out, but no one outside the car could see the interior. In other words, anything could happen to me in here and no one on the street would be the wiser. I felt a thin trickle of perspiration slide down my side.

They say the last thing one should do when faced with a menacing situation is show fear. I jutted my chin and prayed no one would notice the tremble in my hands. "Just where are you taking me?"

One of my captors, for that is what they now seemed, began a hushed conversation on his cell phone. The one beside me whipped a bandanna out of his pocket. "Put this on," he commanded.

Seeing little choice, I did as he asked and the world outside disappeared altogether. We drove in circles for a while, then came a series of left turns, which I counted. Finally, judging from the echoing noises and the change in the quality of light, we pulled into some kind of underground structure—a parking garage, maybe. My teeth had actually begun to chatter. I remembered all the gangster movies I had seen in which someone gets offed in a dimly lit, deserted parking garage.

The blindfold was removed and we exited the car and entered a freight elevator. I got the sense as we rose past floor after floor that we were in one of the larger hotels, maybe out on the Strip. Finally, the doors opened and we stepped into an ornate foyer. The stillness was deafening. The carpet must have been a foot thick; air conditioning thrummed in the background. One of the men opened a double oak door and beckoned me to follow him. Inside the room was a massive desk. Floor to ceiling windows let in light and afforded a gorgeous view of Vegas and the desert beyond, not that I was much in the mood for dazzling views.

A smallish man with stark white hair and a prominent chin sat behind the desk. He spoke very softly, indicating with a nod that the others were to leave the two of us alone. He was nattily dressed in a well-tailored suit, shirt and tie all in the same shade of soft gray. When he stood, he invited me to take a seat in one of the deep leather chairs in front of the desk with a gesture that was almost courtly. "I'm Lonnie." He smiled, smoothed the flawless nap of his lapel and sat. He was almost lost behind the immense desk. "My boys tell me you're a friend of Sonny Witherspoon's."

I gulped and realized that, as the saying goes, I was now in over my head. I had never in my wildest dreams expected that I'd get mixed up with organized crime figures. And if these guys weren't criminals, they were putting on one hell of an imitation. But having come this far, I could see nothing for it but to proceed. "Friend is a wee slight stretch of the term. A family friend would be more accurate. You see…"

I launched into my pitch about the family and its desire to look into a little scrape of Sonny's. "I'd just like to verify that Mr. Witherspoon…Sonny…was not gaming with you on the evening of October fourth. It would mean so much to the fam—"

"Where is Sonny?"

"Right now, that's not the issue."

"Oh, yes it is. More than you know. Where is he?" Lonnie's blue eyes glinted in my direction.

"Well, I'm not entirely certain, you see. I'm merely a friend of his aunt's. Do you remember the evening in question? It's very important."

"I'll decide what's important and what's not. Mr. Witherspoon and I have a business matter to settle." Lonnie paused and let his eyes drill into me. "You help me, I'll help you. You tell me where he is and I'll tell you whether or not he was at my establishment on the evening of October fourth. Deal?"

"Would you be willing to swear to it, or put it in writing?" I negotiated.

Mr. Street smiled. "You drive a hard bargain." I could tell he was playing with me. I felt foolish for even asking the question. Lonnie Street leaned over his desk, his ice-blue eyes piercing. "I don't swear to anything. And I never put things in writing. My word is my bond."

This was it. No turning back. "I'm sure that's true. However, under the circumstances, I really want something in writing that says Sonny was not here on the evening in question. Give me that and I'll reveal his whereabouts."

Lonnie's eyebrows shot up. "Did you say *not* here?"

"Yes. That he was not in your establishment, or with you that evening."

Lonnie crossed his arms over his chest and regarded me for a moment. "Can't help you, lady. He was here. All night."

I felt the wind go out of me, just as surely as if someone had punched me in the stomach.

"You want me to write it down? Now, where's Sonny?"

"Uh, no. You won't need to write it down. And as for Sonny, I don't really know where he is, exactly."

Lonnie frowned. "Look, it's not my habit to rough up old ladies but money is money. Just tell me what you know and we'll take you back to your car."

Even at this age, I find it difficult to be called old. Old has so many negative connotations. Although I have no shortage of gray hair and certainly a few wrinkles, I really don't think of myself that way. Old is what happens to someone else. Apparently considering me that way was no problem for Lonnie and, in this case, it was probably just as well. It might just have saved me from a beating. Or worse.

Finally, I informed Lonnie that the last time I had seen Sonny he was staying in a small motel on Route 66 outside Barstow. Good as his word, Lonnie had me again loaded in the dark sedan and soon I was traveling through Vegas, blindfolded, on my way back to the Lucky Dog.

I couldn't remember ever feeling so low. My prime suspect was now not a suspect at all. But if not Sonny, then who?

CHAPTER ELEVEN

The information provided by Lonnie Street had dealt a fatal blow to my case. Mr. Street and his cronies had also managed a serious threat to my heart rate and anxiety levels.

All was not entirely lost, I mused as I opened the door to my Airstream back at the Knight's Rest. Sonny might have hired a hit man to do the deed for him. From the looks of the hangers-on at the Lucky Dog Casino, he could have taken his pick. But Sonny needed a cash infusion badly and hit men are usually rather expensive, or so I've learned from the movies. With deep regret, I moved him to the bottom of—although not entirely off—my list.

That left Myra, her about-to-be-indicted husband and Otis, of course. And though David had an airtight alibi, what about his young associate, speaking of hit men?

Myra had been at home the evening that Claude's body was discovered. I knew, because I myself had telephoned her there. She could have paid her aunt and uncle a visit, setting into motion the events that would lead to Claude's death, then gotten back home before my call. But how would she have known where Claude and Janet were? By Sonny's own admission, he had followed his aging relatives using a high-tech tracking device, ostensibly because he was looking after their welfare. Myra had no way of knowing their whereabouts, however, unless Sonny had communicated with her. I took out my pad and pen and wrote a note to myself to ask Sonny whether or not he had called Myra after locating his aunt and uncle. Of course, if the two of them were in this together, he might not tell the truth.

As if on cue, when I glanced outside I spotted Sonny leaning against the side of the café, lighting a cigarette. He was now low on my suspect list, but might be willing to divulge a little information about his sister.

I walked outside and threaded my way to where he stood. Heavy gray smoke curled in front of his face. Sonny's eyes flitted back and forth between the road and me. He took several quick pulls on the smoke, then ground it out under his booted foot. "Yeah?" he muttered.

"Excuse me, Sonny, but I was just wondering about, ah, your sister, Myra. I'm a bit concerned. She's been holed up in that cabin for hours. Should we be worried? She seems to be taking her aunt's death rather hard." I thought that if I could get him to talk, perhaps he would let something slip, something I could use.

"Myra? Fat chance!" Sonny again cast his glance along the deserted highway. "Myra only cares about three things, besides herself, of course." He looked away and didn't offer any further comment.

"What are they?" I prodded gently.

"Money, money and more money." He fished another cigarette from his pocket and lit it. An old blue Ford came into view as it crested the top of the rise and made its way in our direction. Sonny stepped back so that he was hidden from the road by the corner of the café. Lengthening shadows fell across his face. He pulled down his sunglasses and inhaled deeply on his cigarette. He looked so frightened I almost wished I hadn't told Lonnie Street Sonny's whereabouts.

"Ah…listen," Sonny mumbled. "On your business card it says you're a doctor. Is that true?"

"Yes. But not a medical one. I'm a clinical psychologist."

"Yeah, yeah. That's what it says. I was wondering…uh," Sonny pressed his lips together and wiped his palms, "do you, like…talk to people who have, ah…problems? See, I got this friend who gets obsessed, can't stop this thing he does."

"Tell your friend that I applaud his courage. Changing a destructive behavior is very hard. I'd be happy to give you the name of a good psychologist if you'd like."

"Naw. Nothing like that. It's probably nothing, anyway." Sonny shrugged and looked away.

Even though he might not be going to jail for murder, Sonny's future struck me as cloudy at best. I wasn't fooled for an instant and really hoped he would seek help for his issues. But right now, Sonny Witherspoon was not my problem...finding a murderer was. As the Ford passed without turning into the Knight's Rest, some of the tension fell away from Sonny. "As you were saying," I reminded him, "all Myra cares about is money, money, money?"

He threw down the cigarette and jammed his hands into his pockets. "Forget it," he said. "It's none of your business anyway. Her finances are her stupid husband's problem. She drinks because she likes to. And when she drinks she shacks up with whatever pair of pants wanders into her web. I've called her husband. He'll be here to scoop her up soon." Sonny glanced toward the cabin where Myra was keeping company with Mr. Smirnoff. A look flitted across his face and was gone before I had time to fully register it. Was it concern? Compassion? "She's his problem, not mine."

"But I'll bet you keep tabs on her, just like you did on Janet and Claude. Am I right?"

"Yeah, I do." Anger crept around the edges of his words. Sonny pushed his sunglasses onto his head and squinted at me. "You're too nosy. Why don't you just butt out? I'm not saying anything else."

"I was just wondering, Sonny," I began, plunging ahead despite Sonny's warning. "When I telephoned Myra to tell her that Claude was dead, she didn't know where your aunt and uncle were. I'm surprised you didn't keep her posted as you followed them. You seem so...well, so adept at keeping tabs on their whereabouts."

"What would I do that for? Myra doesn't give a hoot about them." Sonny stalked off in the direction of the café, signaling an end to our little tête-à-tête.

I watched him go, feeling on the brink of exhaustion. It had been a long day with Janet's murder and me the prime suspect. Then trying to clear myself, I had sought out and been threatened by gambling crime thugs. The day was ending with more questions than answers. I was grateful to climb into my rig, lock the door and fall thankfully to sleep.

The next morning I arose rested and with a renewed determination to keep myself out of the sights of the police by finding some solid answers.

I walked the few steps to the beat-up Winnebago and, once again, entered the crime scene. This time I ignored the living area and, instead, slid into the driver's seat, the one area I had not searched. The dashboard of some of these rigs today resembles that of an airplane. The newer the motor coach, the more sophisticated the instruments arrayed before the driver. Many of the bigger rigs come equipped with a dash-mounted video camera aimed at the rear end to assist the driver in backing the thing up. The older versions are less well endowed with electronic gadgetry, but impressive nonetheless. However, the machinery before my eyes here was rudimentary.

I tried to put myself in Claude's head as he got ready to leave—on a trip he was taking on short notice and, from all reports, a trip he was making in an angry frame of mind. In Claude's thinking, he was moving permanently to Friends in Need and it stood to reason that he would bring any important papers along with him. Claude must have loaded the rig with a few changes of clothes and perhaps some food...though I saw little evidence of fresh groceries. Maybe he and Janet had eaten in cafés on their short and ill-fated journey.

After picking up his sister from the nursing home, Claude pointed the rig east, not intending to stop again until they reached Friends in Need.

I checked the side pockets on the seat and the little pouches built into the door panel, convenient places for drivers to stow maps and other documents. Nothing there. A plastic cup holder was anchored to the area between the seats and had compartments for music tapes, pencils, loose change...whatever. Two empty drink cups from a hamburger stand sat wilting in the cup holder. One of the little compartments had a flip-up lid. I opened it. Inside, several items lay piled on top of one another, but the topmost item was a shiny new key.

I picked up the key and examined it. It didn't appear to be a door key, though it could have been. Nor was it an ignition key. I eased out of the driver's seat and shoved it into the pocket of my jeans. I had seen a key like this somewhere before, but where?

On impulse, I leaned forward and pulled down the driver side visor over the windshield. Held to the visor by a rubber band was a folded piece of notebook paper. Slipping it out, I opened it and smoothed the creases on the dash. The lined paper contained a map, hand-drawn and rather clumsy. I continued staring at it, trying to decipher the information. After a moment, it became clear. The paper contained a map to the Friends in Need Sanctuary.

No wonder Claude had gotten lost. The drawing was crisscrossed by a great many turns, several onto roads without signs or names. The diagram merely bore instructions, such as to turn left on the third dirt road after the lava field. David, or whoever had drawn the map, indicated the turns by giving the mileage from the last turn, or describing any outstanding features at the intersection. I slipped the map into my back pocket alongside the key.

Halfway between the Winnebago and my rig, I remembered where I had seen a key like the one I'd just found. Sudie rents a box at one of those private mail establishments. Such a box works best for her, as she is always sending off manuscripts. A couple of months ago, she'd had the flu and asked me to pick up her mail that day. She handed me a key very similar to this one.

At last I had something to go on. What if Claude had rented a mailbox somewhere near here? It would be easy enough to do by phone and credit card. Then, before starting out, he could have mailed important papers to himself at his new address, and the post office, with a simple card, would forward all recent mail to the same place. I felt excitement tickle at my scalp. Once Claude and his sister had arrived, they could have dropped by the mailbox company, picked up their key and retrieved their mail. Now all I had to do was find the right establishment.

Taking out a mailbox too far from the sanctuary would have made no sense. I had certainly seen no mailbox rental business here and I doubted such a business existed anywhere between where I stood and the town of Barstow. With any luck, the mailbox would have been rented there. And, indeed, a quick check of the area phone book in my room turned up three mailbox rental businesses in that fair city. Once again, I got in the car.

At the first place I drove to, a disinterested young girl sat on a stool behind the counter, filing her nails. She barely looked up when I entered. A rack of greeting cards stood in the middle of the floor. I pretended to peruse the stock, picking up a birthday card and glancing over the top of it at the store. The walls down each side were covered with small to medium-sized mailboxes. Behind the counter in back, racks held mailing envelopes, tape, and small boxes for purchase.

I put back the card and picked up another. The young girl still did not look up from her nails. The key in my pocket was engraved with the numbers 1347. I edged closer to the wall of mailboxes to my left. The numbering began with 001. If the sequence was kept, no way a box here could reach the number 1347. Still, it didn't hurt to check. I walked over to the adjacent wall. The numbers here began with 227. Disappointed, I realized this was not the right place. Two more to check. I still had the birthday card in my hand so I walked to the counter and paid for it. "Do you know of anyone in town who rents storage space for papers, files, that sort of thing?"

The young girl looked up. She considered my question for a moment, and then shook her head. "Nope," she said and returned to her nail filing.

"Nope as in you don't know? Or nope as in there aren't any?"

"As in I don't know."

The second mailbox rental place was smaller than the first and like the first had no boxes with numbers high enough. This time I didn't even bother to buy a card.

The main drag of Barstow is really the old Route 66, all cleaned up and sterilized. As for the old-time motels, the El Rancho still exists, with its tiled roofs and '50s kitsch. The cabins, lined up and waiting for the next night's guests, looked as though they hadn't had a paint job or even an airing since Marilyn Monroe stayed here back in the '40s. I drove past without another glance. The rest was just fast food joints, chain motels offering Jacuzzi tubs in every room and brand name gasoline stations.

The last mailbox business sat cheek by jowl with a hamburger joint, the same hamburger joint named on the soft drink cups in the Winnebago. I felt a chill run along my arms. Claude and Janet had stopped here, gotten a couple of sodas and gone inside to pick up their key and check the mail. I got out of the car and started for the door of Mail Boxes 'R' Us.

Key number 1347 slid into a medium-sized mailbox bearing the same number. A slight twist to the right and the door swung free. The inside was crammed full of envelopes, several letters and a large manila mailer. I glanced over my shoulder at the clerk. He was busy helping a customer. Without another thought, I scooped the contents of the box into my shoulder bag and casually headed for the door. I'm sure tampering with the U.S. mail is at least a felony—add that to my growing list of criminal activity.

When I got back to the Knight's Rest, I still saw no sign of Ramey. The clang of hammering and the insistent buzz of a circular saw, however, let me know Hazel and Billy were already hard at work on the Murder Museum.

Though it was nearing lunchtime, I had lost my appetite for cooking and instead fixed a sandwich and took it with me into the bedroom. I dumped the contents of my bag onto the bed. The newspaper article about the Witherspoon bequest lay open on top.

I perched on the comforter, munching the sandwich and flipping through the various envelopes from Janet and Claude's mailbox. A flyer advertising the services provided by Mail Boxes 'R' Us was included among the papers. I stuffed it back into my bag. You never know.

I set aside envelopes that had been forwarded to Mail Boxes 'R' Us, bills, advertising letters for insurance, a couple of magazines. Instead, I focused on the large manila envelope addressed to Claude Witherspoon. The handwriting was wavy and looked to have been written by a feeble hand. The return address was also Claude Witherspoon. That explained it. Claude had been crafty enough to mail his important papers to himself at his new address, thus protecting them while he and his sister were en route.

After cutting through the clear tape sealing the envelope, I unwrapped the twine from the little round tab and shook out the contents. I found four documents. A brief glance confirmed that two of them were the much-sought-after wills. The other two were letters from David DiMarco to the Witherspoons. One was in a regular envelope, the other in an Express Mail envelope from the U.S. Post Office. I examined the wills first.

Both documents were in the same handwriting—probably Claude's, and dated September first, but Janet's had her own signature as far as I could tell. Each bequeathed one-half of the assets of their estate to the Friends in Need Animal Sanctuary. The remainder was to be divided equally between Sonny and Myra.

The third document was a letter from David DiMarco to Janet and Claude Witherspoon, dated September fifteenth. It read:

Dear Janet and Claude.

It is with deep gratitude that I acknowledge your bequest to the Friends in Need Sanctuary. Your generosity will mean so much to our efforts on behalf of the animals we care for and rehabilitate. Of course, I hope that we will not see these funds for a good long time to come. I value your friendship and counsel and look forward to many more years of our continuing relationship.

Your sincere friend, David DiMarco

I opened the second envelope and read the letter sent by David DiMarco on October second at eight am and signed for by Claude Witherspoon at two pm the next day.

Dear Janet and Claude,

I am so sorry to hear of your difficulties. You must try not to think too poorly of your relatives. Doubtless, they feel they have your best interests at heart. However, I'm sure it is not easy to face the prospect of a hearing such as you described. I understand your frustration.

In response to your request, of course you are welcome at Friends in Need. You have been most generous in offering your estate to us in return for your care. We look forward to your arrival and our mutual efforts toward our goals. Once you arrive, our attorneys will be available to assist in drawing up new wills, ones that will assure your last wishes are carried out to the letter.

We have a lovely Spanish-style home on the property. I believe you and Janet would be quite comfortable there. I feel you both have much to offer our work on behalf of suffering and abused animals. I will be honored to have you as my guest. No, as a member of our family. Please advise me by return mail if these arrangements will be satisfactory.

On Behalf of the Animals,
David DiMarco

I looked back and forth between the wills and the two letters to the Witherspoons. The newspaper article had been correct in reporting that Janet and Claude had bequeathed half of their estate to the animal sanctuary upon their death. What the paper had not reported, because it hadn't happened yet, was that Janet and Claude intended to make new wills, leaving the entire estate to the sanctuary in return for their care while still living.

Looking over these documents revealed one thing and one thing alone. The only people with a motive for murder were Sonny Witherspoon and his drunken sister. Once the siblings reached the sanctuary, David DiMarco would control everything. Half of something is something. Half of nothing is just that.

CHAPTER TWELVE

I hastily stuffed the contents of the envelope back inside and was struck with a realization. Two murders had been committee because of what the wills contained. I had no wish to join that elite number.

Neither did I trust anyone enough to just put the folder back in the Winnebago. I picked up my cell phone. Ramey was not in so I left a message for him stating that I had uncovered something that might prove very useful in apprehending a killer.

I dialed David's number, immensely pleased with myself, happy to be the bearer of good news, a commodity in seriously short supply of late. David would be thrilled that I had located the wills, and, as for me, I just wanted the damned thing out of my possession and fast.

Handwritten wills are a risky thing. Unless someone knows of it, or its location, the document might as well not exist at all. Most people who make them either have a deep distrust of attorneys, or they haven't the money to retain one. Usually they stuff these handwritten wills into metal storage boxes and hide them in a closet or they rent a safety-deposit box at the bank. Some even bury them between their mattress and box spring. Claude and Janet had chosen to have theirs mailed to them at a rental mailbox in Barstow.

If Sonny or Myra had found the wills first, they could have merely torn them to shreds and no one would have been the wiser. In the absence of wills to the contrary, any probate court in the land would award the estate to surviving relatives. Could Claude have known, or suspected, that Sonny would try and follow him? Clearly, he had taken the precaution of making sure the expression of his and his sister's wishes was kept safe. Sonny and Myra might possibly endure a long and costly probate of the wills, but that would be far preferable to losing out to Friends in Need.

I could not shake my suspicions that Sonny was somehow involved in the murders, even if he had not committed the deed himself. Then there was Myra. Perhaps my remaining task was to establish an alibi, or lack of one, for her and her husband.

David's phone rang unanswered, and finally a recorded voice advised me to try my call again later. I left a brief message, telling David I had located the item he so eagerly sought, and turned my attention to learning more about Myra and tracking down her whereabouts at the time of the first murder.

The newspaper article about the bequest was spread out beside me on the comforter. I glanced at it again, hoping for inspiration, and, after a moment one came. The article carried the byline of an Amy Bowen. She had interviewed Claude and Janet for the piece. Perhaps she had gotten to know other members of the family as well. I dialed information for the number of the newspaper.

Like so many of the fibs I had told over the last few days, the one I was about to tell skirted the truth, close enough so that I could feel the edge of it as I blew past.

Amy Bowen answered on the fourth ring. I introduced myself as an independent reporter, which, in a way, I was. Did she really need to know that my beat was travel pieces, not murder? "I'm doing a follow-up story on the deaths of Janet and Claude Witherspoon," I said boldly into the receiver.

"They're dead?" Her voice sounded incredulous.

"Sorry, I assumed you would have gotten notification by now."

Amy Bowen let out her breath in a long sigh. "Both of them at once? Was it an automobile accident?"

"No, unfortunately. The police are investigating. I'm afraid there is the possibility of foul play. Actually, I'm calling to check on a few facts. You interviewed them a couple months back, didn't you?"

"More than that. I kind of got to know them a bit. Who would want to harm those two?" When I didn't respond, Amy plunged ahead. "My God, they were just a couple of harmless do-gooders—frail old folks." She let out a long sigh before continuing. "I'm an animal lover, too, and—well, we had quite a bit in common. This is really terrible. I'm so shocked to hear this." Amy paused and blew her nose. "I'm sorry. Who are you again—and what paper are you with?"

I explained again about my status as an independent. I wanted to use the term "stringer," but decided it sounded too official. "As I said, the police are investigating. I'm interested in an accompanying article and thought you might be able to tell me a bit more about the family. The Witherspoons have a long history in California—old family passing into extinction—you know, that sort of thing."

Amy didn't answer right away. I heard her rearranging papers on her desk. She coughed into the receiver. "Sorry. I've got a head cold. You know, I really shouldn't say this. It's not pure reporting. But what happened to them really gets my goat."

"How so?" I held my breath, waiting for her to say something of interest.

"First off, it's the old story of—well…of neglect, if not elder abuse, or just this side of it. I'm afraid it's far more common than any of us knows. Our older citizens—nobody really wants them. Not while they're still alive, at any rate. It really makes me angry. I think I'll do a human interest piece on the subject." She paused for breath. "What kind of world is this?" she asked at last.

What kind, indeed? Two innocent people lay dead. Not only did they have no one to care for them, or protect them, but someone had murdered them in cold blood. "What about the nephew, Sonny?" I asked. "And isn't there also a niece? Weren't they involved with their aunt and uncle somehow?"

"Minimally, I suppose. But neither of them really cared all that much. At least that's the impression I got. Sonny lived in that old mansion with them. Perhaps he did care for them, after a fashion. But Sonny's an odd duck. I don't know how effective he is—or I should say—was.

"I interviewed them at home. Man, you should have seen the place. Talk about your musty mausoleum. I don't think anybody ever took a mop and broom to the place. Bills, papers, all kinds of junk piled to the rafters. And the two of them just roaming around in that drafty old house. All I saw in the kitchen was canned soup."

I thought about the Winnebago and the messiness. "What do you know about the niece?"

"Not a lot, really. She married into another old money family, the Hamptons. Rumor has it that she has a major drinking problem. Rumor also has it that she would torture or kill her own grandmother if she stood to gain a buck or two. Altogether a pretty unpleasant sort of gal. Now that I'm thinking of her, I remember an article we ran recently concerning her husband."

"Oh? Please, go on." I congratulated myself on sounding completely uninformed.

"Well, the paper is reporting that Jack Hampton, Myra's husband, is in a bucket full of hot water. The federal boys have sealed his office and taken all his records. Stock fraud and the allegations are pretty ugly. The SEC is charging that he ran a fraudulent investment operation. Sold stocks in phony companies, then covered investors demands for money by taking it from the accounts of other investors. That kind of thing. He'll go to the federal pen unless he can prove he didn't seek to defraud—or unless he can pay back all the investors. But that would take a wad of money. I think I read the sum was around three or four million." She blew her nose again, as if in appreciation of the significance of such a sum.

"Do you happen to have access to that article?" I asked quietly, my heart rate accelerating.

"Sure. Want me to fax it to you? What's your number?"

I quickly dug into my bag, extracted the flyer from Mail Boxes 'R' Us and gave her their fax number.

She said, "I'll put the article over the wire right now. Hey, keep me posted, OK?"

I retrieved the fax from Mail Boxes 'R' Us a half hour later and returned, without anyone noticing my absence. I didn't take time to read the fax, but instead shoved it into my bag.

When I pulled the Honda into the parking lot, I saw at once an aging Camaro parked just beside Myra's cabin. I stared at the beat-up vehicle for a moment. It looked oddly familiar. Where had I seen it before? Probably just a trick of the eyes, or an overactive imagination, I told myself. Old sedans with dented fenders and ripped tonneau roofs were hardly unique.

I parked next to my motor home and jumped out. To my surprise I saw Johnny Rocket, David's employee, emerge alone from Myra's cabin. He did not look nearly as pleasant as he had the first time I had met him. A lit cigarette dangled from his mouth, his face a scowl. Myra, I surmised, was up to her old tricks, to coin a phrase.

Johnny started toward me, but, as he did, Hazel appeared out of nowhere and planted herself between the two of us.

She had obviously been hard at work on her renovations. A leather carpenter's apron circled her hips, hammers, pliers and other assorted tools dangling from it, so that she more or less clanked when she walked. Hazel's cheeks were inflamed, veins standing out in her neck.

"You know this guy?" she asked me, jerking her thumb in Johnny's direction.

"Not really," I replied. "We've met."

"Well, he owes me four-fifty for the pie and coffee the other day. Slimeball pulled a dine and dash. Walked out without payin'."

Johnny ignored Hazel and instead leveled his gaze on me. "DiMarco says you got the wills." He extended his hand. "Give 'em to me."

When I hesitated, he snapped his fingers a couple of times. "Come on. I ain't got all day."

Johnny's face had lost its youthful charm. Something about him frightened me.

"I'm afraid, Johnny, that I can't do that," I replied calmly.

He glared at me, his lips parted slightly. I couldn't tell if the open mouth was due to words not yet spoken or to being dumbfounded that

I had refused his request.

"'Scuse me?"

"I was asked to help in finding the wills. I've done that. David instructed me to give them to him should I find them. I intend to do just that." I pulled myself to my full five foot eight, squaring my shoulders.

Johnny's eyes narrowed to slits. The muscles of his jaw rippled. I thought for a crazy instant he intended to slug me.

Once again Hazel interrupted, glaring daggers at Johnny. "Didn't you hear me the first time? You stiffed me, asshole. Now pay up."

The last thing I needed was an altercation between Hazel and the suddenly disagreeable Johnny Rocket. My mind was totally focused on getting back to Amy Bowen's fax. That one article should contain enough information to establish a strong motive for Mr. Hampton and wife to commit a murder. I hugged my shoulder bag closer to my chest. I couldn't wait to get the dirt, so to speak.

Rocket ignored Hazel and her accusation, turning to focus his steely gaze squarely on me. "I'll make sure Mr. DiMarco gets it."

Again I refused. For all I knew, the man might have had a falling-out with David. He seemed the type. He was perfectly capable of ripping the wills to shreds in spite.

Johnny harrumphed in disgust and half turned at Hazel's tap on his shoulder. "I asked you to pay up. Pie and coffee is four-fifty. And, while you're at it, quit harassing my friend here."

He turned back to me. His right hand eased toward the inside pocket of his windbreaker. I had a vague sense he might be reaching for a gun.

Hazel whipped a heavy metal T-square from the tool belt, and, without the slightest hesitation, whacked Johnny across the face with it.

He howled in pain, and most likely with a fair amount of justifiable surprise. "Bitch," he screamed, holding his hand to his lip where a trickle of blood had appeared. With the other hand, he pulled a small, snub-nosed .38 from his jacket, moving so that he stood facing both Hazel and me.

"Shut up about the goddamn pie and coffee. Tasted like shit, anyway. I ain't payin'. Not now. Not ever. As for you," he brandished the weapon, waving it in the air, "Mr. DiMarco don't like trouble. Just give me the paper he wants and nobody gets hurt."

What Johnny didn't see, because he doesn't have eyes in the back of his head, was that Billy Ray, all three hundred pounds of him, was fast closing the distance between his bulk and the gun-pointing Mr. Rocket. I have never before been so happy to see a fat man on tiptoe.

Billy Ray landed on Johnny's back with the force of a black bear jumping down from a tree. Johnny fell to the ground, emitting a loud whoosh as the air went out of him. The gun skittered across the asphalt to land at my feet.

Before the startled Johnny Rocket could disentangle himself from Billy's girth, I reached down and retrieved the weapon. I had never held a gun before. I was surprised at the weight of it. Rather than point it at anyone, I merely held it at my side, aimed at the ground.

Billy punched Johnny in the jaw and drew back to land another blow when Myra stumbled from her cabin. "Hey! You! Get off of him," she screamed, rushing toward the prone Johnny Rocket. Johnny struggled to his feet. Myra stared down at him, then hissed, "I heard her. She has the wills. Get it from her. Now!"

Johnny stood, rubbing his hand across the place on his chin where Billy Ray's blow had landed. He looked first to me, then to Myra and then to Hazel who, judging by her countenance, had not forgotten about the purloined pie. "Look—don't shoot, OK?" Johnny held both hands out in front of him. "I'm not armed."

It took several seconds for me to grasp that his plea was directed at me. Slowly I raised the gun, hoping no one would be able to tell that I had not so much as held a gun before today.

Johnny raised his hands in the air in the universal gesture of surrender. "Put that thing down," he rasped. "Look, just let me go. I won't bother any of you again. And I'll pay up for the pie and coffee, OK?"

"Coward," Myra roared, beating her balled up fists against her thighs in frustration.

Hazel walked over to Johnny, her face almost touching his. "Keep your hands in the air and answer me a question. Which pocket holds your wallet?" she demanded. "'Cause I'm gonna get paid, one way or the other."

Johnny indicated his right rear pocket and with surprising grace and speed Hazel extracted it and began searching through a wad of bills. After a moment she shoved the wallet back into his pocket. "I'm takin' a fiver. Alls you owed me was four-fifty, but you ain't got any change. Just calculate that you're payin' interest." Hazel frowned and shoved the bill into a pouch in her carpenter's apron.

"Now, here's something else for you to think about. Billy and me don't like it when someone acts mean to our friends. So I think it would be for the best if you just hightailed it outta here. And don't you plan on coming back."

Requiring no further encouragement, Johnny fled to his car. He scrambled inside, slammed the door and locked it quickly. The engine refused to turn over. He cranked again and finally a third time before the thing started. Thick black smoke ballooned from the exhaust pipe of the aging sedan. Johnny gunned the engine, burned rubber, and sped away.

Myra stared slack-jawed at the retreating automobile. "Shit," she spat, then went back inside her cabin, slamming the door behind her, the atmosphere thick with her displeasure.

Hazel watched Billy, who had walked to the road's edge to make sure Johnny didn't return, stride back to where we both stood, love gleaming in her eyes. "My baby," she murmured as he enveloped her in a sweet embrace.

Charming as this all was, and I was thrilled for Hazel, I was unnerved in the extreme by the incident with the gun. My knees had turned to water and my legs felt weak as a newborn colt's. Would Johnny Rocket really have shot me? Truth be told, I could not answer that question. And what did the episode say about David DiMarco? Had Johnny brandished a pistol on David's orders, and, if so, why the desperation?

These unpleasant thoughts were interrupted by the appearance of a sleek gray Mercedes pulling majestically into the parking lot. The driver, a rather short man, balding, dressed in jeans and a silk shirt, sat for a moment before getting out, staring at the motel and café. He slowly removed his sunglasses.

The man appeared to be in his middle forties, though worry lines ran along his forehead and beside his mouth. "I'm looking for Myra Hampton. I'm her husband. She here?" he asked in a dull, matter-of-fact tone. The man's demeanor and tone indicated that he was no stranger to searching third-rate bars, motels and God only knew where else in search of his errant wife.

Hazel didn't miss a beat. She disentangled herself from Billy's arms. "She's in cabin three and it's after check-out time. She owes me for another night."

Myra's husband never questioned Hazel, but instead drew a pile of bills from his pocket and began peeling off twenties. "How much?" he asked, without betraying a single emotion other than boredom.

During these transactions, I took the opportunity to size up Mr. Hampton, my newest suspect. He didn't look like a murderer either, but then who does? He was well-dressed in a casual sort of way, jeans and an expensive silk polo shirt. I was sure the leather loafers were Gucci. Mr. Hampton was clearly a man who wore wealth well—his clothes, his car, his very bearing. Were I in his position, I, too, would be loath to give any of it up. Prisons are so spartan.

Business completed, Mr. Hampton wasted no time in striding over to the cabin containing Myra and the vodka bottle. He pounded on the door and in a second quickly disappeared inside.

Hazel returned to Billy's embrace, then arm in arm they went back to the task of renovation. Soon the noise of energetic hammering rang through the air. This sound was quickly joined by loud arguments blasting forth from Myra's cabin.

I stood where I was. No telling what the Hamptons might let slip in the midst of a heated domestic dispute. I could hear every word. In fact, the words could probably be heard from across the street and down the road. A round concrete base encircled the metal pole holding up the Knight's Rest sign. I sat on the edge, my ear cocked toward cabin three.

Accusations flew. Mr. Hampton cursed his wife as a floozy. No argument there. On the other hand, Mrs. Hampton reminded her husband that he was a loser and a fool. Back and forth it went. I was about to give up. Other people's arguments are so difficult to endure.

"You slut! Is there anything you can do besides whore around?" Mr. Hampton bellowed.

Myra made another garbled response, boozily claiming to have had her dear husband's best interests at heart. A moment later the door to the cabin flew wide open. The Hamptons emerged into the sunlight.

Myra leaned against her husband for support, clutching the vodka bottle in her hand. Her mascara ran, her vivid red lipstick was smeared, her carefully coiffed hair tumbled wildly around her puffy face. She was hardly the picture of the society matron she so wished to portray.

She hesitated just outside the door, blinking her eyes. All at once, she screamed and pointed her finger at me. "Look out. She's got a gun." Myra ducked behind her husband and continued screaming. "She knows where the wills are hidden. Get her, goddamn you."

I raised my hands in what I intended to be a gesture of innocence. Only then did I realize I still held the pistol in my hand. I dropped the gun as quickly as if I'd found myself holding a rattlesnake.

Mr. Hampton showed no interest in Myra's information and instead wrestled his wife around so that she again was by his side. "For the last time, we don't need your relative's musty old money! Got that?" He grasped Myra's arm tighter and propelled her toward the waiting Mercedes. "Don't mind my wife," he appealed, through gritted teeth. "She's the original drama queen." He opened the passenger side and poured Myra into its swank interior. He slammed the door and strode around the car. "I don't know what you're doing with that gun, but you should be careful. You could hurt somebody." He slid into the driver's seat, started the engine and sped out of the parking lot.

The commotion had brought Hazel running, Billy panting a few paces behind her. The three of us stood like sentinels watching the Mercedes disappear over the rise. "Good riddance," Hazel snorted. "By the way, what the hell was that all about?"

"Nothing, really. I hadn't realized I still had Rocket's pistol in my hand. I'm afraid it frightened her." I reached down and picked up the gun.

"If I was you, I'd hang on to that thing. Way things are going around here you might need it. Folks are dropping like flies." She chuckled and elbowed Billy in the ribs. "'Course that could be good for business, I reckon."

After Hazel and Billy wandered away I went to my rig, taking the gun with me. I laid it carefully in my purse between a wad of Kleenex and my wallet. The very fact of its presence provided a measure of comfort. Hazel did have a point.

CHAPTER THIRTEEN

The message screen on my cell phone told me no one had tried to call. The thought crossed my mind to put in yet another call to David, but if he hadn't responded to the first two, I had little reason to suppose a third would prove the charm.

I eagerly pulled Amy Bowen's fax from my handbag and began to read. By the end of the article, no doubt lingered in my mind but that Myra's husband was in deep financial trouble. So deep, in fact, that a cool several million was probably the only thing between Mr. Hampton and a stiff jail sentence. Of course, if he committed a crime no amount of money would keep him out of jail.

Next, I pulled the envelopes containing Janet and Claude's forwarded mail toward me and began rifling through them. Most of the mail was in the form of bills, all of them opened and stuffed into an envelope for forwarding to the new address.

Bill-paying has never ranked high on my index of preferred activities. I often find myself in a rush, paying stacks of bills at a time, some of them dangerously close to their due dates. By habit, therefore, I began sorting bills according to urgency.

It wouldn't have taken a professor of economics, or even a middling homemaker, to discover that most, if not all, of the Witherspoon bills were overdue—seriously so. The pile with dire warnings and downright threats grew by the instant. Janet was in danger of losing her place at the nursing home. There was a large second mortgage on their home, and, according to the stacks of bills arrayed on the bed, Claude had even been in danger of having his television and VCR repossessed, along with a refrigerator purchased just last year.

What was going on here? Were the two of them so addled, or infirm, that they could no longer take care of the ordinary business of living? If this was true, Myra and Sonny would have had little trouble making a case for guardianship, to David DiMarco's great unhappiness. While my loyalties certainly lay with Friends in Need, I, nevertheless, felt I had to press on.

Several months' worth of bank statements were included in the package. Taking a look at the balances would soon solve the mystery. The statements had not yet been opened. Without the slightest hesitation, I decided to break the law again and open them. Hopefully, tampering with the mail is less of an offense if the addressee is deceased.

The first of six statements was dated April of this year. The beginning balance stood at one thousand eight hundred and ninety-three dollars and thirty-six cents. Claude had written checks totaling five hundred and sixty-one dollars and seventy-eight cents. I remembered the statement Amy Bowen made about canned soup in the kitchen and little else and felt a pang of sorrow. Anger flared again. Those poor, doomed souls. Myra and her shiftless brother deserved a public hanging.

The next statement was even more depressing. The one bright ray of hope was a transfer into the account from a certificate of deposit at the same bank. Still, the checks written far exceeded the deposits. The Witherspoons ended the month of May in the hole by one hundred and two dollars and forty-seven cents.

June and July and August also contained small deposits from the CD account. September, however, was a different story.

This month, no deposits from the CD account had been recorded. In fact, no deposits at all were registered. The Witherspoons ended the month with a balance of three hundred and forty-seven even.

I fumbled around in the mass of envelopes, looking for a statement from the CD account and finally found it. The deposit to checking in August had wiped the account clean. The balance in the CD was zero.

I continued searching through the financial papers. Claude had included a number of old passbooks and bank statements. Though some were dated several years before, all were overdrawn or showed a zero balance.

If the information spread out on my cozy purple and green comforter was to be believed, their asssets might not even cover their debts. Janet and Claude had been dead broke! Actually, the Witherspoons were dead—and flat broke, too.

The newspaper article about the bequest to Friends in Need lay somewhere in the jumble of papers on my bed. I shoved bills and bank statements and the like aside until the page emerged from beneath a stack of old flyers. Amy Bowen's story was datelined September of this year.

I gave the account of the Witherspoons' bequest another quick read, and, as I did, a question began to take shape. If Janet and Claude Witherspoon were penniless, and it appeared they were, then wouldn't they need to turn to someone? Someone like their old friend David DiMarco? Had this entire scenario been a setup from the beginning, the Witherspoons promising David a sizeable portion of their estate in return for their care? The fly in the ointment, of course, being that no estate at all was left to bequeath.

Suddenly, instead of eagerly awaiting David's call, I dreaded it. I had found wills all right, but wills with nothing to bequeath. This would be a major blow to the Friends in Need Sanctuary.

I didn't have long to consider this development, as a loud knock slammed into the door, followed by Hazel's hearty bellow. "Open up!" she shouted, exuberance adding volume to her already full-throated voice.

Hazel stood at the door looking quite radiant. She had traded her signature cotton shirt, jeans and work boots for a stunning little number, black with spaghetti straps and a side slit from ankle to thigh. Her dark hair was almost tamed into a French twist. Carmine red lipstick and dangling rhinestone earrings completed her ensemble.

Billy Ray looked resplendent, too, in a dark suit. His red face was at least three shades darker than normal and was lit by a huge grin, the kind that begins somewhere near the toes and, assuming a life of its own, radiates up and out from there. He fiddled with the natty handkerchief in his pocket, while he gazed adoringly at Hazel. "We're gettin' married," he proclaimed and put his beefy arm around her shoulder. "We gotta get goin'. Vegas, here we come."

The shiny gold watch glittered at his wrist.

I may not have distinguished myself as a sleuth. The murders of my friend Janet and her poor brother remained unsolved. But Hazel and Billy Ray's happiness was something I had helped to accomplish. I felt like a proud grandma.

"We'd like to ask you to stand up with us," Hazel looked into Billy's eyes and I was put in mind of a starstruck teenager gazing at the captain of the football team. "You know, be the Best Man, or, in this case, the Best Woman."

One of the more astonishing things about life, I've discovered, is the array of situations that have the ability to touch you deeply, sometimes quite by surprise. I beamed at the about-to-be newlyweds. "Congratulations," I cried and threw my arms around first Hazel, then Billy, then both of them together.

"Will you come with us?" Hazel asked after the round of hugs.

"Oh, I'm afraid I can't. Deputy Ramey ordered me to stay put. I probably should decline—crossing state lines could only add to my problems."

"Shoot! In all the excitement of Billy's proposal I plumb forgot." Hazel snapped her fingers. "Deputy Ramey stopped by here. I guess you must have been out on an errand."

"Did he say anything?"

"Nope. Just asked for you and when I said you weren't here, he kinda frowned and said he'd stop by later."

"Well that settles it. I'd better stick around. He probably wants more information about Janet or Claude. I can keep an eye on things here. You have my blessings. Now scoot."

Hazel and Billy Ray were out the door in a second and on their way to Vegas and marital bliss.

I, on the other hand, was destined to spend my time alone, puttering around in the solitude of a thirty-two-foot Airstream with nothing to do but wait for a police officer to come and let me off the hook...or arrest me.

Melancholy is no stranger to me. After Kat Oscar left, I had rather a bad case of the Black Mariah's. Nothing seemed worth the effort—activities that usually brought me pleasure just seemed boring and drab. I remember a particularly bleak afternoon, when, as I looked at my hands, I mused that the only way I knew I was still among the living was that my fingernails continued to grow. Then the news of breast cancer. I don't remember ever feeling so scared. Eventually though, as time and the healing process wore on, I began to resurface, slowly taking up the life I had once known, and knowing that life is a gift, every single moment of it.

I have known other such times, too, times without so specific a cause. Usually, the depression begins the same way. I start to feel as though a mist is settling over me, pressing me down and blotting out light.

Sitting in my motor coach, staring out at the now deserted parking lot, I felt the first tentacles of that familiar fog bank moving toward shore. As if on cue the cell phone rang. I was sure it was David returning my call, so when I heard a woman's voice it took a moment to realize that the famously disappearing Kat was herself on the other end of the line. "Kat? What—"

"Bet you can't guess where I'm calling from."

Even though her tone was light and airy I detected the slightest tinge of anxiety. "Having heard little to nothing from you for over a year I am not in the mood to play guessing games."

"Right. Well, I hope you'll be happy. I'm in Albuquerque. I've always wanted to see that Balloon Festival myself. I'm here at the RV resort with a couple of our old friends. They thought it would be better if I called to let you know I'm here. It'll be great to see you. When are you arriving? A few of the gals were starting to worry."

My voice stuck in my throat. Glad to hear from her? Glad to see her? Would I be? I would certainly have been thrilled to hear from her several months ago. But now? "Kat," I began, not bothering to keep the anger out of my voice. "First of all, what makes you think I would be happy to see you? Second—oh hell. I don't know what second is." I switched the phone to my other ear. "What about Lynn? Is she with you?"

The line was quiet for a moment. "No," Kat finally said. "We broke up a few weeks ago."

Ah, so that was it. "Look, Kat. I would like to talk with you…someday. We could use a bit better closure than we had. But I'm not ready for that in Albuquerque. In fact, I'm not even sure I'm going there after all. I've really got to dash. I'll give you a call some time, back in Long Beach. Maybe we could go for coffee."

I pressed END with shaking fingers. Not a word from good ol' Kat since the day she moved out, unannounced, to take up with Lynn, a golf pro in Palm Springs. I had yearned to talk with her then—have her tell me what had gone wrong, why she had done this to our relationship. Then I wanted to call because I missed her, and then to tell her about the cancer. But I didn't and she didn't. Till now. What else could happen while I was marooned out here?

Restless and more than a little overwhelmed, I sprang from my chair and began to pace, not an easy task in an RV, let me assure you. I called Sudie. Not home. I called an old friend, Sandra. Ditto.

A walk was in order. Not a long one, though. I might miss Deputy Ramey again. The call from Kat had certainly dispelled the encroaching gloom, if only by firing up all my adrenaline. Now I needed a walk to sort out my feelings for Kat.

I also had a pair of murders to think about. As yet I had failed, miserably, to find the killer. How on earth would I be able to investigate Jack Hampton? Did Hampton have an alibi? Had he hired someone to stuff a piece of insulation into the Witherspoons' heater vent? Slit Janet's throat? My head began to ache from all the unknowable.

The Knight's Rest had, to my knowledge, never been a hub of

excitement and activity. Even so, the empty parking lot looked desolate and forlorn when I stepped out onto Route 66.

The sun hung just above the western horizon as I began my much-needed walk. The incredible shades of violet and blue that adorn the desert sky at sunset had started to float across the landscape. Woven through the blues and purples were the orange rays of the setting sun. A magical time, and a perfect time for a stroll. Just me and the desert, and an old road taken on a whim. Something would come to me—an avenue, a piece to the puzzle so far overlooked. As for Kat, I knew even before taking the first step down Route 66 that she and I would never again be lovers. Maybe in some unseen time in the future we could become friends.

Ancient lava fields lay along both sides of the road, fingers of molten rock halted in their descent from a volcanic eruption over six thousand years ago. The black beds of rock were the picture of desolation. No vegetation grew among them. I doubted even rattlesnakes could survive such a hostile environment.

In places where the lava had not covered the desert floor, stubby shrubs, creosote bush and sagebrush, struggled to exist. A Joshua tree thrust spindly arms toward the purple sky.

The sun dipped toward its nadir, but the heat remained steady. Even the breeze blew hot, lifting swirls of sand into frenzied dust devils. I felt as if the desert were trying to suck the last drop of water from every living thing, including me. I could almost feel my skin shrivel.

Long legs make for a long stride and I had covered a fair amount of ground by the time I looked back. I could barely make out the GAS sign on the defunct station. One or two cars passed, slowed, and then moved on down the road. Otherwise, the evening was still and absolutely quiet.

I began spinning out all the adjectives appropriate to my surroundings: sterile, arid, sere. I came up with quite a long string of them, and by the time I headed back to the Knight's Rest had added barren, parched and scorched.

A car approached from behind. It wasn't traveling fast. As the vehicle gained on me, I froze in my tracks. I stared at the landscape, at the desolation, the lack of anything green. Behind me, the car, or maybe it was a truck, gained ground.

An idea, unpleasant and frightening, fought to gain a foothold in the deeper recesses of my mind. I sensed something about the sound of the car approaching, something very much not OK.

After a moment, the car drove past, and I saw it was not a car but a battered pick-up truck. I had never before laid eyes on the vehicle or the driver, a balding man with a scraggly red goatee. But the sound of an engine out of tune—now that was a sound I had heard before. Then, in an instant, I remembered when. And where.

The truck disappeared over a rise and I stood in the silence left behind. I shivered despite the heat and rubbed my upper arms with my palms.

I knew the identity of the murderer. Beyond all doubt. All I had to do now was prove it.

CHAPTER FOURTEEN

I had no time to lose. I ran to my RV and grabbed my bag, stuffed in the hand-drawn map I had found over the visor of the Winnebago and flew toward the door.

It was going on toward dark, but there was no help for it—not with so much at stake. Luckily, I carry a flashlight in my bag and a small camera in the glove box. You just never know when something picturesque will turn up and I always try to be prepared. Thus provisioned, I plunged ahead.

Hazel had asked that I keep an eye on things while she and Billy were away. Good as my word, I glanced at the Knight's Rest establishment just to make sure all was well. The sign at the office read CLOSED. Likewise the café. I started my engine and was just pulling out of the parking lot when I happened to look into my rearview mirror.

Damn! In their haste to leave, the lovebirds had forgotten about poor Sugar. She was loose, sitting on the doorstep of the office, her big eyes focused on my every move. Now what? I had no key so I couldn't let her in, yet I couldn't leave her unattended. She might wander off, get hit by a car. I swung back. Maybe I could urge her into my Airstream. She would at least be safe there. I prayed she was housebroken.

"Here, Sugar," I called. The bulldog ran toward me with a speed I would never have dreamed that clunky body possessed. Unfortunately, I had left the door to my car open and instead of stopping at my feet, she dashed into the Honda and settled herself into the passenger seat.

She turned her bejowled face toward me with a look of unabashed triumph. Her expression told me all I needed to know about the potential success of removing the creature to my rig. Such an activity, if undertaken at all, would consume valuable moments of surveillance time. I slammed my door and headed out.

The map lay unfolded on the passenger seat, Sugar's rump directly upon it. I extricated it without ceremony and spread it out across the steering wheel. According to the handwritten directions, an unmarked road about a mile east on Route 66 would lead me to the right path. A left turn there would take me past several smaller lanes, all dirt, toward a fork in the road. Fortunately, with a full moon on the rise, I had just enough light to see where roadbeds had been cut into the scrubby desert floor. The map showed the Friends in Need Sanctuary to be located another quarter of a mile past the left branch of the fork.

It's a bit of personal silliness, I'm sure, but I think I can see better with all the windows down. I flipped off the air conditioning and opened them, letting in the stll-hot desert air. I strained my eyes into the gathering gloom in search of the first turn. Sugar, it seemed, wished ardently to help. She placed her front paws on the dash And alongside me, peered into the night.

No wonder Janet and Claude had gotten lost. The landscape was virtually empty—no farmhouses, no trees and no cows serenely munching their pastures. Finally, a dirt road led off to the left. I took the turn, hoping it was the right one, and began a bone-jarring ride down a trail that was more a wash than a road.

A jackrabbit scurried across the track and for a panicked moment I was afraid he would be paralyzed by the lights and freeze just before my tires crushed him. But he sped off into the darkness, unharmed.

An interminable time seemed to pass and still I did not come to the fork in the road. The washboards of the road had only gotten deeper and deeper. I wasn't sure either my tailbone or my bladder could withstand the torture too much longer. But I needed to hurry—Ramey said he was coming back to see me later. I pressed harder on the gas pedal. I wanted to be there when he arrived.

It's funny how the mind works. I had been merely taking a stroll in the country and thinking up all the words I knew that would describe a landscape like this one. How could I have known that a truck with a bad carburetor coming down the road at just that instant would solve a mystery?

The brochure of Friends in Need had painted a lovely picture of the environment. I remembered the lush green pastures, the graceful palms, and the courtyard with a handsome fountain. Pretty, indeed—but fake. The green grassy lawns, the stately palm trees—none of that could grow out here. Not without massive amounts of irrigation. And the irrigation projects ended back on the other side of Barstow. This was pure desert sand, tumbleweeds and rattlesnakes, some of the latter of the two-legged variety.

I would have realized this all by myself in time. But hearing the vehicle had suddenly made it clear to me. I had heard that sound before, perhaps not that exact truck, but certainly a car with bad timing. The first night, as I sat in Janet and Claude's Winnebago, I had heard it. The killer was obviously coming back to destroy evidence, perhaps even to call the police to reap the rewards of his evil deeds by finding two people dead in an old washed-up RV. The sound I had heard outside the Winnebago was probably the murderer trying to extract the piece of insulation from the heater vent, which is why I had seen a corner of it flapping in the breeze the next morning. My yelp from inside the rig surprised the killer, and he had sped away before completing his task. He had even had the nerve to order pie and coffee at the café the night he murdered Claude and tried to murder Janet. I could see it now. Johnny Rocket had probably gone inside the Winnebago, maybe even with David present, and certainly at his behest, and had a nice little tête à tête with Janet and Claude just before their bedtime. Then while David had tea and cookies with them, or whatever, Johnny went outside and stuffed the heater vent full of insulation. It was probably David who had turned on the heater just before bidding the doomed pair a pleasant good night. No wonder the propane tanks were empty.

Then I had heard that same misfiring engine again in what I thought was a dream the night Janet was murdered. And, finally, the last time an engine with a poor carburetor played a role was only an hour or so ago, when Johnny Rocket had driven out of the Knight's Rest parking lot.

Little things began to make sense. It must have been Johnny Rocket who had been at the Knight's Rest searching for the wills, while I was at the hospital with Janet. Then, when he and David had appeared that night—of course he had known where to find a lighter. He had already rifled through every drawer. He then went to the café and pulled the dine and dash—stiffing Hazel for the pie and coffee.

It had not occurred to me to feel fear, at least up to this point. All I intended on doing was finding the so-called sanctuary, and then taking lots of incriminating pictures. Thank God my flash attachment was in good working order. Who knew what I might find. It was possible that no one had set foot on the property in years.

Of course David DiMarco couldn't allow Janet or her brother to get as far as the Friends in Need Sanctuary because there was no sanctuary. Anger curled around my spine and rose in my throat, tasting acrid. I could think of no punishment too severe for the fraudulent Mr. DiMarco and his gun-toting, baby-faced pal, Johnny Rocket.

Thinking of guns reminded me that I carried Johnny Rocket's pistol tucked into the recesses of my bag. Though I've never actually fired one of the things, the knowledge of its presence was comforting. However, if all went according to plan, the only thing I would be required to aim was a camera, then I'd be gone before anyone was the wiser.

I fished in my bag for the flashlight. Even with all the moonlight, I would need it to continue to read the map. But in reaching for the flashlight, my fingers didn't make contact with any of the familiar items, the odds and ends of life that had taken up more or less permanent residence in the depths of the bag. Perhaps most alarming, I couldn't even find my wallet. Had I taken it out at some long-forgotten checkout counter and neglected to put it back? Visions of frantic calls to credit card companies and the Department of Motor Vehicles flashed in a brain already on overdrive.

I willed myself to remain calm. With firm resolve and a deep breath, I thrust my hand again into the recesses of the bag. This investigation turned up worse news than before. Not only did I find no wallet, I could locate no wad of Kleenex, no sticks of gum and, worst of all, no revolver. My fingers alternately clamped around a trial-sized bottle of shampoo, a half-squeezed tube of toothpaste and my battery-operated hair dryer. In my haste, I had picked up the wrong bag.

What a fine mess. I knew I had felt comforted by the presence of the gun. I just didn't know how deeply until I realized I didn't have it any more.

Turning around right here and now presented itself as an option. I should be home in my rig, settled comfortably in front of my TV, watching reruns of *Law and Order*, a glass of chilled wine in hand. I asked the empty air, why should an unarmed woman, one just a tick or two past her prime, put herself in harm's way in the first place? Because she is suspected of being a murderer, my mind whispered back frantically.

I gave the gas pedal a tiny nudge. The Honda hit a bump and quickly sailed over another just like it. No need to worry, I tried to reassure myself. Friends in Need was nothing but a scam. If a sanctuary for abandoned animals had once been out here, and, according to Hazel, it had been, the place had folded long ago. My guess was I wouldn't find anything there at all. Just my little digital camera and me.

At last, a fork divided the road ahead. I took a left and began searching the barren landscape for any sign of civilization, of human intervention in the seemingly endless desert. If anything, this road was worse than the last.

Abandoned buildings, some of them collapsing, others barely maintaining their upright posture, loomed into view at the end of a long drive on the left side of the road. I stopped the car and turned off the lights. No need to announce my presence, just in case someone was about.

A wooden sign crossed the drive, held up by posts. The lettering had fallen prey to the heat and wind, but I could still make out a few of the words. I think I made out Noah, and possibly an Ark, but nothing even close to Friends in Need.

A circular drive fronted long concrete block buildings, probably kennels with attached runs. Just in front of the gated entry was an unfinished building, construction debris lying scattered around its periphery. I could barely make out a hand-lettered sign reading Adoptions. Down either side were the collapsed remains of more kennels separated by fenced exercise pens. I grabbed the camera and stepped out of the car. By force of habit, I grabbed my bag.

Moonlight illuminated the abandoned grounds as if a floodlight had been trained over them. The night was completely still—no birdsong, no rustle of wind, no sign whatever of any presence other than my own. Still, I walked forward on tiptoe.

The pictures included on David DiMarco's beautiful brochures had by no means been taken here. I spotted no fountain. No white picket fences, no graceful Spanish-style buildings with barrel-tiled roofs and whitewashed adobe walls. He could even have downloaded pictures of some sunny nirvana from the Internet. Instead of being a paradise, the place was dilapidated. Even in its heyday, whenever that might have been, it could only have been a pathetic, heartbreaking attempt to do good without having the proper financial support. Everything was homemade or jury-rigged. Ramshackle would be a good choice for a one-word description. And to that one could now add derelict.

Under the arched gateway, I stopped and snapped a picture of the ruined sign. I decided to take a photo of the circular drive and began walking carefully, picking my way along by the glow of the overhead moon.

Just at the side of the unfinished adoptions building I spied several rolls of insulation. Inching off the road to take a peek, I wasn't surprised to see the brand was the same as the piece of insulation that had been stuffed into the heater vent. A small scrap lay on the ground, which I picked up and shoved into my pocket. Even though the piece that I had found in the heater vent had mysteriously gone missing, perhaps some kind of test could match the fibers left from that fragment with the one I had just picked up.

My case was building by the minute. Nothing succeeds like success, they say, and I felt downright cocky as I headed toward a large, barn-like structure at the rear of the property. Deputy Ramey would immediately drop his suspicions about me once he was in possession of the information I was gathering. I raised my digital camera and snapped a picture of the fallen-down kennels on either side of the driveway.

Just before the barn, to the right of the drive, was a boarded-up single-wide trailer, probably staff housing. The closer I came to the rear of the property, the stronger I smelled something malodorous. I couldn't quite place the scent at first and then it came to me. Dung. Lots of it, which stood to reason. Judging from the number of kennels and runs, as many as a couple of hundred animals could easily have been here at one time, probably mostly cats and dogs. These cats and dogs had to eat. Then, of course, these same cats and dogs had to excrete waste. Figure a pound of food each and a half-pound of excrement per day per animal. That adds up to a lot of dung. A pit must be somewhere on the property, used to bury the stuff.

These ruminations brought me just alongside the rundown trailer, where I stopped to get my bearings. Suddenly, my breath caught in my throat and my heart skipped a beat.

From somewhere behind the sagging structure, I saw light. Maybe it only came from a motion sensor or maybe a night-light, but why would anyone care? Was someone else here? I edged closer and peered around the corner of the trailer.

Blocked from view of the road stood a small concrete building attached to the right side of the barn. Another hand-lettered sign proclaimed the office. A light inside shone through one of the front windows.

I walked the length of the trailer and peered around the opposite corner for a better look at the office building. From this vantage, I could clearly see not only the light in the window, but also David's Toyota and

Johnny Rocket's rust-bucket sedan parked next to one another at the side of the building. I crept forward. I had to know what was going on inside. And if it was something nefarious, I wanted to snap their picture *en flagrante delicto*, as it were.

The building was small, probably just two rooms—maybe three. It was made of concrete block with a flat roof and had been painted with varying hues of leftover paint. The edifice was, by far, the most colorful feature in the whole place. The door was open, as was one of the windows, it being much too hot, even at night, to leave doors and windows closed. I bent down and inched forward on my hands and knees, grateful I had worn jeans instead of shorts.

David DiMarco and Johnny Rocket were seated at a battered wooden desk. On the desk were stacks of envelopes, some of them opened, others sat waiting. Two other piles rose on the desk, one for cash, and another for checks. None of the piles was inconsequential in size. A canvas mail sack sat empty at the foot of David's chair. His tassel loafers shone in the light from a single kerosene lamp. David sat tilted back in an old-fashioned office chair, his hands working quickly to separate checks from envelopes, ankles crossed on the desktop. Johnny Rocket sat across from David, a similar pile of unopened envelopes stacked before him. Johnny picked up a stack of envelopes and began opening them, stacking their loot into tidy piles.They worked quickly substituting the occasional nod or grunt for actual conversation.

By the looks of it, neither was particularly happy, bent over mounds of papers. David pulled deeply on a cigar, slowly expelling the smoke in perfect little rings. I could have over-heard every word, had they been having a conversation.

I knelt directly underneath the window and, with the fingertips of both hands on the sill, rose up just enough to better observe the occupants of the room. David and his sidekick were in the lighted space; I was outside in the darkness. I felt sure they would not be able to see me though I could make them out clearly. Still, I was very cautious. I scarcely dared to breathe.

David had told me he solicited funds through direct mail and, by the look of it, his fund-raising plan was a success. Hundreds of innocent animal lovers had been duped. But the only thing these victims of David's scamming had lost was money. Janet and Claude Witherspoon had paid a far dearer price for their trust.

It would not do to take a picture. The flash would alert them to my presence. I froze the scene in my mind. I intended to recount every last detail for Deputy Ramey: the empty mail bag, the stacks of checks and cash, the scattering of brochures lying on the dirty floor. The same brochures had almost taken me in, too. My reaction was visceral as I recalled that day in David's car. I had been a mere whisper away from taking out my checkbook myself. Imagine! What a liar DiMarco had turned out to be. The expense of good veterinary care for abused animals indeed. My snort of disgust was actually audible.

I really had no reason to linger. My camera was filled with incriminating pictures, plus I had witnessed the counting of gains from obvious mail fraud. Even without a murder charge, that could get Messieurs Rocket and DiMarco sent to prison for a considerable stretch. I felt positively gleeful. Now to get back to the car in one piece.

I turned to go, starting my return trip along the front of the trailer toward the driveway. I could see no point in even trying to make my way back in a straight line. As near as I could figure, I was directly above the spot in the road where my car was parked. However, the maze of fenced exercise pens between my current position and the car would make such a short exit impossible. Just as I neared the opposite corner of the trailer, my foot banged against something metal, a pail maybe. The object skidded onto the road with a sound only an empty bucket bouncing on rock can make.

The single-wide trailer blocked my view of the tiny office, but I was sure both David and Johnny were on their feet, scanning the darkness for the cause of the commotion. I flattened myself against the trailer and in a moment I heard voices. David directed Johnny to check out the long drive to the road. I heard his footsteps start toward me on the gravel, while David's footsteps came toward me from the other end of the trailer. I was trapped.

My back was plastered to the aluminum-sided trailer, my heart pounding in my ears. I had the terrible urge to urinate. They say one's life flashes before one's eyes when death is imminent. However, nothing flashed in front of mine but the excruciating need to get the hell out of that place in one piece. The only thing on my side was timing. David approached from my left, while Johnny's heavy tread grew closer on my right. If Johnny passed the trailer first, I could skirt around behind him and dash for the cover of the fence at the back of the property. What I would do after that was anyone's guess. But at least I wouldn't be caught between the two of them like a frightened animal in a hunter's crosshairs.

Johnny, well-illuminated by the moonlight, passed so close to my hiding place I could have reached out and touched him. He held a gun pointed at the darkness ahead. I held my breath as he passed, still gauging David's progress on the opposite side of the trailer. Johnny stopped and called out, "Who's there?"

That gave me exactly the chance I needed. Before David could round the corner, and just after Johnny passed on the drive, I sprinted toward the fence, wedging myself between the sagging gate and the side of the barn. I don't know if Johnny heard me. I could no longer hear his steps. But David was aware of something. He turned around and walked slowly back toward the rear of the property. "Who's there? Show yourself," he bellowed. His slow, steady footsteps drew closer.

My breath came in ragged pants. My choice of hiding places had brought me face to face with whatever was causing the awful smell. From where I stood, the stench was overpowering. It only took a moment to see why. The fence I had squeezed behind hid a large open pit, ten to fifteen feet across. I had no way of knowing how deep it was, but the surface water came to about four feet below the top of the pit. Clearly, this had at one time been used to dump the feces from the kennels. What with the rain over the last few days, the pit, probably long dried in the sun, had turned into a stinking, muck-filled pond. It had a ragged, hand-dug perimeter and the edges looked crumbly from the moisture. I wanted to hold my nose, but drawing breath while keeping quiet was already difficult enough.

From my vantage point at the rear fence, I could see only desert beyond where I stood. Maybe I could strike out into the open land, then cut back down to my car once I had gotten clear of the maze of kennels and exercise pens. I set my bag on the ground, abandoning it as too great a weight. I checked to make sure I had my car keys and, on impulse, pulled the battery-powered hair dryer from the bag and thrust it into the front pocket of my jeans. At least it had a barrel and a trigger. That alone was comforting.

I edged slowly along the fence, keeping to a patch of ground between the edge of the cesspool and the barn. If I could make it across, I could slip behind the barn and hopefully disappear out into the desert. I reached the end of the fence and stepped onto the swath of ground. A few more steps and I would be safely behind the barn.

I looked down as I walked, to make sure I did not step off into the manure pit. Just then I looked up and saw David sliding effortlessly and silently from the side door of the barn toward the pit. He was carrying something heavy probably intended to throw at an intruder. I looked around to see if Johnny was also close by. When I looked back David stood squarely in front of me, blocking my way. I let out a cry of equal parts surprise and fear.

David wasn't armed except for a cement block, I noted with huge relief. He kept staring at me, a half-question ready on his lips. "How did you?—"

"Never mind that. The bigger question is how you planned to get away with the murders of two innocent people."

"Hey, what are you talking about? I didn't kill anyone." He looked genuinely alarmed at the accusation.

"Oh sure. You could hardly allow them to arrive at your sanctuary, now could you?"

"Well, that did present a problem. A big one. But I swear I never killed anyone." David stared at me, a little mirth showing around the corners of his mouth. "But I can't say I wasn't relieved when they both got offed. Boy, I had my bags packed, ready to blow this joint. Johnny went to town one day and saw the ambulances. He came back and told me the old duffers were dead. Figured I'd stick around awhile...see if I could lay my hands on the wills. I'm a con man, after all, and money is money."

"Speaking of cons, here's a good one for you. The Witherspoons were completely broke. They were on their way to you because they no longer had the means to care for themselves."

"No kidding. Pretty clever for a couple of old farts." He took a step closer to me. "But, hey, I don't give a rat's ass. Things have gotten way too hot here. I'm packing up my brochures and my money and I'm gone. There is the little problem of you, though. I sure as hell didn't kill anyone, but wouldn't want you complaining to the authorities about the nice living I make defrauding the public." He stood at the top of the oval cesspool, each step toward me bringing him closer to the ragged edge. Suddenly, I knew what I would do. It was my only hope.

"You are a true slimball, bilking decent people. I'll see to it you get nothing for your efforts, but a stiff sentence. Too bad I can't pin the murders on you, too. You deserve worse."

"Bitch!" He continued toward me, the block raised, his face menacing.

When he got close enough I drew the hair dryer from my pocket just like a cowboy draws a six-shooter and aimed it. A blast of hot air hit him in the face. He lost his footing, from surprise more than anything, and teetered on the edge of the cesspool. For a long instant he seemed to dance there on the edge of the stinking muck. First, like a crane, one leg up, his arms out, then the other leg up he dropped the block and his arms flailed. He looked almost graceful. But, the ragged edge, unable to bear his weight, crumbled and in he went.

I turned to make my escape, the night air rent by David's loud howling. But Johnny Rocket, drawn by our voices, ran toward the fence. I couldn't exit down the drive and he would surely be able to follow me if I ran toward open desert. A small side door of the barn was ajar. Just before Johnny reached the fence, I slid inside. Outside, I heard David screaming and gagging and splashing.

The interior of the barn was dark and filled with shadows. Just enough moonlight shined down from two high windows for me to see that the place was mostly empty. Assorted debris lay on the dirt floor. Along the back wall, someone had built a wooden loft about six feet off the ground, running the entire length of the barn. The clever, if crude, arrangement allowed for more storage. A handmade wooden ladder led to the loft. When the last occupants had left, they had not bothered taking the large bags of pet food stored up there.

I quickly took in the remainder of the interior, including a large, front entrance made of metal, the kind that opens like a garage door. Good for unloading supplies, bad for hasty escapes. I could only imagine the creaking of rusty steel springs as the door slowly rose upward on its metal tracks. I could spot no other exits, save the tall windows and the door I had used to enter.

David, who by the sound of it had extricated himself from the pool, was engaged in a loud conversation with Johnny. "Crazy old bitch thinks I killed those two old geezers. Shit. That's bad enough, but worse she's uncovered our little scam."

"Your little scam, you mean," Johnny huffed. "I'm just the hired help around here."

"Try that on the D.A.'s office, chum."

Instead of turning back to search for me among the jungle of kennels and runs, to my horror David snarled, "Check out the barn, asshole."

I sprinted for the ladder, scrambled into the storage loft and flattened myself behind a stack of several one hundred pound bags of dry dog food.

Johnny entered the barn first, his gun drawn. David followed, his face a mask of sudden anger. I tried not to breathe. They stopped just beneath where I lay pressed against the Alpo.

"Jesus, man. You stink."

"Shut up! Just be quiet. I have to collect my thoughts."

"Screw that. I say let's grab the dough back in the office and get the hell out of here."

"Use your head for once. If she gets away, we're dead meat. Bunco is a felony. We've got to get rid of her. Come on, we can't let some little old woman outsmart us. Where the hell do you think she went?" David scanned the empty barn. "She can't have gotten far."

Johnny pulled a cigarette from his pocket and lit it. "We could go find her car. She must have parked out on the road. We'll wait there for her and when she shows up—Bam! Bam! You're dead."

"Fool. We have to make it look like an accident." David's voice was low and like a growl. "Shooting her is too obvious. Let me think a minute."

It was just then that I realized two important things. One, I had to get out of here now—or wind up dead. Two, the hundred pound bag of food on top of the stack was tilted slightly over the edge and positioned exactly over both their heads. One push. That's all it would take. I didn't wait for another inspiration and, instead, gave the bag a mighty shove.

It fell like the proverbial ton of bricks.

I shinnied down the ladder in a heartbeat, skipping the last two rungs altogether. I sped past David and Johnny, both of them prone on the floor, covered in kibble. One of them groaned, so they were only stunned, probably just the wind knocked out of them. I skittered a couple of times on the spilled dog food but was soon on the driveway and running, my knees pumping higher and faster than I thought them capable. I had been a pretty good lacrosse player back in college. Long legs and the daily practice of yoga carried me streaming toward my car like a runner half my age. Of course, you should never underestimate the restorative power of adrenaline either.

Near the end of the drive, I jammed my hand into the pocket of my jeans and pulled out my keys. No time to waste scrabbling for them when I got there. It was then that I heard the sound of a car starting up. I believe I'll remember that sound until my last day on earth.

My breath was coming in quick pants. I felt as though my chest might explode on the very next inhalation. Even after I reached the end of the drive, my car was still parked a good city block away and Johnny Rocket's car was gaining on me. I heard the groan and clank of rusty springs and loose metal parts and the awful noise of tires chewing up gravel and growing louder. Try as I might, I could not make my legs pump a millisecond faster.

At the arched gate, I swung left, my speed causing me to lose time by making a wider circle than was necessary. I was out onto the road, but so was Johnny Rocket's car.

A fiery pain burned in my chest and I had a terrible stitch in my right side. In a desperate last-ditch sprint, I reached my car and threw open the door, just as Johnny applied the brakes and skidded to a stop not twenty feet from where I stood.

To my horror, Sugar bounded out of my car. I had completely forgotten about the dog. "Sugar!" I yelled. "Get back here."

Sugar was in no mood to mind her manners. Just then, Johnny swung out of the car and started toward me. From the darkened interior, I heard David say, "Don't shoot her, Johnny. Just get her into the car. Hurry."

We couldn't have been more than ten feet apart. I brought my hands up in the classic fighter stance, even though it was all for show. Johnny Rocket had at least fifty pounds on me, considerably more of it muscle than my weight consisted of. It's just I didn't quite know what else to do when facing certain death from a madman.

I believe in God, but not the way many do. I have a whole theory that involves God as infinitesimally small, residing at the core of all matter, as opposed to the larger version with beard and long list of dos and don'ts. Scientists recently discovered the hitherto unseen world of the smallest particle ever dreamt, the boson particle. Since these particles form the stage for all other particles in the subatomic play, they call the boson the God particle. However, facing death with only a boson particle for comfort was downright unappealing. I began a short prayer.

At that moment, Sugar flew past me on her way toward Johnny. As he closed the gap between us, Sugar threw herself at his left leg, grabbed his trouser cuff in her generous mouth—and yanked. Johnny

Rocket tumbled to the ground, slamming his head into the hard earth with a sickening thud. He tried to rise but fell back, his eyes glazed.

Sugar, having quite a field day, refused to let go of the trouser leg, and, rump in air, she growled and tugged, actually pulling the prone Johnny Rocket a short distance in the sand.

"Sugar!" I called, but she was deaf to all but her mission. Johnny rose to his knees, trying to shake off the insistent dog. David had opened the passenger door and, cursing Johnny as a fool, started for the middle of the road where the Sugar drama was taking place. Something fell out of the car—a dark ball of material—but I couldn't tell what it was,. Before I had time to register what had happened, David kicked Sugar full in her face, knocking her backward into the night.

"Some animal rights activist you turn out to be," I screamed at him. The door to my car was still open and I wanted to leap inside, start the engine and be gone. I could save my own life. But what about Sugar? The pooch let out a howl as she was kicked and now whimpered, huddled into herself at the side of the road. I took a step toward her and David followed me. I'm sure his intent was to bodily force me into the car.

Sugar was having none of it. As soon as David put his hands on my arms and began pulling me toward him she leapt from the shadows and hurled herself against his legs. This time David was the one who buckled. Sugar, her snarl deep and menacing, pounced onto his chest, baring her crooked teeth at his throat.

"Get the gun, Johnny. Shoot this dog before it kills me," David screamed, while fending off Sugar's slobbering jowls with his hands. Johnny managed to limp to the car and leaned inside. Sugar had about thirty seconds to live by my calculations. I stepped forward and grabbed her collar. "Come, Sugar," I said sweetly. "It's time to go home."

Returning sweetness in kind, Sugar bounced off David and started toward me. Then, to my horror, she stopped and sniffed the dry grass at the side of Johnny's Camaro. Good grief! This was no time for a potty break. "Sugar!" I yelled. "Come!" She clamped her massive jaws around the dark object that had fallen from Johnny's car, and then ran toward me, jumping through the open door of the Honda as if she were this year's poster girl for advanced obedience training.

Thank God for automotive accessories designed to make driving simple. I pressed one button on the driver's side door panel and all the locks clicked reassuringly into place.

Johnny screamed, "The bitch has got the..." I couldn't hear the rest. David picked up a rock and drew his arm back to heave it at me. At that moment the engine fired and I gunned it, gaining the road in a wide U-turn, leaving a plume of dirt and gravel in my wake. I could still hear them cursing as I headed back the way I had come.

A moment later the headlights of Johnny's car appeared in my rearview mirror, following me closely, then almost riding my rear bumper. Then suddenly Johnny gunned his engine. The old car wheezed and huffed in protest, but in a short time he had pulled along-side the Honda. He was driving on the desert because the road was really only wide enough for a single vehicle. He intended to run me off the road.

Just then, Johnny turned his wheel toward me and both our cars skidded off the dirt road and onto the sandy desert floor.

We bounced along over brush and rock and some very uneven real estate. My teeth chattered, not from fear, though I felt plenty of that, but from the drumming the desert floor gave my poor springs and shocks. You see TV commercials where they put these SUVs in every conceivable kind of driving hazard—mountain peaks, flooded river beds and the like. I felt for a wild instant as if I were starring in one of those adventures.

Johnny kept turning in a circle, pushing me in an arc back in the general direction from which I had just come. We flew past the gated entry of Friends in Need, me holding steady to my steering wheel, Johnny turning hard to the right. We bounced back over the road and headed for what looked like a dry wash.

The ditch wasn't deep, maybe two or three feet from the lip to the bottom. I hit it first, nosediving into the gully and landing with my front tires in the deep sand at the bottom. The Camaro dove in right beside me and Johnny gunned his engine, which only served to dig his tires deeper into the sand. He gunned again with the exact same effect.

I pressed the gas pedal in an even, measured manner and, with hardly a blink, I was up the other side of the gully, and driving again on level ground. And to think, I had once considered all wheel drives a frivolous doodad for pretentious yuppies.

Looking in the rearview mirror, I saw David and Johnny throw open their respective doors and hop out of the disabled vehicle. The car was hopelessly mired in sand up to its axle.

Moments later, I sped along the road leading back to Route 66 and the Knight's Rest, though I needn't have gone quite as fast as I did. DiMarco and Rocket would need some time to hike out of that gulch.

Sugar's lip sported a bright drop of blood, but otherwise she appeared to be unhurt. She assumed her position on the passenger seat, eyes forward, ears up, and smiling.

CHAPTER FIFTEEN

By the time the sign over the Knight's Rest loomed into view, my breathing was almost regular, but I still had a stitch in my right side. I pulled the Honda alongside my Airstream and parked, my shaking hands clamped to the wheel.

At first I thought I was alone at the motel, but just when I felt I had enough strength to open the door and limp to my rig, I spied a flicker of movement inside the office. My stomach clenched. After a moment, I realized that DiMarco and Rocket were probably still marooned in a sand gully somewhere. No way could they have beaten me back to the Knight's Rest.

I must have been weaker than I imagined, for, as I placed one foot on the ground, my knees buckled and down I went onto the rough pavement. In an instant, Billy Ray was standing over me. Hazel flew outside and stood beside him. "What happened?" they exclaimed in unison. Married only a few hours and already they sounded like two peas in a pod. "Are you hurt?"

"Only my dignity." I struggled to my feet and dusted off my pants. "But have I got a story for you. You won't believe it."

"Come on in the office, we'll get you cleaned up." Instead of arguing, I followed her. The three of us marched into the office and after a call the sheriff's office, Hazel said, "First off, you shouldn't have been out there all alone. You coulda' gotten hurt worse." Billy Ray hung on her every word, nodding gravely in the background while Hazel sponged off the desert dirt and applied tincture of iodine to my skinned knee, then blew on the abrasions.

"I know, I know." I scrunched up my face at the sting. "But everything fell into place as I walked along the road earlier this evening." I breathlessly recounted my adventure—the phony sanctuary, the mail fraud, even my escape from certain death. "So you see," I said at the dramatic conclusion, "I've caught a murderer, David DiMarco. He claims he is innocent but I don't believe him."

"Sounds to me like you caught yourself a con artist," Hazel offered in that strident tone of hers.

Hazel had just thrown cold water onto my parade, but I continued. "And, Rocket, that employee of David's—today I remembered where I'd seen him before. It was the night after Claude died. He must have come back to the Winnebago to remove the insulation stuffed in the heater vent. That's the sound I heard. That and his car's engine."

"Yeah. And that's when he stiffed me for the pie and coffee," Hazel offered. "Pretty careless, too, if you ask me. Leavin' evidence lying around like that."

"Or dumb. After he removed the insulation and tidied up a bit, he could call the police to report a dreadful accident." Of course, David DiMarco claimed he was innocent of murder. But, if so, what possible connection did Johnny Rocket have with any of this?"

"Seems to me you haven't proved that DiMarco fella did anything other than separate a bunch of folks from their money. Meanin' he's a jerk all right. But a murderer?" Hazel fixed a questioning gaze on me. "You can't prove it."

"All along, I thought David DiMarco was the least likely to have committed murder. He didn't have a motive as far as I could see. But with all I've discovered...I don't know." I laughed. "Did you know I even suspected poor Otis, for heaven's sake? When I saw that new bike...well..."

"Aw, you got that one really wrong. A 'Nam vet came along the other day, a swell in a Cadillac, and shelled out a wad for Otis. He just took the painted rocks to make Otis feel better." Hazel laughed her deep laugh. "Gotta hand it to you, though. You were determined."

"If what you say is true, then it was probably this jerk who loosened your lug nuts the other day." Billy Ray crossed his massive arms over his chest. "I'd say you're next on his list of victims. Better let the sheriff deal with this." He nodded with finality.

"I've already tried to let them handle, and I'm afraid all I did was dig myself in deeper."

Just at that moment, Sugar lumbered into the small office. I had forgotten all about her in the excitement of telling my tale. She plopped down at my feet and, to my surprise, dropped something onto the faded linoleum, something dirty and bloody and utterly gross.

I nudged the dropped tribute with my toe, gingerly uncurling the sticky wad. I could barely make out the original colors because of all the blood, but I soon realized that the yucky item on the floor was Janet's yellow scarf. The murderer must have covered his hands with it as he plunged the knife into his victim. Maybe he even used it to wipe his hands after the deed was done. And Sugar, God love her, had retrieved it from the dry grass, just after it tumbled from the floorboard of Rocket's car.

As if on cue, a sheriff's car pulled into the parking lot just as all three of us stood staring at the bloody object.

Ramey unfolded himself from his vehicle, never taking his eyes from me. I gulped and started to speak. "You see—"

He cut me off. "I came around earlier to tell you that you're no longer a suspect. Got a call from a Sudie Marshall. Said she was your sister and she was worried about you. I've been cruising by here every fifteen minutes or so just to check on you. Are you all right?" He didn't give me a chance to answer but plunged ahead. "We got the prints back from the lab. The knife had no prints on it. But we did lift a partial from the dresser. Guess what?" Ramey pulled his mustache and grinned.

"Don't play games, officer. You have no idea what I've just been through."

"Prints belong to one John Rocket, alias Johnny Rocket, alias, alias, alias. He's got a rap sheet as long as my arm. Still not a lot to go on but at least it's something."

"Wait a minute," I yelped. "Maybe we have more than we think." I pointed at the bloody scarf. "This scarf has to be loaded with the murderer's fingerprints. It's the only piece of solid evidence linking the killer to the crime."

Billy Ray stooped to pick up the scarf but Ramey stopped him. "This is evidence in a murder case. Let me get my evidence bag." A short while later Ramey had picked up the scarf with a pair of tongs and deposited it into a plastic bag without speaking.

I said, "Somebody is certain to want that scarf back—Johnny or David, or whoever. I think Johnny knows I have it. Just as I was pulling away from the sand gully, I heard him scream into the phone something about..."the bitch has it."

"What gully?" Ramey asked. "Who do you think he was calling?"

"I have no idea who. Nor why he still had the scarf. Any decent criminal would have burned it. Oh, officer, in all the excitement I forgot to tell you your number one suspect is mired up to his axles out at that old abandoned animal sanctuary. You'll find one David DiMarco there as well, along with tons of evidence of mail fraud, and maybe even more evidence pointing to the murderer."

Ramey spoke into the mike clipped to his shoulder strap. A bevy of police vehicles would soon be on their way to the stranded Mr. Rocket and the former animal sanctuary.

Why couldn't I let my mind just rest? I was safe now and out of trouble, but something still gnawed at me. The murderer? Could it be Johnny Rocket? Or had David been lying when he said he was innocent? After all, he is a con man and lying must be a tool of the trade.

"Hey," I yelled suddenly, "I have a plan." My sudden yelp brought an end to a silence that bordered on reverential. "But we must hurry."

At just past midnight, a car pulled slowly into the darkened parking lot. The Knight's Rest was deserted. Even the lone bulb in the motel office had been extinguished—all the better to see me with the lights ablaze in my motor home and my mini-blinds up. I couldn't see the car, however, only hear its smooth whine and the sound of tires crunching gravel. Timing is everything, they say. Tonight timing was all that and more...my life depended on it.

I lay stretched out on the sofa in my rig, a book held open though I could not really concentrate on the words. Around me, inside the motor home, everything looked normal—dinner dishes on the counter to dry, TV flickering, a cup of tea on the small coffee table. Everything, except for one detail—Janet's bloody scarf crumpled inside a plastic bag lying on a section of paper-towel on the dinette. Here was the only piece of solid evidence linking anyone with the crime. The murderer would surely want that back.

'Sitting duck' is not an expression I'll use again without thinking of the moment the car door closed with a thunk and the footsteps drew closer.

The book trembled in my hands as my late night visitor click-clicked across the pavement. At the Airstream, the visitor stood under the dinette windows and all was quiet for a moment. Brief shuffling in the gravel just outside the door, then a knock—loud—insistent.

"Who's there?" I called sweetly.

I prayed silently that everything was in readiness. I stood, walked the few paces to the door and opened it. My jaw dropped. There stood Myra, her lips garish red, every hair in place, in a minimal sleek black dress, her feet elegantly encased in expensive dark pumps. She surged forward, stepping toward me, pointing a small, yet very deadly pistol at my midsection.

"Myra!" I exclaimed and stared at her in open-mouthed shock. I backed up and allowed her to enter. What was happening here? How on earth did she know about the scarf, or did she?

"You know what they say," she sneered. "If you want it done right, do it yourself. God, men are assholes!" She stared at me, never lowering the gun.

"It is an understatement to say I'm surprised to see you," I managed. "Why don't you put that gun down? I won't hurt you."

"Oh, I know that. It's just that I see you have something I want." Still training the gun on my gut she took one backward step and grabbed the scarf. With a grimace she shoved the thing into her hand-bag. "I stopped and peeked in at your cozy little home just now. I rather thought I'd find the scarf. That wretched dog grabbed it and the dog was with you." She grinned evilly at her clever deduction.

"But how did you know about the scarf? You were nowhere near."

"My former friend, Mr. Rocket, called from a sand dune some-where. Actually, I got a kick out of his predicament though he deserves much worse. What a screwup. Should teach me a lesson. Just because they have cute buns doesn't mean they can think." Myra laughed, hard-edged and shrill. "Can you believe being so stupid as to leave that piece of insulation for someone to find? And I hate to think what might hap-pen should that scarf fall into the wrong hands. Johnny's prints are all over it. My guess is that he would crack after less than an hour of inter-rogation, naming me as his employer in a murder for hire. So you see, the scarf simply must remain in safe hands, namely mine."

"So, Johnny Rocket worked for you? I always thought—"

"Worked for me?" She grinned. "Well, not in the sense you mean. I met him on a visit that jerk DiMarco made to my dearly departed aunt and uncle. We...umm...got along very well, if you know what I mean."

I think I did know what she meant. But so many unanswered ques-tions remained. I took a stab at one of them. "Then when you found out your aunt and uncle had left Pasadena, you called Johnny and asked him to help find them, is that it?"

"You're close. The nursing home called to say Aunt Janet was missing. That could only mean they were on their way to that fool DiMarco. I called Johnny...told him that if he stopped them, I'd see to it he got a nice payment after the wills were probated. My mistake was in assuming he had a functioning brain."

"I see. So David DiMarco was never part of your little scheme?"

"Of course not. I didn't realize until Johnny called from the sand dune that his operation was phony—though I should have spotted the scam. More's the pity. My dear aunt and uncle would be alive today. Oh, well."

"So you had your relatives murdered. My, my. How extreme."

"Ummm. Well, pleasant as our little chat is, I must be going. I told my husband I was attending a meeting of the Junior League. Wouldn't want him to grow suspicious. Now that I know that Friends in Need is nothing but a swindle, the wills are a non-issue."

"Actually, more of a non-issue than you know." I started to spill the story of Janet and Claude's empty bank accounts, but stopped myself. She'd find out soon enough...most likely from a prison cell.

"Just one last task before I have to toddle off." Myra brandished the pistol, indicating the settee. "Lie down on the sofa, my dear. You are so much larger than me I'd never get you onto the thing after I've shot you." Myra smiled like a snake might, if it could. "Get along, now. I haven't got all night."

"You'll get caught, Myra. Why add another murder to the list?" My voice came out sounding surprisingly firm.

"Oh, not murder. Suicide. How unfortunate, but the poor old thing felt such remorse for the killings she took her own life. I'll just wrap your dead fingers around the gun and be off."

My next sentence was the cue. "You are a fool. I hope they throw the book at you."

I held my breath. Myra cocked the trigger. Where the heck was Billy Ray?

Seconds later, Ramey pushed into the living area from the rear bedroom, his pistol drawn. A loud crash sounded through the rig, then a curse. We had hidden Hazel in the bathroom, which in my motor home contains only a toilet and washstand. Billy Ray, we had squeezed into the shower stall just across the aisle—in hindsight, perhaps a mistake.

Myra jumped at the sound and I managed to grab her arm so that the bullet she fired shot out through the roof. Not too costly a repair, I hoped.

Billy Ray charged into the narrow aisle, wearing the aluminum shower frame around his girth. Hazel careened out of the tiny bathroom just behind him, screaming, "I got the whole thing on tape, scumbag."

Myra twisted away, flung open the door and ran out onto the asphalt, Ramey right behind followed by Billy Ray still trying to extricate himself from the door frame. Within moments, Myra was subdued and spread-eagled on the fender of the police vehicle. Myra would be very late indeed to her meeting of the Junior League.

I woke in pain the following morning. Although I thought I had acquitted myself admirably in last evening's hundred-yard dash, my muscles protested. Most RV resorts have exercise equipment somewhere on the premises. I vowed, in the future, to make better use of them. Groaning, I lifted an edge of the blind and peered out. Hazel and Billy Ray stood side by side, watching a huge truck with a crane attached to it pull into the Knight's Rest parking lot.

By the time Deputy Ramey had left last night—tires squealing, blue light flashing and Myra handcuffed in the back—I had been bone-tired and in no shape to travel. I decided to stay one last night. Hazel and Billy Ray had retired right after last night's close call in the rig and I wanted to say a proper goodbye. This morning, I dressed as quickly as possible, under the circumstances, made a quick cup of coffee and joined them outside.

We chatted and watched, fascinated, as the crane hauled down the old Knight's Rest Motel and Café sign. Somehow, I felt sad to see it go. Then the new sign was attached to the crane and the workmen began hauling it up into place. HAZEL TUTT'S MURDER MUSEUM, it read in dignified white lettering on a black background.

When nothing was left to see, I hugged first Hazel and then Billy, wished them well and turned to go. I had missed the Balloon Festival by a mile but I had gotten a much more powerful idea for the article. What better subject than the Mother Road herself, in all her gaudy if faded glory? Much more interesting, and just as colorful, too, in her own way. And, as if I needed any extra urging to return home to Long Beach, I was pretty anxious to see a certain redhead with a sexy Southern drawl.

I had one foot on the steps and was ready to swing into the rig when Hazel called after me. "Ain't you forgettin' somebody?"

She hitched her thumb over her shoulder, indicating the office. In the window stood Sugar, her front paws on the sill. Those eyes! That look! I am quite sure the dog knew exactly what she was doing when she lifted her right paw as if to wave goodbye.

I steeled myself against her outrageous display. The nerve! Then the picture of her knocking Johnny Rocket to the ground in the nick of time flooded my vision. "OK, damn it," I said out loud.

"All right, all right," I said as Sugar was freed from the confines of the office. She came lumbering toward me across the parking lot, her bejowled face split in a huge grin of victory. Responsibility is a good thing, I reminded myself. So is loving. Maybe a little of both will do my old heart a world of good.

In a trice, Sugar bounded through the open door of the Airstream and, without need for instruction, hopped into the passenger seat, her comical face eagerly pointed toward the highway. "What are we waiting for?" she seemed to say, "Let's hit the road."